PRAISE FOR THE JOHN HENRY CHRONICLES SERIES

"D.M. Herrmann's…John Henry Chronicles takes us to the post-apocalyptic aftermath of an electromagnetic burst that leaves the survivors bewildered, dazed and disorganized. Tribalism reigns. It is every man for himself, where the bonds of family face off against the remnants of government power in a struggle for supremacy."

—Charles DuPuy,
Author of the EZ Kelly Mystery series

"*Innisfree* is an interesting read, and a fairly accurate portrayal of human nature in extreme circumstances. Set in current times, with much of the unrest of the world today, D.M. Herrmann captures a possible future for us."

—Brian Oppermann,
U.S. Marine Corps Combat Veteran of
Desert Storm/Desert Shield

"A dystopia in our not so distant future. Excellently conceived and written. *To See the Summer Sky* was both entertaining and frightening, a wild ride."

—Joseph E. Mosca,
Author, *Scorpion Wind* and Retired Sergeant,
Florida Highway Patrol

"D.M. Hermann has written a great series. *To See the Summer Sky* is engaging and enthralling, and it is non-stop action through the entire John Henry Chronicles series. I haven't been able to put any of them down!"

—Elizabeth Visgar,
United States Army Veteran

"*Innisfree* confronts the terrifying reality of a world without conveniences we've so heavily relied upon and just how far you would go to protect your family. This novel will keep you reading until the very end, securing its place among the top necessities you would grab if the world would crumble."

—Callie Trautmiller,
Author of *Becoming American*

"The novel, *To See the Summer Sky*, continues the intriguing story of the Henry family as they try to survive following catastrophic events; a very well written third installment in the Henry family's adventure. The character development throughout the series and attention to detail by D.M. Herrmann is unmatched by other authors. I eagerly await *Fire of Death* and would be pleased to see a film adaptation of this series in the future."

—Clint E.,
Chief Warrant Officer Three,
United States Army

FIRE OF DEATH

D.M. Herrmann

FIRE OF DEATH

Book Four of the John Henry Chronicles

D.M. Herrmann

Green Bay, WI

Publisher/Executive Editor: Brittiany Koren
Copy-editor: Maria Connor
Cover Art Designer: Ed Vincent/ENC Graphics
Interior Layout Designer: Amit Dey
Ebook Interior Layout Designer: Amit Dey

Category: Post-apocalyptic Military Science Fiction

Description: John Henry and his extended family continue to stand up to the threats of guerilla warfare in Northeast Wisconsin, which requires unthinkable actions they never imagined or losses they ever expected.

Hard Cover ISBN: 978-1-951375-90-4
Paperback ISBN: 978-1-951375-91-1
Ebook ISBN: 978-1-951375-92-8

LOC Catalogue Data: Applied for.

First Edition published by Written Dreams Publishing in October, 2023.
Ebook Edition published by Written Dreams Publishing in October, 2023.

Green Bay, WI

BOOKS BY D.M. HERRMANN

Innisfree,
Book One in the John Henry Chronicles
If Their Star is Their World,
Book Two in the John Henry Chronicles
To See the Summer Sky,
Book Three in the John Henry Chronicles
Fire of Death,
Book Four in the John Henry Chronicles

Books written as Evan Michael Martin

Sorceress Rising, Book 1, A Clio Boru Story
Sorceress Revealed, Book 2, A Clio Boru Story
Sorceress Resurrected, Book 3, A Clio Boru Story

NOTE FROM THE AUTHOR

This is a work of fiction, or is it. Much of what you will read here is either true or fact. Of course, the characters and the storyline are not.

The story contains information that anyone wanting to be prepared could use. But that isn't the main purpose of this story. The story is about people. People who call themselves family. More than biological family, it is about how people come together and become family. Through deed and circumstance, they form a bond.

This is the story of one such man. Divorced and living apart from all of his family, he struggles during a time of enormous crisis to bring them together, keep them together and protect them. He longs for peace, and the dream of a forest glade, where he is safe, and so are they. He faces the reality of great evil and the natural tendencies of man. This is the struggle of all who cherish their families; this is the struggle of John Henry.

This book is dedicated to families, families together, families apart, families created by circumstance. Families are drawn together for good and bad, families driven apart because of words. Families reunited because of hurt. Cherish those families regardless of where you are. The family is the very root of our existence.

Some may find parts of this story disturbing. It should be. However, all of the so-called experts agree that our civilization on any given day is about three days away from completely breaking down, if the right circumstances occur. The inability to provide the necessities of life will quickly degenerate, and as the animals that humans are, the violent tendencies we all naturally have will return then if for no other reason than to survive. Unlike some books in this genre, this story contains profanity. I felt it was a more accurate portrayal of life in stressful times and did not want to paint an inaccurate or unrealistic picture of the environment. Much of what you can learn in this book can be put to use to help your family survive and possibly thrive in any short or long-term breakdown of essential services or society. We've seen it following hurricanes, both the good and the bad.

Fair warning, this book has several graphic scenes that may upset some. They are used to show how low human behavior can go when society breaks down.

So, enjoy the story, enjoy the will and struggle to survive during challenging, terrible times. In the words of a childhood cartoon character…Let's get dangerous!

"Fed with his unrevealing reticence
The fire of death we saw that horribly
Consumed him while he crumbled
and said nothing."

—Edwin Arlington Robinson
Avons Harvest, 1921

To my Readers,

You make writing enjoyable, and your enthusiasm for these stories fuels my efforts. Thank you!

Gary, you've been a loyal fan. Thank You!

To my new fans, the soldiers of the 3rd Infantry Division who have read and liked my stories. Some of them have been invaluable to me in ensuring I don't commit grievous errors in tactics or equipment. To each of them, "Rock of The Marne."

To 2-14 Infantry, 10th Mountain Division – "Right of the Line!"

And of course, to my Brothers and Sisters in the 3rd U.S. Infantry, The Old Guard. Many of you have read these books in support of one of your own. Thank you – "Noli mi Tangere."

To the Eighth U.S. Army Headquarters, Camp Humphreys, "why in my day…" you don't know how good you have it. "Pacific Victors."

To Ed Vincent, you have designed many covers for me, and I have never been disappointed. A true artist and partner in this journey. Thank you.

As I was writing this book, I learned that an old comrade in arms had passed. RIP Scotty, till Valhalla. He was a good guy who had a smile I will always remember and a bushy head of hair that always needed cutting.

Dedicated to Cecil "Scotty" Plouse, 1959-2022.

PROLOGUE

The soft gray shades of evening began to envelope what remained of the day. The two men, one a few years older than the other, sat on the porch. Each lost in his thoughts, neither with anything other than a slight grin. As had become our practice so many years ago, we still gathered on the porch of the cabin to reflect on the day behind us and the days in front of us. It was our town hall or meeting place—the place where we gathered.

"Won't be long and the leaves will be turning colors," the younger man said. "It's always been my favorite time of year."

"I like the cool weather in the fall. Winter is what I don't like," the older man replied. "My dad liked the fall. Said it was his favorite time of year."

"I still remember the day I first met him. I thought he was going to shoot me."

"We thought you were going to shoot us," the older one replied with a chuckle.

"He wasn't too happy that my grampa stopped you guys on the road."

"Ya' think," the older one said with a chuckle.

The creak of the screen door opened and announced the arrival of someone else on the porch. The two men stopped talking.

A larger, physically fit man, clean-shaven and bald, came out onto the porch carrying a glass filled with a brown liquid. He stopped and stared at the two men sitting side by side in the now old and weathered Adirondack chairs. "What are you two conspiring about?" he asked.

"Nothing," the older one replied. "We're just talking about the weather."

"Yeah, fall is coming," the bald man said almost absently. "He would be full of energy right about now. Telling us we need to make more wood, get more meat, just about everything we would need for winter."

"We were just talking about that," the older man said, his voice a bit melancholy.

Dragging a chair from across the porch toward the two men, the bald one sat down, took a sip from his glass, and said, "Then let's talk. I like telling stories."

CHAPTER 1

"When neither their property nor their honor is touched, the majority of men live content."

—Machiavelli

I sat in my chair on the porch of my cabin in Lake View, Wisconsin. For once, Max and King, my two German shepherds, were alongside me lying on the floor. I was enjoying an ice-cold glass of water fresh from the well. We had the best well anyone could have. Its water seemed to be about one degree warmer than freezing, and for once, I was enjoying the peace and quiet. It was a different world now. Had been for since the EMP hit. Everyone else was doing chores when a rider galloped into the yard on a brown horse.

"Hello, John Henry," Jake Kook shouted, waving his hand in the air. Jake was from the Menominee Reservation, known as "The Rez" in these parts. He and some of his men had come to help us out as things started to get a bit more than we could handle. He wore a faded blue denim shirt, dark jeans, a green ball cap complete with a farm implement logo, and a pair of brown army boots. A huge warm grin crossed his face, but his eyes told a different story.

"Hello, Jake," I shouted back, rising from the chair. I started to put my glass of water on the porch floor but remembered the dogs were there. They'd most likely drink it. They had a bucket over on the other end of the porch where they could drink. This glass was mine.

The weather was still warm enough that I was comfortable in a tan t-shirt, jeans, and boots. Most everyone except Nancy, my son Brian's wife, were wearing army boots. The younger kids were now wearing moccasins we had made from deer hide or went barefoot. It was becoming a challenge to keep them in shoes. We were experimenting with cut-up car tires as soles and using canvas or deer hide for the rest.

Walking up to Jake, I shook hands with him. "How did it go?" I asked.

"About as shitty as you could expect," he replied. "Carl's mom isn't angry. She said she was proud of her son for dying a warrior's death."

"That's not the reaction I would have expected," I said.

"Me, either," Jake said. "I was surprised, but then her family tended to cling to the old ways in some things, so I shouldn't have been."

"By the way, did you see who was guarding out front?" I asked. "No one called in and said you were coming in."

"Those two boys, Sajan and Allen," Jake answered. "I told them not to call."

I gave him a look. "They should have called in anyway."

"You getting grumpy at me, John?" Jake said with a grin.

"They aren't letting me do much of anything else right now. Might as well be grumpy. Brian and Rahn are running our teams; Sam is on the radio, the ladies are making medicine and stocking up on veggies by canning everything, and everyone is taking turns on guard. The guys are running patrols, too. Gary is having a hard time with Arthur."

"Arthur?" Jake asked. "We get someone new?"

"Oh, we got lots of new people. I need to fill you in. I'm talking about Arthur-itis."

"Man, that's gotta suck."

"Well, he's in his seventies now, and this hard life is catching up to him. He was supposed to be enjoying himself, retired, hunting and fishing. Instead, we're back in the pioneer days. He's trying, but it's wearing on him bad."

"Can we do anything for him?" Jake asked.

"Linda made some willow bark tea. It's basically aspirin tea. Helps some. Donna made some heating pads out of some cloth bags filled with sand that she sewed together. She boils them, wraps them in a towel, and he uses them that way. Problem is, they don't stay warm long. It's going to be tough for him come winter."

"Let me put my horse up, and you can tell me about the new people. I'll send one of my guys back to the Rez and see if they can find one of our medicine people. They may have an idea that will help Gary."

"Thanks, Jake. Talk to you in a bit."

··✦✦◆✦✦··

Lieutenant Nelson King of FEMA strode into Colonel Wayne Harrigan's office inside the Antigo National Guard armory building. King wore the standard black jumpsuit that all FEMA para-military personnel wore. He had a leg holster on carrying a Browning 9mm pistol. Harrigan was the commander of the FEMA forces sent into the area to deal with a rebellious lot.

"Colonel, this is the sorriest collection of people that I have ever personally experienced," King announced.

Harrigan, seated at his desk, looked up from the papers he was reading. Dressed identically to King, the only distinction between the two uniforms was the silver eagles on Harrigan's collar and the silver bars on King's.

"What do you mean, Lieutenant?" Harrigan asked.

"That sergeant, Thomas is his name, has been moving these men through patrolling exercises straight out of the *Army Field Manual*. These men can't get their movements straight. They get into each other's lane of fire; they can't comprehend overwatch. They are a sorry lot, Colonel."

"Get me Wolfe," Harrigan ordered. "And bring his sergeant along with him."

"Yes, sir," King replied as he turned and left the office.

He returned a few moments later, followed by Major Elias Wolfe and Sergeant Mark Thomas. Wolfe was a young man, about 6 feet tall with tight, curly brown hair. He was dressed in the standard black FEMA jumpsuit with black rubber-soled high-top boots. The man had formerly commanded the National Guard Infantry Unit based in the armory. He had moved to the FEMA Camp in Wausau and had been sent here to help with ending the insurrection, as Harrigan called it.

Mark Thomas was of average build with blonde hair and sharp blue eyes. He, too, was dressed in the standard FEMA uniform. Like Wolfe, Thomas had also served in the military, having been a U.S. Air

Force Security Police Officer. The three men now stood in front of Harrigan's desk.

"I would like an assessment of how the training is going," Harrigan began. "A way to get to the root of the issue I learned in my military career was to start with the most junior person and work my way up the rank scale. That ensures no one is intimidated by rank or by their senior person. Sergeant Thomas, you start. How is training progressing?"

"These men aren't soldiers, Colonel. They don't know the basics. They've been thrown together and are expected to work as a team," Thomas said. "Some have prior military service, but they were mostly, like me, rear-echelon types. They don't know how to fight or act like a fighting unit, so the training is very slow, Sir."

"I see," said Harrigan. "Major Wolfe, what's your summation?"

"Sir, shouldn't the lieutenant go before me?" Wolfe asked.

"Wolfe, I've already heard from the lieutenant. And don't forget, in this mission, you are subordinate to him. I don't give a good god-damn about your rank. This is about skill and ability. Now answer my question."

Wolfe regained his composure, but not before Harrigan saw the anger in his eyes. Harrigan's words had hit him hard, and he was not pleased. "Sir, I agree with Sergeant Thomas. These men may be able to guard a detention or refugee center, but they aren't combat soldiers. They haven't had that kind of training or experience. It isn't in their DNA."

"In their DNA, Major?" Harrigan said with a tone of sarcasm. "Explain that to me."

"I should have been more clear, Colonel. They weren't trained to be combat soldiers, and most of them have never even been part of a sports team. They don't know how to be a unit," Wolfe explained.

"I see," Harrigan replied as he leaned back into his chair. Rubbing his chin with his right hand, he sat silently. Then, he leaned forward, resting his elbows on the desktop. "How long do you need, Major, to turn these people into an effective force?"

"At least six to eight weeks, Colonel," Wolfe answered.

Harrigan's eyes traveled toward Sergeant Thomas, and he fixed his gaze on the man. "And you, Sergeant, how long?"

"I agree with the Major, Sir. Six to eight weeks," Thomas replied.

Using his desktop to push himself into a standing position, Harrigan slowly rose to his full height, almost five feet, eight inches. He leaned his stocky body forward across the desk. "You men have two weeks. I'm not running a basic training outfit. We are here to suppress an insurrection by military deserters and civilian criminal terrorists. Two weeks, gentlemen, and then we strike."

⋅⋅⋆◆◆◆⋆⋅⋅

Brian Henry was teaching a class on terrain features and how to use them to a group of his soldiers and a few of Jake's people. Dressed in his customary army camouflage uniform pants with his tan boots, the pants bloused over the top of the boots, his daily weightlifting built upper body straining in the tan t-shirt he wore.

A Regular Army Warrant Officer, Brian, my middle son, had been visiting when the EMP hit the North American continent. He was using a sand table built for mission planning and formed the sand inside of it to demonstrate the different geographic features they would find around Northern Wisconsin.

I walked up on the class and stood far enough away so I wouldn't interrupt his lecture. Brian was a natural teacher, and the way he shared his knowledge with the men and how he drew their questions and comments clearly showed how much he enjoyed what he was doing.

"If you remember to use the military crest of a hill or rise in the earth, you can stay concealed while approaching your target. These natural terrain features don't have to be very prominent to help you," he explained.

"You really think we will be doing more on foot, Chief," PFC Bennet, one of the National Guard soldiers that had joined us, asked.

"You're grunts, aren't you," Brian responded with one of his familiar grins. "You're supposed to fight on foot. Besides, you still haven't fixed those motorcycles you scavenged from the field. We won't always have enough fuel to use the Humvees."

The others in the group began to laugh. Bennet had been working hard at getting the motorcycles to work. He'd gotten the engines running but still had to fix other parts to make them usable.

"I'm almost there, Chief," Bennet answered back. "You'll see. Then, we'll be better than horse cavalry," he added, elbowing one of Jake's people standing next to him.

"Yeah, till you run out of gas. Then our grass-powered horses will run circles around you," the man replied good-naturedly.

The fun poking started to get out of hand at that point as soldiers jibed at the Oneida Native Americans, and vice versa.

"Alright, men, at ease," Brian said.

The group instantly became silent.

"Anything you want to add, Dad," Brian said, seeing me standing back from the group.

I took the opportunity to walk up to the table and look at the features he had built in the sand. "No," I said. "You seem to have everything covered. Well, except for the snowbanks we'll most likely have in a few months."

"I don't want to think about that," PFC Chuck Travis, another National Guard soldier, said. "I hate winter."

"I used to like the snow," I said in reply. "This winter, I'm not so sure. We will be working in it with limited resources, and we need to start thinking about getting some white sheets or something to help camouflage ourselves."

"That's racist," Jake Kook said as he walked up behind me.

The group erupted in laughter.

"I don't know about you, John, but I can't see myself running around in the woods wearing a white sheet," Jake said.

The men were all laughing now.

"Yeah, yeah," I said, rolling my eyes. I hadn't meant it that way. "We ain't burning anything but the FEMA boys, so it will be fine. Besides, you can't wear white anyway, Jake." Jake was the only one that got my joke. I *must be* getting old.

"I don't get it," Brian said, feeding my pain.

"He means only virgins can wear white," Jake said.

The men erupted in laughter again.

"Any questions?" Brian asked, taking control before things completely degenerated into a joke fest. The men slowly calmed down, and no one asked anything.

"Okay, then. Check the patrol and guard schedule before you take off to whatever you will be doing. Dismissed," Brian said.

The men broke up into their groups of friends and walked away. The laughing continued, and I liked that. It said morale was good.

As the men departed, Jake and I moved closer to Brian.

I asked, "Heard anything from Rahn?"

"No, he left at dawn with Johnson and Schwartz. They should be meeting with the guys from Rhinelander about now. I hope this turns into good news. The more men we can get, especially trained soldiers, the better off we will be," Brian answered.

"Does that mean we have a problem?" Jake asked.

"Not at all. It just means I'd like to have more people. Those FEMA boys are growing in strength, and the numbers don't look good. I think we are better off, but we could still use more people and more of everything else."

"How's our ammo?" I asked.

"Right now, it's good; we have plenty for a while. We get into a big fight, and we'll use it up quick. Fire discipline is not yet a strength of our guys, and even if it was, we'd still burn through it."

"Guess we better run those FEMA boys off and requisition their stuff," Jake quipped. "I don't know where else we are going to get any unless those boys in Rhinelander have some."

"It's definitely a concern, Jake," Brian said.

"So, what about those new people you were talking about, John?" Jake asked.

I had explained to him earlier about the refugees who had come from Shawano and that we'd put up in the few remaining homes in Lake View. Brian and I were leaving shortly to go and meet with them, and I asked Jake if he wanted to come along. He liked the idea and wanted to hear from them what had happened. The major roads from Shawano went through the Reservation, and he wanted to find out if any of the golden horde, as we called it or FEMA, were heading that way.

"Let me get Roop and Klotz together, and we'll head out," Brian said.

"We're taking Rambo to meet refugees?" Jake asked. "Aren't you afraid of scaring them?"

"Nope," Brian said. "It might actually help keep them in line. They aren't happy people and want revenge. We need to keep them in line."

"Good point," I replied.

CHAPTER 2

—Sir Walter Scott

Rahn, Johnson, and Schwartz left at dawn. There was a slight chill in the air, so the three men, identically dressed in their Army Combat Uniforms, commonly called ACUs, had their sleeves rolled down. Chris Rahn had been a First Sergeant of the National Guard Unit in Antigo and later at the FEMA camp in Wausau. Disgusted with the situation there, he put together a band of National Guard soldiers and, in a very successful midnight requisition from the FEMA supply depot, ran off and joined us here in Lake View. The equipment and supplies he brought here to the Home Base were invaluable.

Accompanying him were Specialist Felix Johnson and PFC Jay Schwartz. They took the route toward White Lake and then Highway 64 to Langlade, where they headed north on Highway 55. The trip was about an hour long, and they would travel through a few smaller communities—a good chance to see how others may be faring away from the influence of the FEMA operations in Wausau.

"Schwartz, keep your eyes open up there. We don't know what's happened here, and who knows how friendly these people will be about a military vehicle with a machine gun mounted on the top," Rahn instructed.

PFC Schwartz had been one of the early converts from Rahn's unit when they left the FEMA camp in Wausau. He had helped recruit several members, and after he and Rahn had a conversation about the dangers of barracks talk, they got along fairly well.

"Roger, First Sergeant," the young soldier replied.

In addition to his ACUs, he wore a ballistic helmet and goggles. Standing in the turret, Schwartz rested his arm on the M249 Squad Automatic weapon or SAW, which fired a belt of 5.56 caliber ammunition. The same ammunition used in the M4s all of the men carried as a personal weapon.

Each of the men in the Humvee also had an M9 9mm pistol carried in a leg holster. While they weren't expecting any trouble, they were well prepared should anything interrupt their mission.

They continued their drive north, passing through the small towns of Hollister, Lily, Pickerel, and Mole

Lake. As they neared the outskirts of Crandon, Schwartz could see the water of Metonga Lake to his right.

"Sure would be nice to spend a day fishing…" Schwartz said.

"That'd be the day," Rahn said. "I remember once my dad and I went fishing near here, at Quartz Lake. A rustic campsite in the Nicolet; he caught his first musky there."

"No kidding, First Sergeant?"

"No kidding, Schwartz," Rahn said. "I never could catch one."

"Me, either," Schwartz said quietly.

The men continued into the town of Crandon, where Highway 55 turned into Highway 8. They drove past a grocery store, the doors ajar, debris scattered in its parking lot.

"Looters," Rahn said.

"They seem to pop up everywhere," Johnson replied.

"In a way, you can't blame them. Stuff in there was needed, and if they didn't do it, then it would've been wasted," Rahn said.

"Well, they coulda been neater about it, First Sergeant," Johnson quipped. "Now some soldier is going to have to police that up while being yelled at by his sergeant."

"Funny, Johnson. Real funny," Rahn replied, a grin on his face.

A short distance in front of them was a hotel, their destination.

"Stay alert, Schwartz," Rahn ordered.

Schwartz straightened his posture and took a firing position with the SAW. As they drove into the parking lot of the hotel, each of them observed the desert camouflaged Humvee parked in front of the main building under a large, covered entranceway.

Johnson stopped about twenty feet away from the parked vehicle and said, "Now what, First Sergeant?"

"Just sit tight, Johnson," Rahn replied as he stepped out of the vehicle and pulled the charging handle on his M4, chambering a round. "I'm going to see where Charlie is. He had better be here."

"You betchya, I mean Roger, First Sergeant," Johnson said.

Rahn stared at him for a second, saying nothing. "Schwartz, stay alert up there," he repeated.

"Roger, First Sergeant," he replied as he checked to make sure the weapon was ready to fire.

Rahn slowly walked toward the front entrance of the building, his weapon in a low ready position. As he approached the parked Humvee, three men walked out of the building, each dressed in ACUs and casually carrying M4s.

"Hello Chris," a tall bare-headed man of average build shouted. He was also wearing a leg holster with an M9 in it. The two men with him wore ballistic helmets.

"Hello, Charlie," Rahn said, returning the greeting. "How are they hanging?"

"Low as always, one lower than the other," the man replied. First Sergeant Charlie Yerks of the Rhinelander Detachment of the Wisconsin Army National Guard walked rapidly toward Rahn. Tall and thin, with penetrating eyes, Charlie Yerks looked like a soldier. The two men met and exchanged handshakes. "You came armed for a fight, Chris?" Yerks asked.

Rahn nodded. "It's a long drive. Never know anymore what you're gonna run into."

"That's why I brought two of my guys along. We don't have anything, but an old Ma Deuce and our Captain Handy wanted to keep it with him back at the armory. Seems people have been raiding those lately, I hear." The Ma Deuce was the common soldier nickname for an M2 .50 caliber machine gun.

"Yeah, I heard that, too," Rahn said, his arm still healing from an assault he was in.

"Uh-huh, you wouldn't know anything about that, would you?" Yerks asked with a grin.

"I might know a little," Rahn replied, smiling.

"Yeah, it had your name written all over it. I thought you were in with those FEMA boys."

"Not anymore, or I wouldn't be here. They went rogue, and I'm not getting into that. That's why I joined up with the people I'm with. Good thing, too."

"That's why I'm here. Captain Handy wouldn't go in when the units were called up and told to report. We didn't have all of our people report in, and he didn't like the way the order sounded. Said it was kind of hinky."

"'Hinky' doesn't begin to describe it, Charlie."

"Those all the people you brought with you?" Charlie asked, gesturing to the Humvee.

"Why you askin'?"

"I don't mean no disrespect, Chris; it's the times. I need to know who you are with. Captain Handy wasn't exactly in favor of this meeting. He said to be careful."

"This all the people you brought with you, Charlie?" Rahn asked.

"You betchya," Charlie Yerks replied.

Rahn looked around the area before meeting Charlie's eyes again. "If this is going to work, we need to trust each other. I wouldn't be here if I didn't trust you. I'm cautious, but I trust you."

"Me too, Chris. I wouldn't be here either if I didn't trust you. Let's go inside and talk. I'll get you up to speed. You two," he said, pointing at his two soldiers, "go chat with First Sergeant Rahn's boys. You'll be working together, so you might as well get to know each other."

"Roger, First Sergeant," the two men replied as they relaxed and let their weapons hang loose on their single point slings. They headed toward Johnson and Schwartz.

"Johnson," Rahn called, "you and Schwartz get to know these two soldiers better. First Sergeant Yerks and I are gonna go inside and talk."

"Roger, First Sergeant," Johnson and Schwartz both replied.

··✦◆✦··

Brian, Roop, Klotz, Jake, and I headed into town. Klotz was driving, and PFC Rambo—Roop's new nickname because of his aggressiveness—was up in the turret. Jake and I sat in the rear seats, me behind Brian and Jake behind Klotz, and I brought him up to date on the arrival of the Shawano refugees, their condition, and what my plans were. Roop and Klotz were in their ACUs, but Jake and I were wearing blue jeans, tan t-shirts, and denim work shirts.

Brian was in his customary ACU pants with bloused boots and tan t-shirt. He said it wasn't cold enough to wear anything over it. All of us were kitted up with our vests and ARs. Jake was the only one without a leg holster or sidearm. He said he didn't like little guns. I told him that he couldn't shoot worth a damn, and that's why he didn't carry one. He usually mumbled something about small appendages.

Jake questioned my sudden change in helping the refugees.

I told him about the conversation I had with Donna, Linda, and Nancy. They thought it was cruel to not help these people. I tried to explain our limited resources but was quickly shot down by three angry women.

"John Henry, we have plenty, and you know it," Nancy said. "You've got enough food in that basement to feed all of us for two years, and we haven't even begun to process the garden or smoke any of those pigs."

"We have to slaughter them first," I said, trying to get a little humor in the conversation.

"We aren't stupid, FIL. We know that. Your jokes aren't going to change our minds. You *will* help those people," Nancy said with a glare my way.

"Besides, John," Donna added, "we need people. You said yourself that protecting ourselves from those FEMA troops will take more people than we have. These folks will help us if we help them."

I agreed.

We arrived in town and went directly to Carol's house. Coming here always brought back bitter-sweet memories of my time together with her as well as how I last saw her there, gone forever. The pain of those memories was fading, and I had tried to move on. It was hard to forget Carol, especially when she was in my life one second and ripped away the next.

We had put many of the refugees up at Carol's place. Sam's house wasn't too far away, and we used it as well. There were about 25 to 30 of them, and they didn't need private rooms. Several unoccupied homes were in the area, as well as a few farmettes that the owners had either moved on, died, or never returned from wherever they were on the day of the EMP blast. We'd been able to provide housing for them all; feeding them would be another matter.

There were several people in the yard in front of Carol's. I saw a few more coming in and out through the back door. That bothered me a little; I could feel my emotions taking over. Long years of training and experience helped me shove those feelings back down. It wasn't the fault of these people that they were here, and I had to keep telling myself that.

We pulled into the driveway, and Klotz stopped the Humvee.

"Let's do this," Brian said, and we all exited the vehicle almost simultaneously.

A few of the people milling around in the yard looked concerned.

Roop had turned the SAW so that it wasn't pointing *at* the people—*that boy can think*—but I imagine seeing a military vehicle with what, to them was a machine gun, was probably intimidating. In some ways, I thought that was probably a good thing.

The people had seen Brian before, and thankfully they recognized him. The few that had weapons kept them pointed away from us, which also spoke volumes.

"How is everyone doing today?" Brian asked.

There were a few unintelligible mumbles in response, but nothing I could make out. That is until Wendy spoke.

Wendy was a short, round woman and she made her way through the small gaggle of people. She looked all of about five feet tall, and using her elbows, she was able to push those in her way aside. She had short brown hair streaked with gray and wore some brand of khaki pants. At least I think that's what they were as they were covered in dirt, soot, ash, and who knows what else. She had on a purple t-shirt with a crewcut collar, and over the top of it, she had a grey long sleeve shirt. She wore heavy duty hiking boots with bright red laces. Fitting that she wore those here. It was the type of shoe Carol commonly wore, too.

"I have something to say, soldier boy," she said in a firm, commanding voice. Brian backed up a little as she spoke, bringing a smile to my face.

"Yes, ma'am," he said.

"Don't ma'am me," she said.

"Yes, ma'am," was all Brian said.

"What's the army going to do to help us?" she demanded.

"Ma'am, we aren't the army," Brian explained, glancing at me as if to ask, *help me out here.*

"Who the hell are you then? And I told you, don't call me ma'am," Wendy said.

"It would help if you'd tell us who *you* are," I said, coming to Brian's rescue. "My name is John Henry. The tongue-tied man in front of you is my son, Brian. The man on top of the Humvee is Private First Class William Roop, and the driver is Private First Class Dale Klotz. My son was in the army, and he now commands these men. They were in the National Guard but decided to join us to help protect the area from some unsavory types."

"Thought you said you weren't the army," she snapped at me.

"Ma'am, we aren't. They all left over some abuses that were happening. They are here to help, and that is what we are trying to do. If you'd get that chip off your shoulder and listen, we'd get through this much faster," I barked back. "Now, would you be so kind as to tell us who you are?"

She laughed a deep guttural sound, much deeper than I expected from her.

I didn't get the laughter, but I let her enjoy herself. I stood there, hands on my hips, Brian now smirking at me, enjoying seeing me in this woman's crosshairs.

"My name is Wendy Slovack. I was the principal at Shawano High School. Most of these people here were either my students or parents of my students. We don't have a leader, at least in the way I believe you are thinking. You can call me their spokesperson."

"Thank you," I said. "May I call you Wendy?"

"Wendy is my name, and it's better than ma'am. I might look old, but I'm not."

"I understand exactly how you feel," I replied.

For the first time, she smiled genuinely, then said, "I'll bet you do." The barely muffled laugh from Brian beside me was louder than it should've been.

"Wendy, we live in the area. These soldiers have joined me and my family, along with some of the neighbors, to help us get through this time. We've had our share of challenges, too. We've lost people and had to face some pretty bad things. I won't pretend to understand what you folks went through in Shawano. I can only tell you we've had our own pains. What we can do, if you wish to stay, is help each other. Shelter, we have plenty of. Food is going to be the problem as we barely have enough to feed ourselves," I explained.

"How can we help?" Wendy asked.

"We'll get you situated with things in some of the vacant homes in this area. We can also provide some staples, as well as help with foraging for wild edibles. I'll be honest; it's going to be lean for other than game meat and what farm animals can be collected that may be running loose out there. We do find cows and chickens everywhere. I've seen a few goats, too. If we can catch 'em and fence them in, that will help."

"Winter is coming, Mr. Henry," she added.

"Please, call me John," I said. "Oh, don't we know it, and we will all be cold this winter. Most of the vacant homes here have wood-burning fireplaces and wood stoves for heating. That will help, but you'll need firewood. We have tools you can use to cut wood for the winter. Clothes might be a problem. If we can scavenge some of the vacant homes we may find some necessities—clothes, pots, pans, blankets, and so on. I'm guessing you don't have a lot of weapons, so we can help you there, too."

"What about that mob that burned us out," a voice in the crowd shouted. "We want them, you don't know what they did, and we want justice."

"That's what I'm here for," Brian said as he finally joined the conversation.

"Well, what about it?" The man stepped forward. He was young with an unkempt beard, and wore jeans, athletic shoes, and a grey long sleeve NFL shirt.

"What about it," he repeated angrily. "You gonna help us get even?"

Another man stepped forward, elbowing the first one out of the way.

"And you are?" Brian asked.

"Zach, Zach Strayker," he said. He was about 6 feet tall with sandy brown hair. Appeared to be about forty years old. He wore a blue denim work shirt, jeans, and traditional work boots. "They burned down my house, killed my neighbors. I have no idea where any of the rest of my family is. People ran everywhere. They were like crazed animals burning, killing, and raping. It was like they didn't care."

"You didn't fight back?" Brian asked.

He shrugged. "With what? They had more guns than we did. All I had was my shotgun. There were hundreds of them. You weren't there; you don't know what it was like."

"I meant no offense, Zach," Brian said, barely disguising his disgust. "We can help you, but what we can't have is a bunch of you taking what we give you and running off to seek revenge. It will get you killed—fast."

"I've lost everything, soldier. Getting killed is probably the last thing I'm going to worry about. We'll all probably die this winter anyway."

"We're going to try and not let that happen," I said, rejoining the conversation. "There are a lot of

things we have to worry about before we start thinking about chasing down that horde." I stood there,
locking eyes with Zach. The staring contest between
us lasted about five seconds. He dropped his eyes, his
shoulders drooping; he was a defeated man.

"Wendy, let's you and me go sit somewhere and
talk through what you need and how we can help.
I'll let you know what's happening around here and
we can discuss if you want to stay here or move on
elsewhere."

"Okay, John. We've got a few sick and injured,
too," she replied.

"Klotz, get the first aid kit out of the back of the
Hummer and help these people out," I shouted.

"Yes, sir, Mr. Henry."

The soldier still hadn't learned. "Dammit, Klotz,
it's John."

"Sorry, Mr., I mean John," he replied.

"Wendy, let's go have that conversation. Brian,
why don't you and Zach, as well as any of the others
talk about how to survive out here and things like
that."

Picking up on my hunting innuendo, Brian took
Zach gently by the arm and said, "Come with me.
Any of you others that have ideas or who can con-
tribute, come with me. The rest of you sit tight."

CHAPTER 3

*"A man who does not plan long ahead will
find trouble at his door."*

—Confucius

Addie, Donna, Craig, and Nancy were sitting at the kitchen table planning a wedding. Donna and Nancy were carrying on about wildflowers and wishing that they had some way of having music. "We don't want Brian or John to sing," Nancy said.

"Oh, hell no," Donna quipped. "We'll all surrender to FEMA and move into the camps if that happens."

"We don't need a big ceremony," Addie said. "Craig and I just want to be married. We can say some words together, and that could be it."

"Addie, this wedding is as much for everyone here as it is for you. It's a celebration of life and love, and a way we can all unwind and forget what's been going on around here. It's a gift to all of us from you and Craig," Donna said.

"I understand," Addie said. "I just would like to keep it simple, is all."

"Maybe some wedding words," Craig said.

"They're called vows, Craig. Wedding vows," Nancy interrupted.

"Okay, wedding vows. We could say some wedding vows and then have a barbecue or something. We can't have dancing cuz we can't play music, and you already said Dad and Brian aren't allowed to sing."

"We could. I take it none of the other guys are musically inclined," Donna said.

"Not unless you want someone playing a harmonica," Craig said. His tone was not lost on the women.

"Will you be using traditional vows?" Nancy asked.

"I thought we'd write our own," Addie said. "We don't have a minister, so that dearly beloved stuff won't seem right. Besides, it will mean more."

"I like what Addie said," Craig piped in. He reached over and took her hand. "I don't want to sound ungrateful or anything, but we should keep it simple."

"I guess that part is settled then," Nancy said. "Now, the best part. What about food?"

"We're gonna have to feed a lot of people, Nancy," Craig said. "There's like forty of us here, and we can't not invite everyone. Some will still have to be on guard, but they'll have to get something to eat, too."

"We could do a pig roast," Donna said. "That way, everyone will get something. We've got ripe corn in the garden, so we could grill a bunch of it."

"We could," Nancy said. "That would be easy to do. The pig is the hard part. I've never slaughtered a pig, and I hear it's kind of messy."

None of them were raised on a farm. Donna was the only one who had ever processed a large animal, and that was deer. Nancy had cooked plenty of rabbits and turkey compliments of the boys' hunting, all learned recently.

"I guess we know what we're eating then," Nancy said. "I'll talk to John about one of the pigs. We need to butcher some and get them in the smokehouse anyway. Worst case, we have lots of venison. Maybe we could make venison burgers and use some of the pig fat in it."

"I think we'd need a fresh deer for that. All the venison we have has been processed and is in the smokehouse," Donna said.

"Guess I'm going hunting then. I'll take Rick. He knows tm ig said.

"You best be hunting then," Nancy said. "When should we have the wedding?"

"How does two days from now sound?" Donna asked.

Addie and Craig exchanged looks. "Okay," they said simultaneously. They were nervous and it showed.

"I'll talk to John about the pigs when he gets back from meeting with the Shawano people then," Nancy repeated.

"I guess we have a plan," Addie said with a slight tremble in her voice.

Donna put her hand on Addie's shoulder, giving it a light squeeze. "It will be beautiful," she said.

·· ·· ◆ ·· ··

Rahn, Johnson, and Schwartz left First Sergeant Yerks and his team in Crandon and began the drive back to Lake View. Rahn sat silent, his head turned to the right as he gazed out the window at the passing countryside.

"Everything okay, First Sergeant?" Johnson asked.

"Yeah. I'm just thinking about how we've come to this. Yerks wondered the same thing. We're supposed to be defending the state and the country. Neither of us ever expected that to mean we'd be fighting against other Americans."

"Doesn't it say something about all enemies foreign and domestic, First Sergeant," Johnson said.

"You trying to make me feel better, Specialist," Rahn said with a sideways grin. "Before long, I'll have to talk to the chief about making you a Sergeant if you keep it up."

"Oh, hell no, First Sergeant. I'm staying a Specialist."

"We'll see, Johnson. Anyway, when we get back, I need to get with the chief. Yerks and I both think we need to get him and Captain Handy together. Let them work out how we can support each other."

"They joining us, First Sergeant?"

"Looks that way. We could use the help, too."

"Some of the others do good work. Craig is better than many of our guys, and Rick isn't too bad. Most of the Native Americans are top-notch, too," Johnson said.

"We're lucky there. We should work on training the others better, even the ladies."

"I don't think Miss Nancy needs any training. That's one tough woman. I know I wouldn't want to get on her bad side."

"Smart man, Johnson."

· · + ◆ + · ·

As we came back from town, I felt better about the refugees' situation. Brian shared that the ones he talked to were eager to work together. He hadn't told them much about our issues with FEMA other than Wolfe and his crew had done some bad things, killed some people, and weren't doing much except terrorizing people. It was what Brian had learned from them about Green Bay that concerned me.

"They have an operation in Green Bay similar to what's in Wausau, only a bit smaller," Brian said.

"How much smaller?" I asked.

"They've taken over the sports area near Lambeau Field. The refugees inside the stadium are considered the troublemakers. The FEMA leadership are in one of the luxury hotels, and the guards are in some of the cheaper hotels—not that anyone is making money off of them being there. The whole area is barb-wired off," he explained.

"They've seen it themselves?" I asked.

"Zach Strayker said he talked to some people traveling through. He worked with one of them, said they were both carpenters."

"This guy reliable?"

"He's as reliable as anybody else, Dad. Geez, what crawled up your backside?" Brian glared at me.

"What? Sorry. I was thinking about Wendy."

"Wendy? Wow, Dad, you move fast. You just met her. What about Linda?"

"Not funny, Brian. I was thinking about what she told me about their situation and all that we have to do to prepare. I'm not comfortable putting ourselves out there for strangers, but I get it. We have to, or we aren't the people we think we are."

"We can't give them too much of what we have here, or we'll be short. I wish it was spring. Winter is coming, and from what you've said, we'll have frost anytime in the next few weeks, so not much can grow now," Brian said. "Maybe that greenhouse Linda and Nancy built out of old windows will help."

"It won't even put a dent in our needs. We'll have to use some of those long, half-round creations I used to see around here. We can't get that much plastic to cover one up," I said. "However, if these people stay on, we can, maybe, build some smaller greenhouses out of windows for them. It could help with their own food needs, and they wouldn't feel like we are keeping anything from them."

"It could," Brian replied. "We gotta do something, or it will be a bad winter. Are you gonna tell Linda when we get back?"

"Tell her what? God dammit, Brian, I should kick your ass. I told you that's not funny."

"Yes, Dad," Brian said with little remorse. The soft chuckling from Jake, masterfully staying out of the discussion in the back seat, was the only other sound in the Humvee.

"Now, if I may change the subject, when Rahn gets back from Crandon, we all need to get together and figure out how to get these refugees taken care of, maintain our patrols, and probably get your brother married off."

"I can't believe Craig is getting married," Brian said as he turned into the drive toward the cabin. Allen was in the bunker on patrol, and he stuck his arm out to wave as we slowly drove by.

"Time flies," I mumbled, my thoughts still on the refugees and the FEMA problem.

"Well, look who's back already," Brian said.

Turning my head to look forward, I saw Rahn, Johnson, and Schwartz standing by their Humvee.

Brian drove alongside them, and after stopping, pushed the door open on his side. The rest of us followed suit.

Schwartz came to attention when Brian got near, and I smiled. Schwartz was trying hard to fit the part. He was disappointed that Rahn had not taken him along on the recent armory raid and was trying to prove himself. Based on the grin Rahn had when he noticed Schwartz "popping to attention," he was definitely making an impression, but more than likely, not the one he hoped for.

I joined Brian and stood next to Rahn. "Welcome back. How did it go?"

"It was interesting. Zerks wants Brian and his captain to meet," Rahn answered.

"When?" Brian said a bit too enthusiastically.

"Don't get your hopes up, Chief. Charlie said that Captain Handy has no intention of pulling rank. He's an engineer and does engineer shit," Rahn said with a chuckle.

"Thank God," Brian replied. "I was really worried." His dripping sarcasm was lost on no one. "When does he want to meet?"

"The sooner, the better; probably in the next few days."

"We've got a wedding first," I said, "so any time after that should be good."

"Do you know the plans for it?" Brian asked.

"I'm sure they'll let us know," I said. "Chris, why don't you and I go see Sam, and let's try and set it up with our new friends."

"Rahn and I can go do that," Brian said. "I hear Gary's not doing well. Maybe you should visit him."

That message was clear. Brian was asserting himself as the leader, and as much as I didn't want to agree, it was a meeting for *him* and not me. Gary's arthritis had flared up bad, and he wasn't mobile at the moment. He was my friend, and I needed to be there for him. That's what friends do; they look out for and help one another. So I agreed.

"You're right," I said. "You two need to set that up. I have no intention of going. I'll check on Gary, maybe read to him or some shit."

Rahn gave me that *I'm uncomfortable with this* conversation look when I finished talking. As my mom always said, "This, too, shall pass."

•••◆◆◆•••

Harrigan stood in the parking lot observing Lieutenant King lead the mean through a series of movements and exercises.

"Lieutenant King," Colonel Harrigan said. "A word please." He motioned King to join him.

King walked over to where Harrigan stood and said, "Yes, sir."

"What's your view of how the training of these men is progressing?" Harrigan asked.

"It's slow, Colonel," King replied. "They are better than when we started, but it's slow. If those people over in that town are as good as what Wolfe and Thomas say, then we'll need more training."

"Are there any standouts in the group? Those who are better than the others?"

"Yes, sir, about four of them."

"Here's what I want you to do. Take those four and train them apart from the others. I want a guerilla team, one that can infiltrate and raise hell."

"Yes, sir," King replied. "Am I to take them away from this training, or is my training going to be after they complete this?"

"Take them away now. The mission I have for you and them won't involve this group. They won't need what they are being taught here, and we need to move. I don't want to hear anything coming out of Wausau that accuses us of not being aggressive enough."

"Yes, sir," King replied. He saluted Harrigan and walked over to where Thomas was conducting his training. "Sergeant Thomas," he said.

Sergeant Mark Thomas stopped what he was doing and turned toward King. Thomas, like all of the others, was wearing his black FEMA outfit with the black multi-functional tactical vest over it. "Yes, Lieutenant," he replied.

"I need to take some of your men from you to set up for a special mission," King said.

"Which ones, sir?" Thomas asked.

King pointed to four men and said, "These four."

"Those are my best guys, Lieutenant."

"Yes, they are. I said it was a special mission. I need good people."

"Yes, sir," Thomas said. "Jackson, Leonard, Sibilski, Gully, fall out and join the lieutenant."

The four men slowly stood up, looked at each other with some confusion, and walked over to King.

"Yes, sir," Gully said.

"You men come with me. We have a different mission than the rest of the group."

They nodded and followed King as he moved over to a corner of the Assembly Hall. King stopped and turned to face the four men. "We have a mission that we will be conducting. We'll be training to work together as a small group, and when I believe we are ready, we'll execute that mission."

"What's the mission, Sir?" Gully asked.

"Who are you?" King asked.

"Gully, sir."

"I'll give you the details later, Gully. For now, I'll just say that it will be against those people over in that little town."

The men all grinned at King's words.

···◆◆◆···

I'd visited with Gary for a bit. He was in serious pain. His arthritis had flared up bad and he could barely stand, much less sit in bed. Linda had concocted an herbal blend from some turmeric root that I had, but it was in short supply.

We were almost finished with building our greenhouse, and she had said she wanted to try to grow something to ease his pain from the herbal seed packs I had. I had seeds for anise, caraway, chamomile, oregano, cayenne, savory, yarrow, comfrey, and gobo burdock. Each was a medicinal herb, and a couple could be used in regular cooking, which would help make up for the lack of regular medicine. Linda had also been collecting local wild herbs such as wild mint, plantain, elderberry, willow bark, and echinacea. Her herbal knowledge was amazing. There wasn't much more we could do for him except use the heating pads Donna had made.

After I left Gary, I ran into Craig and Addie. They were walking along the cabin row, holding hands and talking a mile a minute. I scared them when I said, "Craig, if you're holding hands like that, how will you get to your weapon if you need to." I hadn't even finished the sentence when Craig nudged Addie behind him and reached for his weapon.

"Geezus, Dad, don't scare people like that," he said.

"I wasn't trying to scare you, son," I said with a small laugh.

"Well, ya' did," Craig replied with that *I'm frustrated* tone in his voice I remembered from when he was younger. "We shouldn't have to be on high alert inside our own homes."

"I agree, but…" I shrugged and looked around as he nodded his head slowly in agreement.

"We need a pig," he said, changing the subject.

"A pig? For what?" I asked.

"For the wedding, Dad," Addie said. "We've planned it for the day after tomorrow, and we thought we'd roast a pig. We have to be able to feed everyone."

"Everyone," I quipped. "Who is everyone?"

"Everyone. We can't not invite others who are living here, and we have to feed everyone," she insisted.

"Okay, I get it. Pick out a pig, not the breeder or the boar. You may have to pick two. Get with Jake. He knows how to butcher and process pigs, and he'll make it happen."

"Thanks, Dad," Addie and Craig said simultaneously.

"Better do it today. It takes time to process them, and it will take a good day to cook them over a wood fire."

"Thanks again, Dad," Craig said.

I watched as he and Addie headed toward the barn where Jake could usually be found. I went to the cabin.

Walking in through the back door, it was quiet. No one was inside. I called out, "Hello," but no one responded.

As I walked through the kitchen toward the dining room, I heard voices coming from the front of the cabin. Stopping at the front door, I saw Donna, Linda, Nancy, and the boys all sitting around in the chairs. Linda was in my chair. Donna sat next to her, and Nancy had pulled another chair over by them with the boys sitting on the ground in front of them. Linda was explaining something to them about a plant she was holding. The loud "creak" of the door as I opened it caused all three women to look toward me, the boys, too.

Mike was the first to speak. "Hi Grampa," he said.

"Hi, Mike. So, what are we learning about today?" I asked.

"Echa, echa. What's it called again, Miss Linda?" Mike said.

"Echinacea. Good try, though, Mike," she answered, then looked at me. "We thought we'd put the boys to work gathering wild echinacea. We can use it for a number of things, and drying it out will let us make teas and we can add it to the compounds I'm experimenting with."

"Well, you must be a good teacher to keep them still for so long," I said.

"Mom said we had to behave, or she wouldn't let us shoot our guns," Caleb piped in.

"Oh, she did," I answered with a raised eyebrow.

"Whatever works, John," Linda said with a smile, the three rows of wrinkles on her forehead becoming prominent when she did so. We teased her often that it looked like a Wi-Fi symbol.

Our conversation was interrupted by the most obnoxious and loud squealing I'd heard in a long time.

Everyone jumped, the boys running across the porch toward where the noises were coming from.

"They're dragging the pigs out, Grampa," Mike shouted.

"Craig must've found Jake," I said.

"Thank you, John," Donna said.

I nodded to Donna.

"Grampa, what are they doing with the pigs?" Mike shouted.

"They're gonna butcher them for Craig and Addie's wedding meal," I answered.

"Let's go watch," Mike said as three boys climbed over the porch railing and started running across the yard. Nancy's hollering for Mike to come back were apparently not loud enough because the boys never hesitated in their dash for curiosity.

"Boys will be boys," I said. The comment did not please Nancy or Donna. The look they gave me explained everything.

With the squealing settling down some, we were once again able to hear.

"Linda, I just left Gary. He's in a lot of pain. Is there anything more we can do?" I asked.

"Sadly, no. We're doing all we can. We have natural anti-inflammatories that we're trying. We do have some medicines that you stockpiled, but I'm not sure we should use them due to the limited supply," she answered.

"I agree, John," Donna interjected. "If we use a proper triage, then we know that all the traditional drugs we have will only give some temporary relief and won't fix the problem. I know he's your friend, but we can't use our limited supply irresponsibly."

"I don't like it, but I understand," I said.

"We'll keep him as comfortable as possible, John. The heating pads Donna made and the other remedies we have used will help ease his pain. If it gets too bad, we'll revisit the decision."

"Shit," I muttered. "Okay, ladies, thank you." I then went down the steps of the front porch and headed toward the barn. I didn't get very far when I saw Sajan walking across the yard to the cabins.

"Hey, Sajan, how are you doing?" I asked.

"Not bad, Mr. Henry," he replied. He had always called me Mr. Henry and I never could get him to change that.

"How'd you like hunting the other day? It was your first time, yes?"

"Yes, sir, it was. It wasn't as exciting as I thought it would be. Maybe because we didn't shoot anything."

"You don't always get something when you go hunting. I've been skunked many a time myself. That's why they call it *hunting* instead of *getting*."

Sajan chuckled. "You like those dad jokes, don't you, Mr. Henry?"

"It's a weakness. But I come by it honestly."

"I hope Craig doesn't start with the dad jokes," he said with his infectious grin.

"He might," I replied.

"Well, now that he's getting married and going to have a kid, I'm sure he'll change," Sajan said.

"You two have been friends since the second grade, Sajan. One of the things I was always impressed by is how, through anything, you guys stayed friends. Even when you went off to school, you always got back together."

He nodded. "You're right, Mr. Henry. Maybe Craig won't change."

CHAPTER 4

"They were going to look at war, the red animal—war, the blood swollen god."

—Stephen Crane

Colonel Wayne Harrigan was sitting in his chair behind his desk. He held a steaming cup of coffee in his hand as he explained his idea for a mission Lieutenant Nelson King would lead with his small team of men. "The mission, Lieutenant, is for your team to infiltrate the Lake View area on foot, find where those people are living and let us know so we can end this."

"Yes, Sir. I understand from Wolfe that they have a pretty good patrol set up out there. They may see us coming," King replied. "That's a long way to walk from here, so getting closer before we head out on foot will help."

"I know that," Harrigan said as he paused and took a sip of his coffee. "My plan is to take you and your men south of their area, put you out somewhere west of there, and then you can move toward the place through the woods."

"Where exactly, sir?" King asked.

"In debriefing Wolfe about his recent escape, it seems they may have scout teams covering the Four Corners area," Harrigan said.

Standing up, he walked over to a map hanging on the wall that showed the area around the fish hatchery. Pointing at the intersection of Highway 64 and P, Harrigan said, "This is Four Corners. You'll be dropped off west of here, just south and east of Evergreen."

King joined Harrigan next to the map and studied the area. "It looks like we can take some of these backroads and get real close to the hatchery. That could save us some time. I doubt they have that many eyes out where they can cover everything. My guess is they have some kind of observation post at Four Corners and another close to the hatchery. They were onto Major Wolfe's whereabouts way too fast for that not to be true."

"I agree, Lieutenant. Just stay out of that damn hatchery. You and your men are going to have to bivouac in the woods. You'll have to make sure they can do that without ending up like the good major and his crew."

"The men I picked are all ex-military, except one, Colonel. I'm sure they've been in the woods at least once. None of them were Navy," King said, emphasizing his last words with a slight smile.

"Any of them infantry, King?" Harrigan asked.

"No, sir, mechanics and supply people, but they'll do okay."

"That seems to be the case everywhere. The only infantry we have are National Guard, and for obvious reasons, we can't use them," Harrigan said. "After that stunt some of the Guard boys did when they deserted the camp in Wausau makes that decision prudent. I don't think those boys would shoot at each other. Well, except for Wolfe."

"Wolfe really hates those people, doesn't he, Colonel."

"Wolfe's an opportunist, Lieutenant, and he's no different than the rest of us that left our oaths behind us to do what we do now. Wolfe took the change a little too personally, is all."

"I can't say anything about that, but I know he wants his First Sergeant and that Warrant Officer hanging from a rope," King said.

"He'll get his wish, Lieutenant. That's your job. Give the major the means to get his wish."

"Yes, sir."

··◆◆◆··

We had all gathered for the wedding in the late morning. Craig and Addie were as dressed up as they could get, which meant Addie was dressed up. I don't think Craig even owned a dress shirt, much less one with a collar. He had on clean denim jeans, his boots, and an army camouflage jacket over a brown t-shirt. Addie wore a dress that Nancy had, and they all had worked together to make it fit as best they could. Neither the bride nor groom was armed, but everyone in the rest of the wedding party was.

The boys had collected wildflowers, and a bouquet was made from them for Addie. It looked a little worse for wear as the boys hadn't been exactly gentle with the flowers as they pulled them out of the ground, but she appreciated their efforts.

The new Mr. and Mrs. Henry had exchanged their vows. Allen and Sajan were groomsmen, with Allen standing next to Craig, and Sajan next to Addie. Donna cried, I had something in my eye, and everything went off without a hitch. We let Rahn conduct the ceremony. It'd started as a bad joke about First Sergeants being next to God, and then it started to make a lot of sense. He did a good job.

I'd started smoking the pigs the night before. After we butchered the first one, we decided it wasn't big enough. I wasn't really comfortable doing that, but it isn't every day your youngest son gets married in the middle of an apocalypse.

The smoked pork was good. So was the potato salad, soup, and greens that had been made to go along with it. The biggest hit, besides the pork, were the cathead biscuits and honey that Nancy had made. Many of the group had never heard of cathead biscuits, and the comments before Nancy explained that it was nothing more than a biscuit about the size of a cat head were bordering on weird. The most common was, "How can you make a biscuit out of a cat's head?" All of the biscuits were eaten. I was glad I had those bags of flour and wheat berries stored. Now that I didn't have to worry about the little-known fact that growing wheat at home was illegal, we'd have to set up an area for growing wheat, especially now that we had the refugees in town to help feed.

As people finished eating and the laughter was beginning to quiet down, Rahn and Brian motioned for me to join them over near the end cabin.

I made my way over to them, and Brian said, "Time to get back to work, Dad."

"What do you mean?" I asked.

"We think we need to hit the armory again," Rahn said, clarifying. "With those new people there now, it's just a matter of time before they come after us. A pre-emptive strike could slow them down or discourage them."

I shook my head. "We don't have enough people for that. We'd be left pretty thin here, and I don't know if Jake's people would be willing to go after the last raid."

"We've got the Guard in Rhinelander. Rahn and I are setting up a meeting with them to talk about combining forces," Brian said, joining our conversation.

"You think they'll go along with it?" I asked.

"Charlie Yerks and I are old friends, John," Rahn explained. "He left me with a good impression that they've got the threat, too, and don't want it hovering in their backyard. I think they'll join us."

"When are you meeting?" I asked.

"Trying for tomorrow. Yerks had to verify with his CO, and once he does, we're off to meet him."

Brian gave Rahn a sideways glance. "Same place as before?"

"Yep, same place as before," Rahn said. "Normally, I wouldn't do that, but we saw very few houses that were occupied or showed signs of being that way. I don't know where the people went, but they aren't in the booming metropolis of Crandon." He smirked.

"It's risky, Chris," I said. "Meeting covertly in the same place twice. I don't know…"

"I'll be there, too, Dad. It's all good," Brian said.

"Okay, Superman, I can't out-argue you both," I said.

Brian grinned. "Damn, I shoulda brought that outfit from home when we came up here. Remember, when I did that in Korea, Dad? Standing in the barracks quad, wearing a Superman costume, hands on my hips, with the breeze blowing my cape. The troops loved it. Chief was Superman."

"You did *not* do that," Rahn said, shaking his head.

"Damn right I did, First Sergeant. Somebody had to raise morale; the officers sure weren't doing it."

"He did, Chris. I have a picture back in the cabin I can show you."

"I see now that apple really didn't fall far from the tree," Rahn said. "It did hit its head when it landed, though."

"Be nice, First Sergeant, or I'll start calling you Top in front of the men," Brian said.

"Uh, huh," Rahn replied.

"What about our patrols?" I asked, taking us back to the more important part of the conversation.

"What about 'em?" Brian asked.

"Is four enough, or should we send out more?" I glanced at Rahn.

"Good point," Rahn said. "With the extra people they have in Antigo, they may try a sneak and peek. You know, send some people in, have them get nosey and look around, maybe tear some shit up while they're here."

"We have a lot of guys sitting on their asses who aren't on patrol. I heard Craig and a few others say they'd like to do more patrols. We can put them in with mine and Jake's guys. Run some foot and road patrols," Brian said.

"I'm not sure we should use up our fuel for these patrols. We have plenty of horses, and with the foot patrols, it would be good for everyone," I suggested.

"I ain't getting on no horse unless I have to put a quarter in it," Brian said.

"What's the matter, Chief, your tender ass special or something," Rahn said with a chuckle.

"Haha, First Sergeant. Just remember, I know where you sleep," Brian replied.

"So we'll do extra patrols, on foot and horseback," I said, taking charge of the rapidly deteriorating conversation.

"Yeah, that'll work," Brian said. "I'll talk with Jake, and we'll get everyone together and put out a new patrol plan."

"Fine. I'll get with Craig and the others and let them know what we'll be doing. Can we start tonight?" I said.

"Yeah, the sooner the better. We can work the bugs out before Rahn and I meet his friend Charlie."

"Good," I replied, and started walking toward the group that was practicing magic by making all of the food disappear. As I left the two men, I heard Brian say, "You know, my ass is special."

The coughing fit from Rahn gave me a good indication of how he took it.

·····◆·◆·◆·····

Lieutenant King had gathered his team—Jackson, Leonard, Sibilski, and Gully—behind the armory near a patch of woods. It was getting dark, and the men were covered in sweat, bits of dried leaves, and dirt. For two days, he had run them through a series of exercises to teach them how to work together as a team and learn the things they would need to know on their upcoming mission. Almost all of it he had learned in SERE, or Survival, Evasion, Resistance, and Escape training he'd attended at a fort a few years ago. Designed for pilots, it was considered one of the most intensive training programs in existence—all based on the experiences of Vietnam War-era pilots who had been shot down and captured.

"Take a knee, men," he ordered.

The men seemed to collapse on themselves as they each dropped to a knee, one of them to two knees. Their heavy breathing could be heard in the otherwise quiet of the woods.

Jackson reached for his water bladder stem, placing it in his mouth, sucking greedily at the water inside.

"I don't believe I gave permission to drink, Jackson," King said sharply.

"I'm thirsty, Lieutenant," Jackson replied.

King removed his pistol from his leg holster and pointed the weapon at Jackson. The action had the desired effect as Jackson dropped the stem from his mouth and fell backward.

"Don't shoot me, Lieutenant," he cried.

The other three men watched in stunned silence—the shock of what was happening showed plainly on their faces.

King lowered the weapon but did not put it back in the holster. "Now that I have your attention," King continued, "we can only carry so much with us when we are on our mission. Water discipline is important because we don't know if we can get any clean water and have no good way to purify any water we may find out there other than boiling it or using purifying tablets, which we don't have an abundance of. The last thing any of you want is the running shits because you drank bad water. We have to learn to conserve what we have and only use it when necessary. Am I clear?"

"Yes, sir," they all replied.

"Lieutenant, when can you tell us what the mission is?" Gully asked.

"We'll be taking a short ride over toward Lake View. From there, we'll head out on foot, kind of a LRRP to see what we can learn about the location of the deserters and the civilians hiding them."

"LRRP?" Sibilski asked. The turn of his head further demonstrating how lost he was with the term.

"LRRP—Long Range Reconnaissance Patrol," King replied. "I thought you were in the army, Sibilski?"

"I was a Supply Clerk, Lieutenant. We didn't do any of that grunt shit, I mean stuff, Sir."

"It's okay, Sibilski, I've heard the word. Yes, an LRRP. We will be on foot, we will be silent, and we will not engage with anyone unless we have no choice," King said.

"How long will we be out there, Lieutenant?" Gully asked.

"At least a week to ten days. Could be more, could be less. Food and water will be our biggest concern. We'll each carry 300 rounds of 5.56 and 60 rounds of 9mm. The MREs don't weigh too much, and maybe we can forage or trap something to supplement our meals. We'll have water purification tablets. Makes the water taste crappy, but no one will get sick."

"There's a lot of deer around here, Lieutenant. I'm sure some farmer's chickens or other animals are loose," Jackson said. He was the youngest of the group and was the only one from this part of the state, having grown up in Wausau.

"If you can catch them by hand or in a snare, I have no problem with that, Jackson. There will be no shooting unless we have no choice. And a venison steak is *not* no choice."

"Yes, sir," Jackson replied.

"Alright, you men, go get cleaned up and have something to eat. I'll let the colonel know where we are with our training. I'll see from him when we should move out."

CHAPTER 5

"Attack him where he is unprepared,
appear where you are not expected."

—Sun Tzu

Craig and I took the pickup into town. We had seeds, a few canned goods, dried herbs, and hand tools in the back. We also had some lumber and carpentry tools to help them begin to build a greenhouse by using some windows we'd strip from garages and other outbuildings.

"You think this is enough?" Craig asked me.

"It's going to have to be for now. We'll get them started and see how well they measure up to the task," I replied.

"Brian said they wanted guns. What are we going to do about supplying them?" Craig asked.

"For now, nothing. They have a few and a limited amount of ammo. I don't feel comfortable letting them know what kind of arsenal we have just yet, and I'm not giving them anything until I do."

"Mums the word, Dad."

"You got that right."

We pulled into the yard in front of Carol's old place. I was not completely comfortable with anyone living here, but it was the right thing to do. My views on strangers had begun to change, and I was realizing we couldn't survive any of this, much less come out of it without helping others.

Wendy came out the back door as we stopped. She waved and said, "Hello, John."

I waved back, and she continued, "Where are the soldiers?"

"Doing soldier stuff, Wendy. We need them to protect us out here," I said as I got out of the truck.

"You think those people are going to come up here after they get done with their mayhem in Shawano?" she asked, stopping near the steps.

"It's not just them," I said. "We've had trouble with others, too. Seems the scum of the earth has crawled out from under the rocks where they've been hiding and want to take everything. They don't care who they hurt."

"We had problems with small gangs and motorcycle gangs in Shawano, too," she said. "We managed to run them off."

"We buried them," I said.

The concerned look on her face when she heard my words gave me a bit of a pause. I turned and looked back at Craig, who was walking around the truck and heading in our direction. He heard my comment, and the slight grin on his face, coupled with a raised eyebrow, signaled he had a similar concern about the look on her face.

"You killed them," she said.

"We did. There's no law out here, and the government people that were supposed to help are just as bad as some of these gangs."

She said nothing, so I continued. "You heard what one of your folks said about the FEMA camps over to the east. There's another in Wausau, and they've been up here trying to force their idea of some kind of perverse new world order, too."

"You bury them, too?" she asked.

"A couple. We've buried some of our own, too." My mind went back to finding Carol. And so many others…

"I'm sorry you had to do that. We couldn't bury our people, wouldn't have been able to anyway; there were too many…" Her voice had a tone of sadness in it as she ended her words.

"We brought you some things to help get you started," I said, quickly changing the subject. "We've got tools, some seeds for after we build a greenhouse, and other things to help start making firewood."

"Winter is coming soon, or so I once heard on a TV series," she said, her voice now a little more upbeat.

"Yes, it is, and without all the modern conveniences we used to have, it will be a tough, cold one too," I replied. "What we have here won't make it easy, but it will help get you through this first winter."

"I harbor no illusions, John. Some of the people may not get through the winter," she said. "Some here don't know what to do, and I don't even know what to tell them to do."

"We'll help where we can. We're all learning. I can guarantee you there are things we don't even know we need yet. If we work together, we can survive. We'll worry about the *thrive* part later."

"What do we have to do," a voice behind me said.

I turned my head toward the person speaking. It was Zach Strayker, the young guy who had voiced his rather strong sentiments when we first met with the Shawano group.

"Zach, isn't it?" I said as I gathered my thoughts for a better reply.

"Yes, Mr. Henry," he answered.

"Let's get you off on the right foot. My name is John, Mr. Henry was my dad and he's not here," I said with as big a grin as I could make. "As to what do we have to do? We have a lot of preparations to make. We've got to get these houses you folks are staying in ready for winter. Check the fireplaces because that's what you'll be cooking in, not to mention keeping you warm. That also means you'll need firewood and *a lot* of it. We don't have enough time to cut enough, but we can start. You'll be chopping it all winter, too.

"We need to build a greenhouse out of windows so you can grow some produce. You aren't going to live all winter off of venison and stay healthy. You'll have to dig a pit for it, too, essentially a basement. Take it below the frost line so you can have a longer growing season, maybe even year-round."

"Seems like a lot of work and a lot of risk, with no guarantees," Zach replied.

I shrugged. "It is. If you want to survive, then what other choice do you have," I said, anger building inside of me.

"Some might want to go to the FEMA camps; they have food and shelter there," he replied.

"Sure, that's an option, and anyone who wants to can exercise that option. I thought I heard you knew about the one in Green Bay and that it wasn't a good place. But if you want to go, I'd suggest starting now. It's a long walk to Wausau or Green Bay."

"Yeah, I said I'd heard that. It may still be better than trying to survive the winter out here," he said.

I could see the man was defeated and wasn't about to argue with him. We'd all gone through tough times with tougher times ahead. "Again, that's your option. If you're going to stay here, I have to tell you, there are no free rides, and the work is going to be hard."

"You have vehicles. Can't you drive those of us who want to go to these camps?"

"To begin with, we aren't a taxi service. Secondly, we don't have the fuel for long excursions like that, and lastly, I don't want to see anyone go to those camps."

"That hardly seems fair," he said a bit too quickly for my liking.

My temper was starting to rise, and I was losing the battle to control it. "Zach, fair used to happen once a year, usually in the fall, and it involved farm animals and good tasting food that wasn't healthy for you."

"Zach, I think John is trying to help us. These are tough times, and you know that. Why don't you go get some of the others and help this young man unload that truck," Wendy piped in.

Zach and I locked eyes again, and like before, it lasted about five seconds. "Yes, Ms. Slovack," he said. He then walked off, presumably to get help to unload the truck.

"Thank you," I said. "I was getting angry."

"I understand, John. I've been teaching school for a long time, and I can tell when boys are measuring body parts in the schoolyard. He's stressed out after all of this, that's all. He'll come around."

"I hope you're right. The last thing we need is that kind of trouble. I don't take to it well, and I don't deal with it in a way that makes a lot of people very happy."

"Let's go get some people together and figure out who can do what," she suggested, taking my arm by her hand and steering me toward the yard to a group that had gathered there.

As we walked, I chuckled and said, "Measuring body parts. You don't mince words much, do you?"

"It is what it is. You just deal with it," she answered.

I was starting to like this woman. This *could* work out after all.

··◆◆◆··

King left Harrigan's office with a spring in his step. It was time for the mission to begin. Walking down the hallway and into the Assembly Hall, he shouted, "Jackson, Leonard, Sibilski, Gully. Get your gear; it's time."

The other men in the hall watched as the four men grabbed their kits, MOLLE II packs or Modular Lightweight Load-carrying Equipment, and weapons.

As they headed out the door, King said, "Each of you stop by the Arms Room, draw 300 rounds of 5.56 and 60 rounds of 9mm. Assemble in the lot outdoors and load your magazines. I'll join you directly." As ordered, the men trooped out in a line and headed for the Arms Room.

He found Thomas quickly. "Sergeant Thomas, I need two vehicles, two drivers, and two assistant drivers for a short trip," King said. "It's mission time, Sergeant."

"Yes, Sir," Thomas replied. "Where are we going, sir?"

"It's mission time, Sergeant. The team and I are heading out for our mission."

"Yes, Sir," Thomas said enthusiastically.

King went to his room, grabbed his kit and weapons, and headed for the parking lot. He had cleaned and loaded all of his magazines earlier in preparation for the mission.

I've not led a mission like this before. I'm glad the colonel believes in my abilities.

Leaving the Armory building, he found his four men where they had commandeered a picnic table for their loading activity. The cardboard boxes of ten-rounds on stripper clips were lying about on the wooden table. The *ziiipp* of 5.56 rounds being pushed through the adapter and into the 30-round magazines, coupled with the light chatter of the four men, gave King confidence that the men were ready.

"You men almost finished?" King asked.

"Yes, sir," the men each replied singularly.

A shuffling of feet on the loose blacktop of the parking area caused King to turn and look behind him. Walking past the charred and twisted hulls of two Humvees that had been destroyed in the recent raid was Sergeant Thomas and four men. Each of them was dressed in the standard black FEMA jumpsuit, boots, and baseball-style caps. The four men carried M4s and wore the Army Tactical Combat Vest.

"Here are your drivers and assistant drivers, Lieutenant," Thomas said.

"Very good, Sergeant. Thank you," King replied. "That's all I need you for."

"Yes, sir," Thomas said and went back toward the Armory.

"You men get your vehicles and drive back here. Once we are loaded, I'll tell you where we are going. Your part of this trip shouldn't take more than an hour. You won't miss breakfast," King said.

Silently the men left and began to conduct their Preventive Maintenance Checks and Services or PMCS prior to heading out. These steps were designed to ensure that everything was in working order as it should be before a vehicle was used for the day. After a brief 15 minutes, the men completed their tasks and drove to where King and his men were waiting.

After a few minutes of loading their equipment into the back of the Humvees, King climbed into the front passenger seat of the lead Humvee and said, "Move out, Driver."

··✦✦◆✦✦··

Rahn and Brian had made their arrangements and were heading to Crandon to meet with Yerks and his commander, Captain Eric Handy. Johnson was once again driving, with Schwartz in the turret. The team had become solid over the last few months, and with the exception of the raid on the Armory that Rahn and Johnson took without Schwartz, the team had done everything together. A natural confidence of the group seemed to radiate from all of them, a confidence that came from the brotherhood of arms, shared risk, and in the words of Johnson, "Living so close together that you can tell when someone has gas just by the look on their face."

"You think this meeting is going to be productive?" Brian asked Rahn.

Rahn was sitting in the seat behind him as Brian, because of rank, was riding in the front passenger seat.

"I think so. Charlie said that the captain was irritated over what he heard FEMA was doing and that's why he made the decision for their detachment to *not* join them in Wausau," Rahn shouted back. The noise inside the Hummer preventing normal conversation.

"We could use them," Brian replied. "We can't sustain any effort against them for too long. Soon, we'll start taking on more casualties, Jake and his people will want to go back to the Rez, and that just leaves us. If we don't end this soon, we're screwed."

"I hear ya', Chief," Rahn answered.

"Is it that bad, Chief?" Johnson asked from the driver's seat.

Brian gave him a sideways glance. "Not yet, but it will be. It's math."

"Math," Johnson said.

"Yep, math. They have more manpower, access to supplies we can't get except to steal, and the essentials—food and water, and all that. So, yeah Johnson, math. I hope you paid attention in school."

"I took general classes, Chief, but I can add and subtract."

"Then you know exactly what I mean," Brian said. *I hope we don't do too much subtracting, either.*

"Those refugees from Shawano going to be any help?" Rahn asked.

"Not really," Brian replied. "A few maybe, but they're going to be more of a burden than a benefit. At least for now. Craig said one of 'em was a bit negative. He thought Dad was gonna punch the guy, but that the school principal quieted things down."

"Just what we need, problems on top of problems," Rahn said.

"It will be no problem. Dad will see to that," Brian said.

Johnson at the steering wheel of the Humvee had entered Crandon and made the turn onto Highway 8 toward a Best Western motel.

A short distance later, they saw a desert camou-flaged Humvee parked under the canopy of the front entrance of the motel. Two soldiers were stand-ing outside the vehicle, one of them waving as they pulled up behind them and stopped.

Brian was the first one out, not in uniform but his standard Army Camouflage Uniform pants with his tan boots, the pants bloused over the top of the boots, and a tan t-shirt under a very worn old school forest camouflage-patterned Battle Dress Uniform or BDU jacket. He had remembered to pin his rank insignia on the tab in front of his jacket.

The two soldiers, both young once-enlisted men, looked at him in bewilderment.

Brian had that effect on people because of his weightlifting. Then, seeing the rank insignia on his collar, they did what soldiers do when they are in doubt, they saluted sharply.

As Brian returned their salute, he heard Rahn come up behind him. "Your first sergeant and com-mander inside?" Rahn asked.

"Yes, First Sergeant," one of the men replied. "Let me go tell them you are here." He turned and went inside, coming out with First Sergeant Charlie Yerks and a man who appeared to be in his thirties with male pattern baldness, glasses, and an overly large nose that looked like he had been a boxer at one time. Both men wore the Army ACU uniform with their rank displayed on a patch in the center of their chest.

Knowing he had to play by the rules today, Brian walked over, saluted the man who he believed was Captain Handy, and said, "Glad you agreed to join us, Captain."

Captain Handy returned the salute and said, "Can't say it's a pleasure, but that's not because of you. It's this shit storm we're all living in right now."

"It does suck," Brian said. "I guess we'll just have to dust off that old saying about embracing the suck and get down to work."

"I'm just an engineer, Chief," Handy replied. "I'm here to listen to you combat experts and see how I can help."

Sensing he was now more or less in charge, Brian said, "I guess we should go inside. We'll bring you up-to-date on what is happening and what we *think* is happening. Then, I'll share our plan with you, and we'll see what you have to say."

Without waiting for a reply, Brian turned his head and said, "First Sergeant, you have those maps?"

Rahn held them up without speaking.

"Well then, let's do this," Brian said, and the men went inside the Motel, their teams remaining outside.

··•◆•··

The two-vehicle convoy of black Humvees stopped on Harmon Road just before Elton Creek. The seemingly abandoned home across the road was the only sign of any habitation. Exiting the lead vehicle, King waved his four-man team to assemble on him.

"Jackson and Leonard, go check out that house and see if anyone is living there."

"Yes, sir," the two men said as they dropped their packs and trotted across the road, their M4s held at a high port.

"Gully," King ordered, "you and Sibilski go ahead of us where the road intersects. Take up positions and watch both directions, left and right. If you see anyone, one of you come back here and let me know. Do not be seen or engage anyone, am I clear?"

"Yes, sir," they replied, and dog trotted up the road toward the intersection about a quarter mile away.

Reaching into the back of the lead Humvee, King removed his pack, placing it on the ground next to Jackson's and Leonard's packs. Leaning into the vehi- cle, he said, "Okay, Driver, you two can turn around and head back to the armory. Don't stop for anything. If you see anyone, try and radio me a message on our Sincgars."

"Yes, sir, Lieutenant," the driver said as the assistant drivers entered the front passenger seats.

King closed the door, and the two vehicles executed a U-Turn and headed west back toward the armory.

As they drove away, Jackson and Leonard returned from checking out the house across the road.

"It's empty, sir. Looks like no one has been in it for a while," Jackson said.

"Very good, Jackson," King said.

"Sir, are we going to set up in the house?" Leonard asked hopefully.

The question caused King to smile, and he said, "Nice try, Leonard. No. We're going to move out and set up a rustic base camp in the woods ahead. I want to be near the fish hatchery, but we will not enter it or use it. Major Wolfe told me there are hand pump wells there, and we may use them for water, but we'll only do that at night. We aren't here to be seen. We're here to get information."

"Yes, sir," Leonard replied, the disappointment in his voice evident.

"Grab your gear, and let's join Sibilski and Gully up ahead," King ordered.

After the team joined up, and hearing no one had been seen or heard down either direction of the road, they moved forward into the woods to their right, finding a game trail to follow. It proved to be a good choice as they passed two farmhouses that appeared to have residents. Their trek lasted a couple of hours, and as the day was ending and the sun started to set, King ordered a halt in a small clearing just across the Evergreen River near a large, cleared farm field.

"Let's get set up here," he said as he dropped his pack and surveyed the area. Each of the men dropped to the ground, their exhaustion after hiking with full packs getting the better of them.

"You men, get up and center on me," King ordered.

With a series of groans and moans, the four men pushed themselves up and joined King.

"Noise discipline is in effect from here on out. We only speak in whispers. At night, I want two men guarding when we are in camp. During the day, we will have one man awake at all times. There will be no fires. Use the heating element in your MREs if you want hot chow," King explained.

"What about coffee, sir," Sibilski asked. "We have to have coffee."

"We'll suffer with cold coffee for now."

"Yes, sir," Sibilski said without much enthusiasm.

"Get your gear unpacked," King said. "Keep your spare ammo handy but covered. I don't want to risk it getting wet. I'm going over to the edge of that farm field up ahead and taking a look. When I get back, we'll make our plans for reconning the area, seeing what's here, and accomplishing our mission."

"Yes, sir," the men replied softly.

"Jackson, get that Sincgars operational and do a commo check. I want to see if we have the range," King ordered.

"Yes, sir, Lieutenant," the youngest member of the team responded.

As King walked toward the farm field, Jackson went through his pack, getting the radio and spare batteries.

I am feeling good right now, King thought. *I am feeling real good.*

······◆··◆·◆◆··

Linda, Donna, and I were at the garden inspecting the herbs they had planted and discussing which ones we should move into our new greenhouse. The six foot by twelve foot building, built with windows scavenged from Quint's old house and some scrap lumber, wasn't pretty, but it was going to work. The late summer weather was already cool, and inside the greenhouse, it was hotter than hell. Come winter that would be good. Right now, it was worse than a sauna, and I was afraid anything we put in there would die from heatstroke. The ladies said I was overreacting. We'd just open a window. The bigger issue with winter was just how warm the greenhouse would get in Northeastern Wisconsin. *Or not.*

They both laughed hysterically at the bad joke.

I suggested we dig out the floor of the greenhouse to below the frost line, line it with rocks to help keep the floor from being too muddy and extend our ability to grow year-round. As we continued our discussion about who would dig the pit and which plants we would keep growing over the coming winter months, Sam came up to us. I was surprised to see him outside of the barn and his radio room.

"Sam, what brings you out here? Aren't you afraid the sun will burn you to a crisp," I said, trying to show the ladies real humor instead of lame window jokes.

"Funny, John, I needed a break and to stretch my legs. I heard something on the radio that has me curious and wanted to tell you about it," he said.

"What's that?" I asked, taking a few steps away from Donna and Linda.

"I was scanning frequencies and picked up a transmission on the National Guard Armory frequency."

"Oh, what were they saying," I asked, my heart picking up an extra beat at the possibility of more stress coming our way.

"It was a commo check. The operator repeated himself several times, 'Antigo Base, this is Team 1, commo check.'"

"Was there a response?" I asked.

"No, just them trying to do the check," Sam answered.

"What do you think," I said.

"Could be nothing. Could be they are sending out patrols and are too far away for Antigo to hear them. It's that last one that concerns me. They may be out here again."

"Did you contact our people?" I asked.

"Yeah, but no one has seen anything. They said they'd be extra observant," Sam replied. "It's about all we can do, and with Brian and Rahn gone, I thought I'd tell you."

Sam's words must've been powerfully loud, because as he said them, the roar of a Humvee filled the air. I saw Brian and Johnson sitting in the front seat of it as it pulled in the driveway.

"Well, speak of the devil," I said to Sam. Sam and I headed to meet them, Linda and Donna staying at the garden.

"How'd it go?" I shouted as Brian was exiting the vehicle.

"Pretty damn good," Brian replied.

Rahn had also gotten out, leaving Schwartz and Johnson to take the Hummer to what had become our small and surprisingly growing motor pool. We had our four Humvees, two black Humvees compliments of the boys from FEMA, a couple of motorcycles that two of the Guard boys, Bennet and Travis, had rebuilt from the battle with the motorcycle gang, the UTV, and my truck.

"Well, what's that mean?" I asked.

"We have another dozen men plus a bunch of combat engineer shit, is what that means," Brian said. He held his hand up in the air waiting for Rahn to "give him five." Rahn left him hanging, and Brian harumphed in mock disgust.

"It went real good, John," Rahn explained. "We have twelve more guardsmen, all combat engineers, plus Charlie and his commander, Captain Eric Handy."

"Very good. What about equipment?" I asked.

"They have mines, coils of barbed wire, pioneer tools, and a shit ton of C-4," Brian said.

"A shit ton? Just how much is a shit ton," Sam asked.

"They have 20 60-pound boxes of C-4," Rahn said. "Charlie told me they were getting ready to train by helping out a state construction project when all of this hit. They were well stocked."

"That ain't exactly a ton, but damn, that's good," I said. "How much do we get?"

"Charlie's sending us two 60-pound boxes and some pioneer tools. I figured those refugees could use some more shovels, rakes, and axes," Brian said.

"Good thinking. What about ammunition, that kind of stuff?" I asked.

"He said they have some, but not much, about 2500 rounds of 5.56 per man and around 500 rounds of 9mm per man. I'm trading them a case of 5.56 for the C-4," Rahn said.

"Can we spare the 5.56?" I asked.

Smiling, Rahn said, "On the one hand, we have a shit ton of 5.56. On the other hand, you never have enough ammo. I figure the C-4 will make up for the ammo."

"Little boys and their toys, Chris," I said, laughing.

"Yeah, now we can blow more shit up. We only had two explosive charges left after the last raid," he said.

"Speaking of raids," I said, "we need to talk about that. We may have some unwanted visitors."

"Visitors?" Brian asked.

"Yep," Sam said. "I picked up a commo check with someone trying to reach the armory when I was scanning frequencies. It mentioned a team. When there was no response from the armory, I figured they were either out of range or I couldn't hear the armory, which I have never had a problem doing. I figure we may have visitors."

"Have the patrols reported anything?" Rahn asked.

"No, and I contacted each of them, and they reported nothing seen. They know to be extra cautious and observant," Sam said.

"I'll make sure we brief the other patrols before they go out. If we have people sneaking and peaking around here, I want to find them and blind them," Rahn said.

"Let's go sit on the porch and talk about this raid," I said. "Sam, you care to join us?"

"Nah, I'm a squid, John. I don't know nuthin' 'bout no snake eater shit. We had clean sheets and hot food. We didn't sleep in the mud."

"Don't say I never asked," I said as I patted Sam on the shoulder.

"Besides, I should visit Gary. He's hurting bad. It's never been this bad before," Sam said.

"Yeah, I'm worried about him, too. Donna and Linda," I said, pointing over my shoulder with my head, "are doing what they can, but Linda says he has rheumatoid arthritis, and there isn't much herbal remedies can do for him."

"I'll keep him company for a bit. I can tell him some Marine jokes," Sam replied as he headed toward the cabin they shared.

"Well, gentlemen, shall we adjourn to the porch?" I asked, bowing at the waist and sweeping my hand as if giving a royal invitation.

"You betchya," Rahn said.

The shocked look on Brian's face over Rahn using what we thought was a despised expression was priceless.

CHAPTER 6

"Liberty, once lost, is lost forever."

—John Adams

The Shawano refugees had all gathered around Wendy Slovack. The short-in-stature-but-strong-personality leader of this small band was assigning work details. She still wore the clothes she had arrived in—dirty khaki pants, a purple t-shirt with a crewcut collar, and over the top of it, a grey button-down long sleeve shirt. Using the same voice I assumed that she had commanded the halls of Shawano High School with, she said, "I need a few of you to grab shovels and start making garden plots. If we mark them out now, even though it's too late to plant, it will be easier next spring. You three, grab axes and saws. You'll be our woodcutting detail. You can start in that patch of woods across the road. Take down only the trees that are lying down and dead or, if you find some that are standing and dead, cut those down. We need dry wood for now. We can cut green wood for curing later."

"Where do you want these garden plots, Ms. Slovack?" one of the men asked.

"Let's put them on the side where the field is, where they'll get good sunlight and be easy to get to," Wendy answered.

"I don't understand why we need to do this now," another man said a bit too loudly.

"Because we have to be ready for spring. John is sending some people here, and they'll help us pick a spot for a greenhouse to grow some produce over the long winter months. We can use some of the garden dirt for in there, too," Wendy said.

The tone of her voice said, don't argue with me and no one did.

"Zach, why don't you talk with them about building the greenhouses? You're the carpenter in the group."

"Okay, sure," he answered. "I don't want to be digging in the dirt or cutting down trees anyway."

Rolling her eyes, Wendy ignored his comment. "Let's get to work, people. We need to get these things done, especially getting that firewood cut. It's the only way we'll be able to stay warm and cook this winter," Wendy shouted as she clapped her hands together rapidly. "Bill, would you get some people together and start planning hunting parties. We'll need meat, and we can't run down to the Shop and Save to get it."

Wendy watched as each group headed out to begin their work. She had to laugh when she noticed that those picking the wood cutting tools were all men and that half of the people gardening were women.

As the workgroups walked away, she heard sounds of a pickup truck pulling into the driveway. It was John Henry, and he was with two women. John stopped the truck, and they got out. Waving at them, Wendy walked over to say hello.

"Good morning, John," she said with a big grin. "Who are these two?"

"Morning, Wendy," I said. "This is Linda Haines and Donna Henry."

"Hello, ladies," Wendy replied, shaking hands with each of them. "Good to meet you. I'm Wendy Slovack."

Donna and Linda shook hands and exchanged greetings. Being the curious type, Wendy said, "I assume you are John's wife?"

"Ex-wife," Donna replied. "My son, our son and I came up to stay with John during all of this."

"Oh, I'm sorry, I didn't realize…" Wendy said.

Donna interrupted her. "It's a common mistake, nothing to apologize for."

"And you, Linda, how are you related to this group?" Wendy asked.

"I guess, like you, I'm a refugee. John and his family took my two boys in and me. We had nowhere else to go," Linda replied.

She was a bit awkward with her explanation, and I could tell she was still uncomfortable with it.

"Well then," Wendy said, "I guess some of us do have something in common. John, you seem to be a collector of people."

"Not as many as you'd think," I answered. "We've sent many on their way. We can't help them all."

"Uh-huh," Wendy said.

As we were talking, Zach came up and immediately turned his attention to Linda. "Hi, I'm Zach," he said, extending his hand.

He and Linda shook hands as she introduced herself and Donna.

"I guess I'm supposed to get with one of you and talk about a greenhouse," he said.

"That would be me," Linda replied. "We just built a couple of them out of old windows, and it's working out good. John thought I could help you guys do the same. You'll need the produce."

"I'm glad it's you," Zach said. "I don't think he likes me very much."

Linda and Donna both laughed.

"John can be a bit gruff at times," Donna said. "You'll get used to him after a while."

"I am *not* gruff," I said, overhearing her, trying to lighten the mood. The man was right. I didn't like him, and that was evident from the last conversation he and I had. There was something about his attitude and wanting everything either handed to him or getting his way. Personally, I wished he'd taken me up on my offer for him to head to the camp in Wausau, though I'd never wish torture on any person.

Sensing another argument, Wendy said, "I've got a crew starting on gardening plots, some heading into the woods across the road to cut firewood, and another group hunting."

"I guess I'll help with the garden," Donna said and headed toward a small group of women starting to dig. "They look like they could use some assistance."

"You and I can talk about the greenhouse," Zach quickly said to Linda.

I wasn't sure how I felt about Zach monopolizing Linda's time, but she was here to help with that project, so there wasn't much I could say.

"Wendy, why don't you and I go see what else we can cook up to get people busy getting ready for winter? We have more tools coming, and we should talk about security measures, too."

"Then, let's get to work," Wendy said enthusiastically. "Idle hands and all that."

········◆◆◆········

King gathered his men together early, just as it was beginning to get light.

"We need to start planning how we're going to search the area," he said to them. "We'll start our patrols this morning. I don't want a lot of visibility by us during the day. All we are doing is familiarizing ourselves with the terrain and the area. We'll do the bulk of our searching in the evening when people are less inclined to be wandering around. Fires will be burning, lamps lit, and so on. We should be able to focus and find who we are looking for."

"Lieutenant, how far out will we be searching?" Leonard asked.

"This morning, I want each of us, less Jackson, who will stay here in the base camp, to head out for two hours and then return. That will give us a good idea of where we are and where we are in relation to that town, Lake something," King said.

"Lake View, Lieutenant," Gully offered.

"Thank you," King said. "We're close, and I want you to look for houses, groups of people, evidence of work in the woods, bridges, places to ford rivers and creeks. Do not be observed, and do not engage. If you see people, observe them, but do not approach them or get too close. Today is a scouting trip and nothing more."

"So where are we going exactly?" Leonard asked.

"Leonard, you and Sibilski will take this route." King pulled out his map of the area, an old tourist map that had been scavenged from a display at the Antigo Chamber of Commerce building. Using his finger, he pointed and said, "We are about here. Leonard, I want you and Sibilski to travel east until you come to this road that crosses the county road we took to get here. Cross that road and keeping it to your left, I want you to patrol for at least an hour. Stay low and slow, don't be observed, and if you see anyone, do not engage them in any way. Am I clear?"

"Yes, sir," Leonard and Sibilski said, keeping their voices low.

"Good," King replied. "We're probably about three miles from the town, so the closer you get to it, the more you need to be sure you aren't observed."

"Yes, sir," the men replied.

"When should we leave, Lieutenant?" Sibilski asked.

"You can go now. Remember, once you cross the county road, you patrol for two hours, then come back," King explained again. "Am I clear?"

"Yes, sir," the two men said as they stood up, put their kits on, and, grabbing their weapons, headed out toward the field and the forest on the other side.

"What about us, Lieutenant?" Gully asked.

"You and I are going here." Taking his finger, King pointed to the area to the west of where the other two men would patrol. We will patrol this area, and head toward this small lake. That lake looks like a good site for either a cabin or our next patrol base. Jackson."

"Yes, sir," the man replied.

"While we're gone, I want you to make some lean-to shelters for all of us. Nothing fancy. My old football injury is telling me the weather is gonna change, and we'll probably get some rain. Don't make noise chopping down trees. Take your time and make sure you stop every now and then to listen. Walk around a little and make sure no one has discovered you."

"Yes, sir," Jackson said.

"Gully, you ready?" King asked as he began putting on his kit.

"Yes, sir, ready as I'm gonna be," Gully responded.

"Let's go. Keep an eye out, Jackson, and stay alert."

"Yes, sir," both men said as King began to walk away.

Gully turned back toward Jackson and said in a whisper, "What a cluster fuck." Then, he turned and followed King.

··✦✦✦··

Zach and Linda walked to the rear of the house, the southside, which opened up to a large unplowed field behind it. Linda stopped, folded her arms across her chest, and slowly scanned the yard. "I think this is the best place to put them," she said.

"Why here?" Zach asked. "And what do you mean by 'them'?"

"Here, because it's the south side of the property, and this area will get the most sun. Them because we won't build just one big greenhouse; we don't have the means to do that. We should build at least two or maybe three smaller ones, about five feet wide and maybe 10 feet long each."

"That's a lot of lumber and windows," Zach said.

"Not as many as you'd think." She softened her words with a smile. "We have plenty of old abandoned houses around here that have the right kind of windows. The lumber we either have, or we can take some walls down inside one of the abandoned homes and salvage the wood there."

"You seem to know your stuff," Zach said as he took a step closer to her.

"Thank you. I always wanted to build one of these, and I studied up when I was back home. After I ended up here, we built two at John's place. They turned out pretty good."

"So, are you and John, um, are you…" Zach stumbled through the words.

"Oh no, we're just good friends. He's really a nice man, and he's been so kind to me and my boys," Linda explained.

"You and your boys? Are you married?" Zach asked.

"No, divorced."

"Interesting," Zach replied.

"Why is that interesting?" Linda asked.

"Well, a good-looking woman up here, and she's not married, you know, it's interesting," he answered with a shrug.

"In case you haven't noticed, this is *not* an environment where people go looking for relationships, and I am one of those *not* looking," she said, a firmness in her voice that was almost cold in its delivery.

He put his hands up in defense. "Hey, relax. All I'm saying is that you're pretty, and any man would have to be blind not to respond to pretty."

Linda glared at him. "I don't like it when people say I'm pretty. Can we get back to the greenhouse projects, please?"

"I was just being friendly. Can't blame a guy for that," Zach said.

"You seem like a nice guy, Zach. Let's keep it that way. If you're looking for something else, I'm not interested," Linda said sharply.

···◆◆◆···

I was with Wendy and Donna as Wendy was explaining her thoughts behind the plots. I wasn't paying much attention as I was watching from across the yard at Zach and Linda talking. Zach made me uncomfortable, and to be honest, I didn't like him. He reminded me of some smarmy salespeople I'd known throughout the years, always looking for an angle to benefit them. I didn't like the way he reacted to Linda, either.

"John," Wendy said. "John, are you listening?"

"Huh… Oh, I'm sorry, I was distracted. What were you saying?"

"I was explaining our placement of the garden plots. Donna thinks a series of smaller plots are a good idea, and I agree. What do you think?" Wendy asked.

"Um, I like the idea of smaller ones because they are easier to access and work. But you're gardening for a larger group, and um, I think a couple of bigger plots might be better. You can use a few smaller ones for things like tomatoes and beans," I replied, my mind still on Linda and Zach.

"I think that's a good idea, too. I see your point," she replied.

"Have you ever considered square foot gardening, Wendy?" Donna asked. She gave me a look as if she knew where my attention was and where I was looking.

"No. What's that?" Wendy asked.

"It's pure genius," Donna said as she began to explain the process.

I tuned them out as I continued to watch Linda. *You're too old to go getting jealous, John. And you really have no call to act like this.* Realizing that's exactly what I was doing, I said, "I think I'll leave you to the expert, Wendy. I'm gonna go see how your woodcutters are doing across the road."

"That's a good idea, John. Why don't you go do that," Donna said.

The look on her face said she thought I should remove myself before I did or said something I would later regret. She'd seen me staring, more like glaring toward Zach and Linda.

"Wendy and I can figure out what to do, and then we can discuss herbs and things they can grow in the greenhouse once that gets built. Somebody should be digging that hole for the greenhouse you keep talking about."

"Once we decide where to put it, I'll have people start digging," Wendy said.

I didn't waste any time and turned quickly to head across the road and get away from a situation that could become embarrassing for everyone if I stayed. Still, I didn't like the way Zach had been looking at Linda.

··◆◆◆··

Brian and Rahn had returned from their second meeting with Yerks and his men. They were unloading the C-4 and putting it in our now well-defined arms room in the barn.

"We should build something away from the barn to store this. If something were to happen, we'd lose everything," Rahn said as he watched Myer, Klotz, and Owens carry cases of explosives into the barn.

"As much as I hate building anything right now, I think you're right. A fire or spontaneous combustion of anything could cause us a problem," Brian replied as he chewed on a long strand of straw he had grabbed from a bale inside the barn. "I'll get a couple of the guys to start on that. We better do it soon, too. Winter is coming, and before you know it, the ground will freeze up. It will be like digging in concrete."

"Might as well build two," Rahn said. "We can store the ammo in one and the other explosives in the other."

We still had a good supply of grenades and claymores, as well as both 5.56 and 9mm ammo. Keeping it separate and away from the buildings we used for people to live in was a good idea. As the weather turned colder, we'd start using the stoves and even firepits to keep warm. We didn't need to add spontaneous fire to the risk as a way of losing what we had.

"The boys are not going to be happy about another construction project, First Sergeant," Brian said absently as he watched the trio carrying the explosives into the barn.

"Better that than one big boom in the middle of the night," Rahn said.

As they continued watching, Mike, Caleb, and Ethan approached. The older two boys were carrying their .22 rifles. Like the adults, the rifles had become a part of them everywhere they went.

"Hi, Dad," Mike said.

"S'up, Mike?" Brian asked.

"We're gonna go hunting for squirrels and rabbits. Wanna come with us?" Mike asked.

"I can't, buddy. I have to do army stuff," Brian said.

Mike huffed. "You're just standing here talking. That's not army stuff."

"Mike, your dad is doing army officer stuff. He's supervising," Rahn said with a smirk.

"Grampa said that supervising is what people in charge do, First Sergeant," Mike said.

Brian and Nancy had insisted on Mike being respectful of military family adults and not call them by their first names. As an army family, using rank in place of mister or missus was common.

"So, you won't go hunting with us, Dad?"

Brian shook his head. "Not today, buddy. Have you asked your Uncle Craig?"

"I can't find him," Mike said. The disappointment in his voice was clear.

"Did you go to his cabin?" Brian asked.

"Yeah. I knocked on the door, but no one answered," Mike said.

"Mr. Brian," Ethan said, "we looked everywhere. Mom said we can't go alone because of what happened to Mike. We want to go hunting and need someone to take us."

"Johnson!" Rahn yelled.

"Yes, First Sergeant," a voice from inside the barn answered. A few seconds later, Specialist Johnson emerged from the barn. Like Brian, he had a piece of straw hanging from his mouth as he approached Rahn and Brian.

"You look like you need a diversion," Rahn said to Johnson.

"That sounds like extra duty, First Sergeant," Johnson said with a bit of wariness.

"It is, soldier," Rahn said. "Go get your weapon and take these boys hunting."

"Sweet," Johnson replied as he turned to get his weapon.

"Is that how you reply to an order, Specialist Johnson," Rahn said with a somewhat serious but humorous look.

"No, First Sergeant. I'll be happy to take them hunting, First Sergeant," Johnson replied with great exaggeration.

"Much better, Johnson, much better," Rahn said, laughing.

The cheers of the three boys and the excited way Johnson ran back into the barn to get his weapon were a reminder of days long ago when things were normal.

"You boys listen to Specialist Johnson," Brian said.

"Specialist Felix is good to us, Dad; we'll listen to him," Mike said.

"Yeah, and he gives us chocolate and candy from his army food," Caleb piped in.

"Oh, he does," Rahn said. "I may have to rethink this hunting guide thing."

Brian laughed and said, "Nah, just a bunch of kids going out and doing kid stuff. Oh wait, a bunch of kids… Yeah, you better rethink it, First Sergeant."

"No, Dad, we'll be good, and we'll listen to Specialist Felix," Mike said pleadingly.

"How'd you learn his name was Felix?" Brian asked.

"Caleb couldn't say Johnson, so he said to call him by that name. I said we had to be more respectful of adults, and Ethan said so, too. So, we call him Mr. Felix. Except I call him Specialist Felix cuz I'm an army brat, and that's what we do," Mike explained.

"Yes, we do, son," Brian said. "I was an army brat, too, remember?"

Before Mike could answer, Specialist Johnson returned and said, "You men ready to go?"

"We aren't men; we're little boys," Ethan said.

"Well then, I guess we can't go hunting. Little boys don't get to hunt; men get to hunt," Johnson said with a mock-serious look on his face.

"We're little men," Mike quipped. Like his dad, he was developing a quick wit and a sense of humor.

"Then men, let's go hunting," Johnson ordered, and the three boys followed him down the path between the cabins and toward the meadow and woods beyond.

As they distanced themselves from the barn, Caleb said, "Mr. Felix, I don't have a gun. I can't hunt."

"I have a gun, Caleb, and if one of these two won't let you shoot theirs, you can shoot mine. How's that sound?" Johnson whispered.

"You are *so* cool, Mr. Felix. Thank you. You're as cool as Mr. John."

"Why, thank you, Caleb," Johnson said.

"What, what. What did you say?" Mike and Ethan chanted.

"Nothing, just me and this little man here talking," Johnson said.

Brian and Rahn watched them as they walked toward the meadow, three little boys and maybe one big boy heading into the woods.

"He'll take good care of them, Chief," Rahn said confidently.

"I'm not worried about that, Top. I'm just thinking how my dad and I never did that, and now my son and I aren't doing it, either. Same reason, different times."

"There's plenty of time for that, Chief," Rahn said as he put his hand on Brian's shoulder. "Like your boy said, he's an army brat. He understands."

"Yeah, I guess you're right," Brian said. "That don't make it right, though."

CHAPTER 7

The day had ended on a good note. The tree cutters worked themselves almost to death and managed to get nearly three full cords of wood cut and piled up. The hard part would be splitting it. Without a power splitter, that meant mauls, axes, and wedges. Then they'd have to stack it so that the inevitable snow and ice wouldn't damage it.

I promised Wendy I'd bring some wedges for them tomorrow or the next day. We'd probably store the wood in Carol's old garage. No one had any cars to keep in it, and they were going to use it as a stable for a couple of horses we'd bring them.

As we drove back to the cabin, I thought I'd send Craig, Allen, or Sajan on horseback. I didn't want to keep using gas as if it would always be available.

I listened to Donna as she was explaining to Linda about the gardens and how we needed to get those greenhouses built soon so that plants could get started there, too. Food over the winter was going to be a challenge for all of us. We weren't going to starve to death, and I could see a big pot of perpetual soup on the stovetop. Fortunately, Carol's house had an old wood-burning cookstove in the cellar, and Wendy said she would have some of the men move it into the upstairs and figure out how to vent a chimney to it. That was good. They'd need it.

······◆◆◆····

King and Gully moved through the woods north of the town of Lake View. Aside from a few houses and a small family farm with some dead animals and a burned-out building, they saw nothing else.

"That place was a mess, Lieutenant," Gully said as he wiped heavy perspiration from his face with the sleeve of his shirt.

"I believe that is the farm where Captain Jamison was killed. It looks like someone came back and removed the bodies of the people who were there," King replied. "We are probably close to where the damn Henrys have their homestead. Keep your eyes open and watch for any signs of people. Living people."

"Yes, sir," Gully said.

The two men, with a new sense of caution, proceeded on their way. They watched for anything moving or any signs that would tell them they were close to their target.

"*Crack, crack,*" the sharp sounds of a small-caliber rifle off in the distance caused both men to drop to their knees. As they kneeled and looked to see where the sounds came from, more sounds followed.

"Bam, Bam, Bam. Bam, Bam, Bam."

"That's rapid-fire, Lieutenant," Gully said.

"Bam, Bam, Bam." Three more shots sounded off in the distance.

"That's a military weapon; sounds like an M4," King replied.

"It's kinda far off, Lieutenant. Should we go check it out?" Gully asked.

"We've got about a half-hour until we have to turn back. Let's move forward and see what we can find. Keep your head on a swivel, Gully, eyes and ears open."

"Yes, sir," Gully replied as they both slowly stood up.

Keeping their weapons in a high port position, the two men moved quickly but cautiously through the woods, each watching for anything that might lead them closer to their objective.

···◆◆◆◆···

"What the hell is that?" Nancy asked aloud.

The sounds of gunfire traveled through the homestead as she stood outside near the garden. A rapid,

"Bam, Bam, Bam" from the woods behind the property made her jump and look around.

Brian and Sajan came running from the side of the house, Sajan carrying an AR and Brian with his always present M9 in a leg holster.

"Where are those shots coming from?" Brian yelled as he came to a halt next to Nancy.

"Bam, Bam, Bam. Bam, Bam."

"Back there, across the field in the woods," she nervously answered, her trembling voice signaling her fear and memories.

"Mike, Johnson, and the boys are back there," Brian shouted as he began to run toward the field and woods behind them. Sajan ran alongside him, both men beginning to breathe heavily.

The roar of an engine behind them caused both men to jump to the side as a Humvee pulled up next to them.

"Get in," First Sergeant Rahn shouted. Brian and Sajan hopped into the backseat of the vehicle as it sped off toward the back of the property.

"I heard nine shots," Rahn said. The intense and emotionless manner of his speech signaled his concern.

"It was definitely an M4 on burst," Brian replied.

Sajan, turning his weapon on its side, glanced down at where the selector switch was located. He saw three settings: semi, burst, and auto. Brian had told him to never use auto, and he knew that burst fired three rounds every time you pulled the trigger.

"Who's out back, Brian?" Sajan asked.

"Mike, Caleb, Ethan, and Johnson," Rahn replied for Brian.

"Can you drive faster, Owens?" an emotional Brian shouted.

With the accelerator already pushed to the floor, Owens pushed harder, willing the Humvee to go faster across the field and towards the woods.

··+◆+··

Johnson and Caleb walked behind the two older boys. The barely noticeable game trail they followed allowed them to move through the underbrush without getting slapped by branches and brambles, which was growing everywhere.

The two older boys were very serious in their approach. They wore ankle-high moccasins that Jake had shown Nancy how to make from tanned deer hide. The tanning process was a smelly and, according to Nancy, disgusting operation, but the outcome was wonderfully soft deerskin leather.

Their pants were cut-down jeans and handmade cotton from bolts of heavy cloth they had scavenged from abandoned homes in the area, which hung loose on the boys. Their shirts were made from small tan t-shirts that some of the National Guard soldiers had. Poor Caleb, the youngest and smallest of the trio, had to make do with hand-me-downs. Linda and Nancy both had laughed over the prospect of the three boys running naked through the woods, knowing full and well they would have if allowed. It didn't seem to bother him as Brian called him the most obstinate and adventurous kid he'd ever met since he met himself.

Now, the only sound in the woods was the crunch of their feet, becoming less audible as the boys' woodcraft skills improved and the occasional breeze that rustled the just-beginning-to-turn colors leaves in the trees. Caleb was his usual quiet self as Johnson tried to show him things as they passed. If he said anything in response to Johnsons prodding, it was "I know" or "My mom told me that."

As they continued through the woods, a smell began to develop that made Johnson's nostrils flare.

"Hold up, boys," he said to Mike and Ethan. He glanced around, trying to identify where the smell was coming from. He surveyed the perimeter of where they stood, searching for any sign or indicator. His eyes passed something that, at first, didn't register to him. When it did, his attention snapped back on the dark object he'd noticed. A black bear, eating something and utterly unaware of their presence.

Ethan and Mike, either not hearing Johnson or choosing to ignore him, had kept walking. They saw the bear at the same time Johnson did.

"Mike, a bear," Ethan said with excitement in his voice. Holding his rifle in both hands, he swung it up and pointed it in the direction of the bear.

Mike, hearing Ethan and seeing what he was doing, swung his rifle up into a shooting position, searching for the bear. He saw the bear about the time it raised its head and stared at the boys.

With a roar, the large black bear charged toward the boys.

"Shit," Mike shouted as he pulled the trigger of his .22.

"Crack."

If the small round even hit the bear, it didn't stop the animal from continuing its charge.

"Crack." Ethan fired almost immediately after Mike.

In an almost rehearsed move, both boys spun around and began running toward Johnson, scream-ing at the top of their lungs. Four short legs had never moved faster as the boys raced to safety, hoping the bear wouldn't catch them.

"Oh shit," Johnson said under his breath as he pushed Caleb behind him and pulled the charging handle back on his M4, chambering a round.

As he raised the weapon to his shoulder, he used his thumb to move the selector switch to burst, allowing him to shoot three times with a single pull of the trigger. He placed the front sight on the bear, but the boys kept getting into his line of sight.

The bear was quickly moving closer, and it was getting more difficult for a clean shot. Caleb was screaming, Mike and Ethan were screaming, and Johnson was shouting, "Get out of the way, get out of the way!"

It all seemed to take an eternity, but it all happened in a few seconds. It was then a miracle happened.

Mike tripped and fell face-first onto the ground, opening up a shooting lane for Johnson. He pulled the trigger. "Bam, Bam, Bam."

Three shots hit the charging bear, causing it to stagger as it continued to charge them.

Johnson fired again. "Bam, Bam, Bam."

The bear dropped to the ground, sliding forward in a tangle of branches, leaves, and dirt. It came to a stop a few short feet away from where Mike had landed. Johnson, with his weapon at the high ready position aimed at the bear, cautiously moved forward. "Get up, Mike," he said firmly.

Mike slowly stood up and dusted his hands and pants off. "Where's my rifle?" Mike asked, swiveling his head around, searching for the gun he had dropped when he tripped.

"You'll find it later," Johnson said. "Ethan, go to your brother."

"He's okay, Mr. Felix," Ethan said.

"Ethan, go to your brother, now," Johnson said firmly as he slowly walked toward the bear.

Stopping a few feet away, he watched the bear. Bleeding in several spots, a large part of the top of its head was gone from one of the bullets that struck it. The bear lay still in the dirt and didn't move, its tongue hanging out of its mouth.

Lowering his weapon slowly and then extending it with one hand, Johnson tapped the bear on one of its eyes.

The bear did not move.

Breathing a heavy sigh, Johnson said aloud, "It's dead." The thunder of three sets of small feet raced toward him as the boys' curiosity overcame any fears they may have had.

"What the fuck," Johnson said a little too loudly.

"That's a bad word, Mr. Felix. You'll get in trouble for that," Caleb said as he timidly approached the bear.

Johnson laughed heartily as his knees began to shake, and he slowly sank to the ground.

·· ⋅ ◆ ⋅ ··

Gully and King moved slowly through the woods. They had heard voices and the sounds of axes ahead of them, and the presence of people nearby had caused them to slow their progress. King held up his hand, signaling Gully to stop. Both men dropped to one knee.

King peered through the underbrush, his eyes taking quick snapshots as he tried to see how many were in front of them. Through the trees, they observed a collection of men standing around, holding saws and axes. The group looked east toward where the sounds of gunfire had come from. Their animated gestures and loud but unintelligible voices were clearly showing that they, too, were interested in the noises.

King needed to find a way around them if he and Gully were to discover the gunshots' source.

Realizing there was no way around the people ahead, he crawled back toward Gully and whispered, "Looks like it might be a large group. There is no way we can get around them in time to find out where those shots came from."

"Yes, sir," Gully whispered back.

"Let's head back about a hundred yards, and we'll figure out what our next steps are," King said.

The two men slowly made their way back down the trail until King signaled Gully to stop. Looking at his watch, he realized they had been away from their camp longer than he had told the other patrol.

"We're overdue. We need to go back to camp. We'll compare notes with Sibilski and Leonard, and then make plans for another patrol. I know we're close. Those gunshots and that work crew ahead seals that."

"Okay, Lieutenant. You want to take point, or should I?" Gully asked.

"You go ahead. I'll make sure no one is following us. Those people are close. I know they are."

··•◆•◆•◆•··

Owens slammed on the brakes as the Humvee just barely entered the woods. Before it came to a complete stop, Brian hopped out of the vehicle and raced into the woods, shouting, "Mike, Johnson!"

"Over here!"

As Rahn and Sajan came up behind Brian, the trio continued into the woods toward the voice.

"Over here," came the shout again. Recognizing the voice as Johnson's, the men rushed in that direction.

Brian was the first to see them. "Is everyone okay?" he asked, desperation in his voice.

"We're fine," Johnson replied. "The bear, not so much."

Johnson stood next to a large black furry mass on the ground. He held his M4 rifle in the crook of his arm, the muzzle pointing skyward. As soon as he saw Brian enter the clearing where they stood, he'd placed his right foot on top of the bear, striking a successful hunter pose. Two boys, Mike and Ethan, were circling the bear, poking at it with their rifles. Caleb stood next to Johnson, hands in front of him, clutching a short thick tree branch.

"Mike, you're safe." Brian ran toward his son.

Slightly startled at his dad shouting his name, Mike jumped slightly, but in typical young boy matter-of-fact fashion said, "Hi, Dad. Specialist Johnson shot a bear."

Brian stood there, staring at his son. Behind him, he heard Rahn and Sajan come to a stop.

"That's a big bear," Rahn said as he caught his breath.

"It's dead," Caleb said, causing Rahn to chuckle.

"Where is everybody?" another voice in the distance cried.

"Over here," Sajan responded.

A short while later, Owens came upon them. Seeing the bear, he said, "Damn, that's a big bear."

"It's dead," Caleb said again. "It was chasing Ethan and Mike."

"It was chasing Ethan and Mike," Brian parroted as he turned toward Johnson, his eyes flashing anger. "You were supposed to be watching them, Johnson. How did the bear end up chasing them?"

"Chief, I *was* watching them, and..." Johnson started.

Brian interrupted him. "How could they have been chased by a bear if you were watching them?"

"Chief, I was."

"Dammit, Johnson!" Brian shouted.

"Brian, let him explain," Rahn said as he put his hand on Brian's shoulder.

No one seemed to notice that he called Brian by his name instead of his rank. Brian nodded his head in response to Rahn's comment.

"Chief, I'm sorry," Johnson said. "We were walking down the trail. The boys were in front of me, looking in the trees for squirrels. I smelled something bad, dead. I looked around and saw the bear over there." He pointed toward where he first saw the bear. "It was eating something. As soon as I saw it, Mike and Ethan saw it. Then, it saw us, too, and charged. The boys tried to shoot it with their rifles, and…"

"Wait," Rahn said, interrupting. "They shot the bear with .22s?"

"Yes, First Sergeant," Johnson said.

"Damn, I'm impressed," Rahn said.

"Carry on with your story, Johnson," Brian said. He had calmed down as he listened.

"Yes, sir," Johnson said. "Anyways, the bear charged, the boys shot, and that just seemed to make the bear madder."

"Piss me off too if you shot me with a .22," Rahn muttered.

"First Sergeant, I'm trying to explain here," Johnson said in exasperation.

"Go ahead, Specialist. We're listening," Brian replied.

"So anyways, the boys shot and ran toward me. I had my weapon up, ready to shoot, but they were in the way, so I couldn't. Then Mike tripped, opening up a shot. So I took it." With the last words, Johnson stood a bit taller, proud of what he had done. "I did my best, Chief."

Brian stood by silently. He scanned Johnson to the bear, to Mike, Caleb, and Ethan, and back to Johnson. "You did good, Johnson. Thank you. You did good."

"Thank you, sir," Johnson replied.

"As for you two," he said, turning to face Mike and Ethan, "you don't shoot large animals with a .22."

"But Dad, the bullets are just as big around as the ones in the army guns," Mike said in defiance.

"Yes, they are, but the ones in the M4 are more powerful. They have more gun powder behind them," Brian explained.

"Yes, sir," Mike said.

"Specialist Johnson was out here to watch you boys, and you're lucky he was here. If you'd have shot that bear and he wasn't here, you could have been killed. Do you two understand me?" Brian said loudly.

"Yes, sir," Mike said.

"Yes, Mr. Brian," Ethan said, his voice trembling. "But Dad…"

"But what?" Brian replied.

"Nobody died," Mike said with a bit of a smirk.

Rahn shoved his fist into his mouth and turned, his shoulders rocking slightly as he suppressed a laugh.

"Excuse me, young man," Brian said.

"Nobody died," he repeated. "That's what the soldiers in the barn always say."

"You need to watch your mouth. Now, get down that trail and head toward the Humvee with Owens and Sajan," Brian ordered.

The three boys took off and headed down the trail out of the woods.

Rahn walked over to Brian and said, "But nobody died. Like father, like son."

"Fuck you, First Sergeant," Brian said, his grin taking up almost all of his face. "But you're right. He is just like me. My dad's gonna love this story."

CHAPTER 8

—Mark Twain

"I don't like this, Wendy," Zach said. "They aren't helping. We won't have enough food for the winter."

"They're helping, Zach," Wendy insisted. They stood in the kitchen of the main house. Zach was pacing, his frustration and anger telegraphed by his constant motion.

"We're supposed to grow food in a greenhouse built out of windows," he shouted. "Where are we getting the windows? How long will that take?"

"They're helping us, Zach. They are giving us tools, seeds, and helping us build what we need to survive."

"Bullshit. Oh, they're giving us stuff, sure, but not enough. They don't look like they're missing too many meals. They can give us more. We need *more* for everyone to survive, Wendy. We need more than tools and some old windows."

"It'll take time. They can't help us to the point that they hurt themselves. Use your head."

"Yeah, use my head. I tried to use it with that woman Linda. She's headstrong, and it has to be her way. I can cure that," he yelled. "She talked to me like I was stupid."

"You're acting stupid, Zach. And I'd leave that woman alone. Don't push her, or you'll bring trouble upon us. There's something between her and John. Don't get in the middle of that."

"He's too old for her. I ain't trying nothing anyway," he huffed.

"You didn't look like it to me. I'm warning you, Zach. Cool your temper and calm down. You've always been a hothead, and you need to stop right now," Wendy commanded.

He glared at her. "Or what?"

"Or you'll cause trouble we don't need. It won't be long before winter is here, and we need the Henrys to help us get through it. Use your head. Leave that woman alone and work with them. We *all* need to work with them."

"They aren't helping us," he shouted and walked out the door, slamming it behind him. "Fuck," he said to himself as he went across the yard and headed into the field behind the house. *They aren't gonna help us, and that girl isn't going to talk to me like I'm some kind of fool.*

··◆◆◆··

Leonard and Sibilski, hiding in the tree line several hundred yards from the house, watched as an angry man came out of the side door and headed into the field toward their location. Leonard, handing binoculars to Sibilski, said, "Check that out. Somebody isn't a happy camper."

Taking the binoculars, Sibilski observed the man as he moved across the field, stopped, shouted something they couldn't make out, and stomped away toward them. "He's obviously pissed about something. He's heading this way," Sibilski commented. "What should we do?"

"The lieutenant said no contact if we see anyone," Leonard replied.

"But if he sees us," Sibilski said. "What are we gonna do?"

"Let's wait and see what he does. If he sees us, we're probably screwed."

Reaching for the sheath knife hanging from his vest, Sibilski slowly drew it out and said softly, "I can take him out with this."

"Oh, the lieutenant will love that. Put the knife away. I doubt he'll come this far."

The words had no sooner left Leonard's lips when the man sat down in the field, resting his head in his hands.

"We may have something here," Leonard whispered. "We may have someone we can use."

"How are we going to do that? You gonna just walk up to him and say, hey, how'd you like to help us?" Sibilski said softly.

"That group King wants to know more about has people working around here. If we can get him alone, maybe we can make him talk; help us out," Leonard whispered back.

"Uh-huh, right."

They continued to watch the man as he sat in the field. After a few minutes, he rose and walked back toward the house.

"Let's get out of here and head back. We're overdue as it is, and we can talk to the lieutenant about this. Maybe he'll agree."

"I think he'll agree you have a hair-brained idea, is what I think," Sibilski said.

They lay there watching the man as he walked back to the farmhouse, stopped, and then went into the garage.

"Let's go," Sibilski said.

Slowly the two men rose and headed back into the woods. They had a long trek, and neither was looking forward to getting chewed out for being late.

··•◆•··

If I had a dollar for every time Rahn and Brian told the story of Mike and how "nobody died," I think I'd have about five dollars by now. They couldn't stop laughing, and all I could think of was my grandson was getting even for all of the smart-aleck things his dad had said to me throughout the years. Karma. That's what it was.

They had gone back out and brought the bear carcass in. Jake and some of his boys knew how to dress it out so that it wouldn't taste too gamey. We were waiting for a verdict on the condition of the hide as well. It wouldn't be long before we'd need to make more clothes, and I was pretty sure we'd find a use for a bearskin besides using it as a rug.

Rahn and Brian had gone off to finalize their plan for attacking the armory again. I wasn't sure how I felt about that. You can only poke the badger so many times before it rises up and takes a serious chunk out of you. Eventually, those FEMA boys would get smart and fight back with some skill. We weren't always going to be as lucky as we had been.

I'd left Brian and Rahn alone so they could plan their operation and went to spend some time with Gary. He was in obvious pain. He'd had these flare-ups of "Arthur" before. He liked to call arthritis Arthur. I had no idea what he was talking about the first time he used the name. Then he explained, Arthur-itis, and I felt dumb. It was so obvious.

Donna thought it was a combination of all the manual work we'd been doing, his age, and our diet. Gary wouldn't take any multivitamins we had found, which left him drinking a lot of echinacea and willow bark tea that Donna and Linda had concocted. He still had a good sense of humor, as he said if anything, his bladder was healthy from the workout it was getting from the tea.

As the sun began to drop below the trees, I knew it was time for me to go sit on the porch. I had a lot to think about, starting with the Shawano refugees and keeping them both alive through the winter, along with keeping most of them here. We'd need the manpower if FEMA came back, and of that, I had little doubt. It was just a question of when.

Jake and his people were going back to the Rez after the next armory raid. I couldn't blame them for that. It was their home, and they had family there.

We all believed that if it was successful, the raid would keep FEMA away from us through the coming winter, and hopefully, into next spring when civilization might start to come back.

Sam had heard over the radio that some groups were stabilizing, but there were still plenty of places where it was, to quote him, "downright medieval," with open warfare everywhere.

Even though I knew it would happen, it still amazed me how fast people could revert to barbarism and leave the civilized world behind.

I rounded the cabin and glanced at my chair. I noticed someone was sitting in it, which had become something just shy of a mortal sin. I was going to have to give a special dispensation for this one.

It was Mike sitting in my chair, actively talking with Caleb and Ethan. What the three of them were plotting wasn't yet clear, but the boys were very engaged in their conversation. They were so focused, none of them noticed me approaching until I stood in front of them and cleared my throat.

"Ahem," I said, trying to act gruff and menacing.

It worked. Fear washed over their faces.

"Sorry, Grampa," and "Sorry, Mr. John" was said simultaneously.

"What are you boys up to?" I asked. I guess I was overdoing the seriousness in my voice because Caleb slipped behind Ethan and Mike, using the older two as a shield.

"Nothin'," Mike replied.

"Yeah, Mr. John, we were just talkin'," Ethan piped in.

"When I was a little boy, and we were talking like you boys, it usually meant we were planning some adventure that would get us into trouble," I said, softening my voice in the hopes I wasn't terrifying them.

"You were a little boy?" Caleb asked, peeking at me from behind Mike and Ethan.

"Sure was, and I got into a lot of trouble, too," I replied, kneeling down so I could be at eye level with them. "I remember this one time when I was living in Florida, and my friends and I captured a wild baby pig. We drug it home with a rope." Those words no sooner left my lips, and I instantly regretted sharing that story. It was a red-haired pig we had rustled from a small herd a local farmer let run in the woods. He was not happy when he found out we had done that. He said he'd shoot us with rock salt if he caught us doing it again. We believed him, too!

"Wow, you captured a pig?" Ethan asked. "I thought pigs lived in pens."

"They do, Ethan. When I was a little boy in Florida, pigs also lived loose in the woods. Usually, we just chased them because they are very fast. The grown-up pigs could be dangerous, though," I explained.

"Do pigs live in the woods here in 'sconsin?" Caleb asked.

"Not yet, but I'm sure they will soon. Farmers will let them loose, or they've gotten loose on their own because they don't have feed for them. So, the pigs will live in the woods and eat wild nuts and berries like other animals."

"We need to go finds some pigs!" Mike shouted and took off at a run, the other two closely following him as the three whooping, shouting boys raced around the side of the cabin.

"That's a good story, John," a woman's voice said from the cabin doorway. The door creaked as she pushed it open. It was Linda.

Oh, darn…

•••◆◆◆•••

After a couple of hours of slow and cautious movement, Leonard and Sibilski made their way back to the basecamp that the FEMA team had created near the hatchery. King was pacing as he saw them approach.

"You're late," King said sharply.

"Sorry, Lieutenant, we had to wait for some guy to leave so we wouldn't be seen," Leonard replied.

"Some guy? What guy?" King asked.

"We got close to that town, Lake View. We were watching some people in a house across a field from where we were. A lot of people, maybe a dozen or so that looked like they were digging in the dirt. While we were watching, some guy stormed out of the house and walked into the field in our direction. We didn't want to move in case he saw us. So, we sat there until he left," Leonard explained.

"He didn't see you?"

"No, sir, he didn't see us," Sibilski confirmed. "We stayed real still, and he went back to the house. He never saw us, Lieutenant."

"You said a dozen people? Is that the group we're looking for," King asked.

"I don't know. I don't think so. We saw an old black pickup truck with a man and two women drive away," Leonard answered.

"Somebody has gas then. They could be the ones we're looking for. Which direction did they go?" King asked.

"They headed east toward town. We lost sight of them pretty quick," Leonard said.

"Good work," King said. He then explained what he and Gully had heard.

"Yeah, we heard gunshots, too, but figured it was people hunting," Sibilski said.

"You men get some rest. Jackson, lets you and me take a hike. See if we can get into radio range with the armory. I need to chat with Wolfe and Colonel Harrigan."

"Yes, sir," the young FEMA soldier said as he grabbed his kit and rifle. "I'm ready when you are, Lieutenant."

· · + ◆ + · ·

"You're good with the boys, John," Linda said as she sat in the chair next to me. We'd all established a bit of a routine, and that chair was often looked at as hers. "They like that you don't talk down to them."

"It might be because I'm a bit of a kid myself," I replied. "I get accused of being twelve sometimes."

"Were you twelve today when you were staring at me and Zach?"

I shrugged a shoulder. "I didn't like what I saw; I'll be honest about that."

"You have no call to be that way. I don't *belong* to you or anyone else."

"I know, and I'm not suggesting you belong to me. I just didn't like it. I don't like him; he's trouble."

She rolled her eyes at me. "I can handle it, John, don't be like that."

"I still don't like him."

"You can be exasperating, sometimes. He's the one I have to work with to help them build that window greenhouse. That's all it is."

"Okay," I said, feeling like I was being scolded. "I'll put up with him for you because you've asked me to. Fair enough?"

"It's better than my telling you to go to hell. I didn't come out here to argue with you, John. I was looking for the boys. Like I said, you're good with them, and they like you."

Before I could respond, I heard someone clear their throat with a loud "ahem." Linda and I looked up at the same time and saw Brian and Rahn standing at the porch steps.

"Is it safe to come up?" Brian asked.

"He's your son," Linda said with a chuckle.

She rose, patted my arm, and said, "He's all yours, guys, have at him."

As she walked off toward the door, she stopped, turned, and said, "It's okay, John, we're fine." And went into the cabin.

"What did you do?" Brian asked.

"Nothin'. What do you two want?" I said.

"We've finalized our plan to attack the armory," Brian said. "Thought we'd run it by you."

I wasn't feeling particularly gracious at the moment and was still stinging from Linda's confusing rebuke, embarrassed Brian and Rahn had heard it. "Why? You planned it," I said with a bit of snark.

"C'mon, Dad, we're asking for your help here. Pick holes in our plan," Brian said.

"Lay it on me."

"It's a two-prong attack. Rahn will take half of the Guard soldiers and half of Jake's people. Using the same route as before, they'll come up behind the armory. I'll lead an assault from the road in front of the armory with three Hummers and their turret-mounted SAWS at a set time. Rahn's team will take care of the vehicles, breach the building, shooting as many as possible before withdrawing, then go back to the rally point before we return here. Our objective is to destroy all of their vehicles, their radio antenna and kill as many FEMA people as possible."

"And the last time you did that, we lost a man," I said.

"It's war, John. People die in wars," Rahn said.

"What's Jake have to say about this?" I asked.

"We haven't run it by him yet. I wanted to talk to you first. You know this stuff, you know, from the olden days," Brian said. His attempt at humor worked as he got a smile out of me.

"The olden days?" I raised an eyebrow.

"Yeah, you, George Washington, all those guys."

"Screw you, Brian." But I started to laugh. "Okay, here's what I think. You're Rat Patrol with the Hummers…"

Brian interrupted. "Rat patrol? What's a rat patrol?"

"Old TV show about World War II from a long time ago. Anyway, your attack using the Hummers doesn't serve a purpose. There aren't a lot of windows on the street side, and all of the FEMA people are bunking in the assembly hall in the back. You're wasting ammo by shooting the front of the building. We don't have a steady source of ammo. What about all that C-4 you guys got? It won't take much to blow their vehicles. The explosions would draw people out, and then a couple of SAWS can engage them, inflicting large numbers of casualties. You only need two vehicles for that, given the SAWS rate of fire, plus your assault team can engage as well. Keep your lanes of fire set so that you aren't shooting at each other. No friendly fire casualties. Should I go on?"

"This is good, Dad. This is why we wanted your input."

"Uh, huh," I said. "You're smarter than this. How much of this is throw away to get me to buy into this plan?"

"Throw away?" Brian asked innocently.

"Throw away. You want to make me feel good, so you put some bullshit into your plan so that I can say 'take it out.' You think I've never done that?"

"Busted. I was feeling bad that we weren't using your strategic skills much, so I told Rahn I was gonna put some stuff in the plan that I knew you'd disagree with. What you said we should do is what we're planning to do," Brian explained.

"I still think this isn't a good idea," I said.

"John, here's the thing. If we don't do it, they're going to keep coming and keep coming. They'll eventually wear us down. If they succeed, we're dead. You, your family, me, all of us. They see us as traitors," Rahn said.

"I know. That's the only reason I'm not saying no, Chris," I said. "We stood up to them, and now. Well, now they have the same *no choice* that we do."

"So it's a go?" Brian asked.

"What real choice do we have, son," I said. "What about your Guard friends in Rhinelander?"

"I haven't asked them for anything other than the C-4," Rahn said. "If we need them to fight, I don't know. No one has bothered them, but they aren't stupid, either. They know they'll be discovered soon and given a choice. Submit or perish."

"Then, for now, it's up to us," I said.

"That's about the size of it," Rahn said, agreeing.

"Then do it, boys. Be hard, don't hold back, and commit."

"Climb to Glory, Dad."

"Right of the Line," Rahn added.

"You 10th Mountain boys ain't right," I said, grinning. "Make it so."

CHAPTER 9

*"Whoever lives for the sake of combatting
an enemy has an interest in the enemy's
staying alive."*

—Friedrich Nietzsche

"Colonel Harrigan," the FEMA soldier said and knocked on the door jamb of the office Wayne Harrigan was using.

Slowly raising his eyes and glancing with some annoyance at the black-clad man, Harrigan paused dramatically and then said, "Yes, what is it?"

"Sir, it's Lieutenant King. He's on the radio asking for you."

"Why didn't you say so," Harrigan said sharply as he jumped up from his seat, brushing the man aside as he entered the hallway and marched rapidly toward the Communications Room.

As he entered, one of the operators pointed toward the table next to him. "He's on that radio, sir."

Harrigan sat down, grasped the microphone, and said, "King, this is Harrigan."

A brief pause followed, and then, "Colonel, this is King. I have a development, over."

"Well, what is it, man?"

"My team observed a large group of people at the edge of town. About a dozen. They said these people appeared to be working around a house. They also observed a pickup truck drive away with three occupants in it."

"Pickup truck? What kind of pickup truck?" Harrigan asked.

"A rusty, old black pickup truck, Colonel. Is that important?" King asked.

"You find out where that truck went, Lieutenant, and get back to me. Harrigan out."

Ending the conversation, he dropped the microphone on the table, and jumping up from his seat, ran from the room. *They came to me in an old, black rusty pickup. It's got to be them.*

· · ◆ ◆ ◆ ◆ · ·

King held the radio handset at arm's length from his face, staring at it with a perplexed expression.

"Let's head back to camp, Jackson. It's a long walk, and we have planning to do," King said to his young companion.

"Yes, sir," Jackson replied.

· · ◆ ◆ ◆ ◆ · ·

I was enjoying the peace and quiet of the porch when Allen came rushing up. "Mr. Henry!" he called.

"What is it, Allen," I said.

"Sam needs to see you. Right away. He heard something on the radio you need to know about."

"What is it?" I asked as I stood up and went with him.

"Not sure. He said for me to…to come get you, and he'd explain," Allen replied.

"Okay." I followed him to the barn. The short walk gave me plenty of time to worry about what Sam had heard. If he sent someone to get me, it wasn't going to be good news. Allen and I trooped up the stairs into Sam's radio room. Sam had his back to us, headphones placed tightly on his ears as we entered.

"What's up?" I said, probably a bit too loudly as he jumped.

Even Allen jumped beside me.

"I think we've got company," Sam said in an unusually serious tone, even for Sam.

"We've got company," I repeated.

"Yup, sounds like it. I was scanning frequencies, trying to hear what was out there. I heard a conversation, skipped past it, and had to scan back to find it. I think we've got company."

"How? Who?"

Sam gave me a concerned look. "I think the FEMA boys are in the area."

"Anyone specific?"

"FEMA boys, John, that's all I know. I think they're in the area and might be on foot," he explained. "I only heard part of the conversation, but they called the armory in Antigo."

"Was it Wolfe? You'd think he'd stay away after the last time," I replied.

"No, he isn't here. Someone else, a Colonel Harrigan. They mentioned seeing a black truck drive from a house. This colonel told a Lieutenant King to find the truck, and to find out where it went," he said.

I breathed a heavy sigh. "That doesn't sound good. They must have seen us near the refugees in Lake View, at Carol's place."

"That's what I'm thinking. But from where? They weren't on the road; you'd have seen 'em."

"They *must* be on foot. This isn't good. This isn't good at all. They must be getting desperate to find us, or smarter," I said.

"We may want to rethink that mission Brian and Rahn are planning," Sam said.

"You're right. Allen, go find Brian, Rahn, and Jake. Tell them to come up here. Now. Sam on the Ham has some important news," I said.

"On my way, Mr. Henry," Allen replied and headed off to find them.

"We can't let them go on this mission if we have FEMA foot patrols in the area, John," Sam said.

"I know, I know, Sam. I'm surprised the scouts we have out haven't seen them. These guys must be good."

"Or just lucky," Sam added. "Jake's people are good, and Craig's out with one of the teams."

"Yeah, Addie wasn't thrilled about that, but Craig wanted to go. He's become quite the warrior since all this started. The gentlest of my boys and the youngest becomes a hard case warrior."

Sam continued to scan frequencies on his radio as we waited for the three men to arrive. Our wait wasn't long. I heard the staccato of feet coming up the stairs before I saw them.

Allen came up first. "They were all in the barn downstairs, Mr. Henry," he announced. Behind him was Brian, Rahn, and Jake.

"What's up, Dad?" Brian asked as he was the first to come into the room.

"We have visitors," I replied. The grim look I must've had surprised him.

"Visitors?" Rahn asked as he entered the room.

"Yeah, a FEMA scout team is in the area," Sam replied. "We think they're on foot, too."

"How many?" Rahn asked.

"Don't know exactly," I said. "Sam picked up a radio transmission that someone sent. They described seeing my truck leaving a house in Lake View. We think the house was Carol's place and the time was when we left Wendy and the Shawano people."

"Shit," Brian said.

"It gets better. Two voices are new. A Colonel Harrigan," I replied, "and King."

"I bet Wolfe is nearby," Rahn said.

"I don't know. Harrigan ordered whoever was on the radio to find where the truck went," Sam interjected.

"We have people on foot. My people should have seen them," Jake said, adding his voice to the conversation. "These guys are either good *or* lucky."

"I think we should figure they are good and *hope* they got lucky," I said. "We've got to find them before your trip to Antigo. We can't have an unknown number of people running around the area hunting for us. I don't want a repeat of the Winston's place."

"I agree," Rahn and Brian said at the same time.

"We need to send out some hunter-killer teams and take these guys out," Brian continued. "I don't want them running around our home, either."

It was the first time I'd heard Brian refer to our place as his home. It surprised me but made me feel proud, too. I now knew my son was *home* and defending that home.

"I'll get some of my boys together and send them out to look. It sounds like they may be to the west of town," Jake said. "You think they're stupid enough to be at the hatchery again?"

"If they're good instead of lucky, I'd say no," I answered.

"Yeah, but there's a lot of woods around there. It would give them access to water, be close enough yet far enough from here—though, they probably don't realize that," Brian said. "It would be a good way to be clever and deceptive. They'd probably think that we'd think they weren't that stupid."

I walked over to the map Sam had made of our corner of Northeastern Wisconsin. Hanging on the wall, it allowed me to look at our entire county.

I put my finger on Carol's place as the others gathered around me. "Here is Carol's," I said. Tracing my finger to the west, I stopped at the hatchery. "And here's the hatchery. I don't think they are between the two places, but I agree they may be close. Jake, can you have a couple of teams start scouting in the area of the hatchery?"

"Yeah, I can do that. Do you think two more teams is enough? I can contact the other team that's in the area already and have them join up. That gives us six sets of eyes looking for these boys," he said.

"We should send out a couple of mobile teams as well," Rahn said. "Say two Hummers with crews of three each. They can patrol the main road and some of the side roads that run off of it. Jake's people can go cross country with their horses more effectively than we can in the Hummers."

"That's a good plan. We need to start ASAP," Brian added. "These patrols need to operate day and night. These guys are probably holing up during the day, moving at night, and then observing during the day. That's what I'd do, and probably how we missed them."

"If they're moving at night, then they've been trained. That means the odds are they are good instead of being lucky," Rahn said.

"If they're on foot, they are closer to us than I thought earlier. We need to make damn sure we cover all of the area between, say, where Lake View Road intersects with the county road and all the way to where it meets, ummm," I traced my finger on the map, "McGee Road." I stopped about a mile west of the hatchery.

Brian moved closer to the map and looked at the area where I was pointing. "That's a lot of real estate, but I agree. I think we'll add another horse patrol and another Hummer. If these guys are serious, they'll figure out quickly we're on to them. Then, they'll either hunker down or get aggressive. We can't afford that. I don't want to lose any more people."

"It's kind of stupid of them to get aggressive if they know we're looking for them," Jake said. "But then, nobody ever said the boys in black were smart."

"I suggest you get your teams together and get going," I said.

"Agreed," Brian said.

"Sam, can you contact the teams out on patrol and let them know what's happening? Have the team near the hatchery stand fast until the others meet up with them," I said.

"Will do," said Sam.

"Okay, let's get moving," Brian said.

The sound of feet down the stairs as the men filed out and the sudden silence in Sam's loft sent a strong message. The hunt was on.

"I'm going to tell the women. We'll have to keep everyone close to the cabin until we find these guys. I don't want anyone getting kidnapped again," I said, breaking the silence that had surrounded Sam, Allen, and myself.

"Will it ever end, Mr. Henry?" Allen asked, looking at me.

"It will one day, Allen," I said, silently hoping I was right.

CHAPTER 10

*"Because night has fallen and the barbar-
ians haven't come."*

—C.P. Cavafy

The teams had stayed out through the night and continued patrols as dawn broke, rotating and searching for the FEMA boys, as everyone realized the seriousness of our situation. Craig had come back in with one of the Hummers long enough for a change of clothes, I suspect for a few private moments with Addie, and then he'd gone back out again. He told me they had arranged a rendezvous with his riding partner, who was enjoying a bit of a nap, at least according to Craig.

Explaining the situation to Donna, Nancy, Linda, Addie, Gary, and the others wasn't as easy as I thought.

I'd finished breakfast and asked Linda and Donna if they wanted to join me on a call with Wendy and the Shawano refugees. Both agreed, and we left after doing the breakfast dishes. Not that we didn't try and get away without doing them, but Nancy caught us. She was a stickler for clean.

Nancy was already nervous that we were leaving, but I had asked Sajan to stay in the house with her, acting as a bodyguard. It made her feel better, but the greater challenge was the boys. A couple of Jake's men had brought the young boys into the barn to help them. Well, *help* is what they called it, but I thought it looked more like playtime. I heard something about throwing axes and hoped Nancy and Linda hadn't heard that.

Compared to what we'd been experiencing, the road into town was a virtual highway of commuters. Between the coming and going of our HMWWVs to the three of us now in my truck, the road was busier than it had been since the EMP hit, and probably even before that.

The drive seemed to be quicker than normal, and as we pulled into the driveway, I saw Wendy talking with a small group. Among them was Zach, who was probably the last person I wanted to see. I had promised both Linda and Donna that I'd behave, even though I didn't like or trust him.

The crunch of our tires on the gravel announced our arrival, and as I parked the truck, a not very happy-looking Wendy stood waiting for me.

I climbed out of the vehicle, as did Donna and Linda. Donna followed me, while Linda, seeing

Zach had a stack of windows and lumber, went to see him. My blood pressure was already rising, and my mind was telling me to calm down.

Donna hip-checked me, which snapped me out of staring.

"Knock it off, John," she whispered as we walked up on Wendy.

I took stock of the situation. "Hello Wendy, you don't look happy," I said, never being one to like beating around the bush.

"Hello, John, Donna," she replied. "Lots of military activity going on. What's happening?"

"Unfortunately, we've learned we might have some dangerous men sneaking around here. Our boys are looking for them," I answered.

"What kind of dangerous men?"

"The people I mentioned to you before," I explained. "We think it's the FEMA group from Antigo that killed the Winston family a few weeks ago."

"I still have a difficult time grasping that FEMA is some terrible organization out here to harm us," Wendy said.

"I understand," Donna interjected. "It seemed hard to believe for me, too. All we wanted was to be left alone, but they threatened us if we didn't go to the camps. That's why we have some of the National Guard with us. Some of the guys with us objected to having to force people into those refugee camps, and if they refused, to execute them."

"That's horrible," Wendy said. "I'm not calling you a liar, but camps, slave labor, summary executions—it all seems so surreal."

"I understand, Wendy. It was hard for me to accept, but it's all true."

"Excuse me a moment," I said as I headed toward Linda and Zach. I saw him grab her arm and pull on her as if he were trying to force her to go somewhere. I didn't like seeing that kind of aggression toward women. She had pulled back, so I knew it wasn't a friendly gesture.

"HEY!" I hollered. "Get your hands off of her."

"It's okay, John. He didn't mean anything by it," Linda said to me when I was within earshot.

"It didn't look okay to me," I said as I got closer to her and Zach. "Just what in the hell do you think you're doing, boy, putting your hands on someone like that."

"You need to back off, old man," Zach said. "This is none of your business. We're just talking."

"It didn't look like just talking to me," I replied, grabbing his arm and pulling him toward me. "How's it feel to be pulled around, tough guy?"

"Get your damn hands off of me!" Zach shouted.

"Knock it off, both of you. You're acting like children," Linda said. "John, I can take care of myself. Leave it be."

Donna and Wendy joined us, and both were breathing heavily from the run to where we were standing.

"What's going on?" Donna asked.

I explained what had happened between Linda and Zach. "You know how I feel about men putting their hands on women."

Zach's eyes projected fire. Apparently, my words stung. I meant them, too. I'd seen too many women battered by men over the years, and I'd been raised old-school that you don't hit girls. My blood was up, and this situation was getting me ready to explode.

"Zach, we've talked about this before. Now apologize," Wendy ordered.

Everyone stood there staring at him, the tension in the air thick. Zach mumbled something that I expect was some sort of an apology and walked off into the field behind the house.

"That was unnecessary, John Henry," Linda said. "I told you last night I could handle things."

"This happened before?" Donna quickly asked.

"No, John just didn't like how Zach was acting toward me. I told him it was nothing and to let me handle it. I thought he understood. Apparently, I was mistaken," Linda answered.

"Zach has always had a bit of a temper, and he's bossy," Wendy said. "I've spoken to him about it many times. Too many times, I'm sure. It comes down to

Zach wants things a certain way, and there is no room for discussion. I'm sorry, Linda. I thought I had this situation under control. I'll speak to him again."

"I think John has pretty well made things clear to him, and I don't think Zach will act out again toward me. It really wasn't much."

"Don't excuse his actions, Linda. I know what I saw," I said.

"John, go to the truck," Donna said sharply.

I looked at her with a rather puzzled expression on my face and started to say something when she said, "I said, go to the truck John. You need to cool off. I know how you get when you get your blood up."

Without saying a word, I did as she asked.

Behind me, I could hear Donna speaking.

"When he was a young kid, John had a friend whose mom was beat to death by her husband. He and his friend saw it happen," Donna explained. "One thing that will set John off faster than anything is violence against women. It is the quickest way I know to see him get violent. When we were married, I saw it once, and I thought he was going to kill the guy. Had the police not shown up before it went much further, John would've most likely gone to prison. When they learned what caused the fight, they let John and the other guy go with a warning. It was then, afterwards, that he shared with me the story of his friend and his mother."

"I didn't know that," Linda said. "I understand, but still, he…"

"Yes, he shouldn't have interrupted. But he likes you, Linda. Everyone knows it and sees it," Donna said.

"We're just friends, Donna," Linda said testily. "I know everyone thinks he likes me, and sometimes that makes me feel uncomfortable, but I don't think he likes me that way."

Donna's look showed she was having a hard time believing it.

"Zach still has no excuse for grabbing someone and trying to force them to go somewhere," Wendy said, finally able to get a word in. "I'll talk to him. We can't let this stew. Maybe we can get those two to behave and at least put up with one another."

"John forgives quickly," Donna said. "He won't trust Zach ever, but he'll forgive and work with him if that's what is needed."

"Men," Linda said. "Sometimes they can be *too* difficult. I know he means well, and at least he isn't a cheat, like some husbands. I'll talk to John later, and we'll sort this out."

"Careful when you talk to him," Donna said, grinning for the first time. "You get that man talking, and he won't shut up. He talks more than anyone I know."

Laughing, Linda replied, "Don't I know it. He said it's because he writes sometimes, and when writing, you have to explain everything, painting word pictures, he calls it. I know how to shut him up, though."

Donna raised an eyebrow but didn't comment.

····◆··

While I sat in my chair on the porch watching guard soldiers train near the barn, four Humvees and four horse patrols roamed the countryside around Lake View. For three straight days, the patrols were out. The men in the vehicles patrolled the roads, occasionally stopping to inspect abandoned homes and outbuildings, looking for any sign of the suspected FEMA intruders or refugees in need. The horse patrols rode the countryside using game trails, the edges of pastures, and any other natural path they could use to get into the woods, searching for what Jake's people had started calling cowboys.

I couldn't figure it out at first, and then he explained it to me.

Jake laughed hysterically. "John, how many times, when you were a kid, did you wander in the woods looking for hostile Indians? Well, we played, too, only we looked for cowboys."

I had to admit it was funny, though obviously not in the politically correct way our world had been going the last several years, but I found it refreshingly amusing all the same.

I stayed at the cabin and let Jake, Brian, and Rahn run things with the patrol. Throughout the day, Allen would come down from Sam's radio room and give me an update. It was always the same.

"Negative report, Mr. Henry," he would say. Then he'd trot back up by Sam.

After a while of sitting and moping around with not much to do, I decided to visit Gary. I felt bad about not seeing him more often as he was pretty much bed-ridden with what Donna believed was a severe flare-up of rheumatoid arthritis. She was certain he was out of remission, and with no medicine to give him, there wasn't much we could do to make Gary comfortable. I almost made it to his cabin, too, except I ran into Nancy and Addie, my two daughters-in-law.

"Hello, ladies, how are the two of you today?" I asked politely, probably a bit too cheerfully.

"Doing as well as we can, worried as we are about our husbands and all that's going on," Nancy replied.

I made eye contact with her as I wasn't sure if she was blaming me or if she was simply speaking a harsh truth. I shifted my eyes to Addie, and as soon as I did, she started to cry.

Nancy quickly put her arm around her and said, "It's going to be okay. He's safe and with good peo-ple. Brian's with him, too, and Rahn. They'll be fine." She paused for a second, and glaring at me, she continued in what to me was an overly compassionate tone. "Won't he, FIL? Craig will be okay."

I've missed a few subtle and not-so-subtle messages in my time, but this one was loud and clear. We were talking about my sons. "Of course he will be, Nancy. They take good care of each other, and they'll all be fine," I said as I reached out and put my hand on Addie's shoulder.

"I'm scared," Addie said, sobbing. "I'm so scared for him."

"Brian and the others are with him," I repeated, masking my own fears. I pulled the two women toward me, wrapping them both in my arms in one big hug.

A moment later, I released them, not allowing myself to think about a bad outcome for the boys.

"Let's go in the cabin, Addie," Nancy said as she took Addie by the arm and steered her toward the cabin. "Maybe we can bake cookies or something."

Addie nodded her head and thanked me.

I watched them as they headed off toward the cabin, and then, turning myself around, restarted my walk to Gary's. The day was quiet so far, and hopefully, it would stay that way.

··◆◆◆◆◆··

"We have a problem, Lieutenant," Gully said as he quietly awakened King.

Rubbing his eyes and slowly rolling over on his side, King propped himself up on his elbow and said, "What's that, Gully?"

"We have a problem, Lieutenant," Gully repeated.

"I heard you. What's the problem?"

"Patrols, Lieutenant. Lots of patrols. We had two different groups come by on horses, and they're looking for something. I think it might be us."

Drawing his legs in, King came to a sitting position and looked around at his patrol camp. It was still dark. Leonard, Jackson, and Sibilski were all asleep. "You on guard?" King asked Gully.

"Yes, sir," Gully replied. "I've been watching these patrols."

"It's just a couple of people on horseback, Gully. Why do you think they're looking for us? They could be hunting."

"I thought that at first, too. But I can hear vehicles on the road. Sounds like Humvees to me. Several of them."

Alarmed, King glanced around his patrol camp again. "Are any of these patrols around now?"

"No. They rode by about 15 minutes ago, along the tree line about twenty yards or so away from us. We were all quiet, and I was good and camouflaged. I don't think they saw anything and kept riding."

"Show me," King ordered as he slowly stood up.

Gully led King through the brush and to the edge of the trees, then pointed across the field in front of them. "They were over there, Lieutenant. Then two of them came from the left and headed off in that direction." He continued to point toward the south. "No one is there now."

"Where did you hear the Hummers?" King asked.

Pointing back in the other direction, Gully replied, "Over that way. I could hear them moving on the road, and eventually, they drove behind us and headed that way."

"Did they go into the hatchery?" King asked.

Gully shrugged. "I don't know, but if they're looking for us, they may have looked there, too."

"Okay. Wake the others up, one at a time. Quietly, and tell them to be quiet. No fires, no smoking, no noise. We need to move."

"Yes, sir," Gully replied.

King squatted down inside the tree line and opened the case holding a pair of binoculars that he had hanging around his neck. Raising it to his eyes, he slowly looked at the tree line across the field, almost five hundred yards away.

How does Henry and his camp know we were here? I can't alert the colonel. I have to figure out what to do myself. Were any of us seen when we were out? Were we followed?

King shook his head. This mission was becoming a more difficult task than he originally expected. He would not fail Harrigan.

·· ◆ ◆ ◆ ◆ ·· ··

Witnesses later said that the argument between Zach and Wendy was loud. Everyone had left for the day when Zach returned to the house. Wendy was waiting for him in the living room, sitting on the sofa, sipping a mug of hot herbal tea that Donna had given her the makings for.

"Come here and sit down, Zach," she said as he entered the room. "We need to talk."

"There's nothing to talk about," Zach replied as he headed for the stairs.

"There is if you want to stay and be a part of this community," Wendy insisted.

Zach stood there for a moment, staring at Wendy. She stared back; the tension in the room was thick. Finally, he gave in, walking into the room and sitting in a chair next to the sofa.

"What?" he said defiantly.

"You know what," Wendy replied. "What were you thinking, grabbing that woman like that? Linda is a friend."

"I didn't grab her. I took her arm and was trying to show her something."

"It didn't look that way, and now you know how John feels about her."

"That old man can go to hell. She likes me, and he doesn't like that," Zach snarled.

"Come on now, has she said she liked you?" Wendy asked.

"She smiled at me, she talks with me, that's how I know," he said.

"Zach, someone smiling at you or being nice to you does not mean they like you. It just means they are being polite. I've explained this to you before. How many times do we have to have this conversation?"

"You weren't there, and you don't know what she meant. She likes me. She said she did," Zach said, raising his voice.

Wendy spoke in her stern principal voice. "No Zach, she doesn't like you that way. You've done this before and almost got arrested. Do you want to risk that again?"

He laughed. "No one is going to arrest me. You're not. And stop telling me what to do. You've been telling me what to do since high school, and I don't like it anymore."

"This has to stop, Zach. If you don't stop, you'll have to leave this community. We can't have you putting all of us at risk because of your behavior."

Both of their voices were raised now, and it wasn't the way Wendy had expected things to go.

"Is everything okay down there, Wendy?" a man's voice yelled from upstairs.

"We're fine," she shouted back. "We're just having a conversation."

Pausing to catch her breath, Wendy said, "Lower your voice, Zach, and please tell me you will change your behavior. This has to stop."

"I'm not doing anything wrong," he said, and his eyes began to fill with tears. "You weren't there, and you don't understand. She likes me."

"I'm sure she likes you, but maybe as a friend. She doesn't like you in the way you think she does. Now stop this before you get in trouble. The Henrys won't play around. These are different times, and this isn't back home in Shawano."

Zach sat there, staring at her, neither of them speaking.

Wendy broke the silence first. "Do you understand me? We need the Henrys' help, and in time, they may need us. We won't get through the coming winter without them."

"We could go to Wausau, to the FEMA camps," Zach said softly.

"No. I believe them when they say how bad those camps are for refugees. Remember what your friend said about the FEMA camp at Lambeau. I think we're better off here," Wendy replied. "Now, behave yourself around women. No more grabbing Linda or trying to make her go somewhere with you. It will only cause you and us trouble."

"Okay," he answered.

"I mean it, Zach. Behave yourself."

"Yes, Wendy. Whatever you say."

CHAPTER 11

*"Let us sit on the ground and tell sad
stories."*

—William Shakespeare

Major Elias Wolfe stood in the lot outside the armory, staring at the burned hulks of two Humvees. They had been destroyed by "those terrorists," as he sometimes called them, when they raided the armory several weeks ago. He was past the rage he had felt then as well as the attack on him and his men at the hatchery. It was now a simmering anger, brought up to a near boil by Lieutenant King's recent call telling Harrigan about the black pickup truck his men had observed. The truck Wolfe knew belonged to the Henrys and that deserter, Rahn. He folded his arms across his chest, pulling the black uniform he wore tight against his back.

A voice behind him startled him out of his thoughts. "You wanted to see me, Major?" It was Edmiston, the only other survivor of his ill-fated team.

"Yes, I did," Wolfe said. "You heard they might have a lead on the location of those terrorists?"

"Yes, sir, I did," Edmiston replied.

"Our revenge may be close. How many of the men can you trust?" Wolfe asked.

"I don't know, Major. I'll have to give it some thought, but Colonel Harrigan said we were to stay here and wait."

"I'm not talking about waiting, Edmiston. I'm talking about getting some people together and heading out there in the next day or so."

"Should we be doing that, Major?" Edmiston asked. Concern showed on his face.

"We should if King finds them, and we can help. We can put an end to this now."

"Yes, sir," Edmiston said, clear doubt creeping into his tone.

"You afraid to go? You don't want to get even for what they did to your friends," Wolfe asked harshly, glaring at the man.

"I'm not afraid," Edmiston replied. "It's just that the colonel said we were supposed to wait, and I'm not sure we should disobey his orders."

Wolfe wasn't convinced Edmiston wasn't afraid. "Consider it as being enthusiastically creative, Edmiston. Victory belongs to the bold and daring."

"Yes, sir."

"I want you to feel some of the men out, the ones you can trust. Those who knew the men we lost, who maybe want to get their revenge, too."

"Yes, sir."

"You with me on this?" Wolfe put his hand on Edmiston's shoulder. "Are you with me, or are you a coward who won't do what needs to be done?"

"I'm, I'm with you, Major," Edmiston replied.

"Then keep this between us and find us a couple of good men. With King's people and a few more, we can hit them and hit them hard. Waiting is not an option."

⋯⋅◆◆◆⋅⋯

I left Gary's cabin feeling down. He was in pain, and there was little we could do for him. Donna and Linda had tried different remedies to help reduce the inflammation and to control his pain, but little helped. Living with constant pain was difficult, and I could see Gary was more depressed than I was. His words still troubled me.

"How are you feeling?" I asked Gary. He was in bed, a book on military strategy near him.

"Not good, John," he replied, the agony of pain written all over his face. "I'm becoming a burden, and that's not something any of us need."

"You're not a burden, Gary. You're just down at the moment. You'll be fine soon enough," I lied.

Donna and I had discussed letting him try marijuana as something to help. Gary was old school, though. He had flat out declined. It was the only humor he'd shown lately when he said he couldn't do that because he'd get the munchies. Apparently, no one had any flavored corn chips for him to munch on.

"John, face the reality. I can't work. All I can do is lay in this bed, hobble to the outhouse and hobble back in here or, on a good day, sit on my porch."

Gary's cabin, a dog trot with a center exposed and covered porch, was connected to another that Linda and her boys had used before we moved them into the big cabin. Now that side was used by Rahn, Johnson, and Schwartz. Gary had been sharing his side with Sam, but we let Gary keep it by himself after Sam moved permanently into the radio room. With Gary's depression, I was wondering if that was still a good idea.

"Knock it off, Marine," I said. "You'll be fine."

"Semper fi and all that, right, John," Gary replied, but his tone was somewhat sarcastic.

"I mean it, Gary. I get you hurt, and I know you're in pain. It'll pass, and you'll be fine."

"We can only hope," he said, looking away from me.

"Yes, hope. Let's keep hoping, and when you're feeling better, I'll tell you I told you so." I stood up from the chair I'd been sitting in, put my hand on his shoulder and said, "Now, rest up and get better. You'll see."

As I left his cabin, I heard him mutter, "Yeah, get better. That's all I'm good for."

Not knowing what else to say to cheer him, I left the cabin and headed back toward mine.

As I walked that way, I could see activity by the barn. A couple of Jake's people were getting ready to move out, and two of the Hummers were being kitted up, too. Reaching them, I saw Specialist Hart chatting with some of the guardsmen.

"Hello, Mr. Henry," he said.

"Do I have to keep telling you people my *name* is John?" I asked.

"No, it's just habit," he replied. "We have a problem."

"What's that?"

"We need to go back to that gas station and get more fuel. We're running low with all of these vehicles out on the road," Hart answered.

"How much fuel do you think is still there?"

"Quite a bit, but sucking it out of those tanks by hand is hard work, and there is no other way. Plus, we only have so many containers we can fill and bring back here. We empty out your two 500-gallon containers pretty quickly."

"So, what's the plan?" I asked, curious.

"Well, we need to see if we can find a couple of 55-gallon drums or larger gas cans to bring more back. I've got a couple of guys out searching some of the abandoned houses around here. You'd think with all the fishing boats and 4-wheelers everyone had around here that we should be able to find some. We've got to store a lot here before winter sets in."

"Yes, winter. That will be here soon enough," I said. Winter was the one threat we had that we couldn't really do much about. Between storing food, making firewood, filling the smokehouse with venison and some pigs we would butcher soon, all that we could do was accept that winter was coming. I was starting to hate that expression, true as it was.

"Have you checked with Sam or Rick to see if they know of any places where the men might find some containers?"

"Yeah, Rick said he thought there might be some old drums at a farm not far from here. I sent some guys to the Winston's old place, too," Hart said.

The look he had in his eyes when he mentioned the Winston's place said a lot about how he felt about what had happened to them. None of us would ever forget that or Emma.

"Just do what you can, Hart. None of us want to face the winter or next few months without fuel."

"I will, Mr. Henry. If we don't get back to normal soon, we'll all be facing this world without fuel. Our weapons won't be any good, either, once we run out of ammo. At best, it will be bows and arrows and swords," Hart remarked.

"Not a pretty thought. Let's hope it doesn't come to that," I said. "Have you seen Craig?"

"Yeah, he's out with one of Jake's teams. Said he'd rather be on horseback this time around. He's a rather interesting person, Mr. Henry."

"He's changed, that's for sure. Hell, we've all changed these last few months. Can't say it's all been bad, either."

"We're figuring out what's really important again. I think somewhere along the way, we lost that. My dad always said we were a confused country. He grew up poor, not too far from here. He used to talk about government cheese and food stamps. He joined the U.S. Navy to get away from all this. When he came back, he moved to Wausau, worked in a mill. I can still recall him not taking a vacation because all he did was work except for Sunday. That was for church and summer barbecues. Packers in the fall, of course."

"Yeah, go Pack go. My old man was the same way, except he joined the air force. Vacations were to come back to Appleton and visit family. I don't even recall any kind of family vacation growing up. When he wasn't working, he was working on other things around the house," I said.

"Speaking of work, I need to get back to it before the First Sergeant gets back and sees me jaw-jacking."

"Hell hath no fury like a First Sergeant, does it, Hart?"

"No, Mr. Henry, it does not."

I left Hart to his work and went to my chair on the porch. I didn't really have any work at the moment, and I was going to talk to Brian and Rahn about that. I wasn't a sit-on-the-sidelines kind of guy.

··•◆•◆•··

King assembled his men in a small circle. With King in the center, the men all faced inward, kneeling and waiting for his instructions.

"It would appear that the enemy somehow knows we are here. They don't know exactly where we are, but they are looking for us," King began. "We will stay here until nightfall, and then we will move. Staying here is no longer safe."

"Where we gonna go, Lieutenant?" Leonard asked.

"I've been giving that some thought," King answered. "That place you two holed up yesterday. Near the town and that house. It's risky, because we are so close to them, but they may not think we would set up that close. I think that's the place to go."

"It's a couple of hours' walk from here, sir," Leonard said. "In the dark, we'd have to go slower. It might take us all night. We could even walk into an ambush."

"All of that is true, Leonard. The fact of the matter is we can't stay here. If we do, they will find us

for certain. If we move, we have a chance of finding them, waiting them out until they decide we
either left or were never here, and *then* we can get
out of here."

"You're in charge, sir," Leonard said.

"That's right, I'm in charge," King replied in a
snarled whisper. "Don't question my orders again.
Am I clear?"

"Yes, sir," Leonard said, raising the inflection of his
voice to emphasize his answer.

King glared at him for a second and then, making
eye contact with the others, asked, "Any questions?"

The men shook their heads from side to side.

"Good. Get some rest, and just before dark, we'll
pack everything up and head out of here. Leonard,
you'll lead the way. You know where we are going."

Leonard nodded his head and then shifted his eyes
toward Sibilski, rolling his eyes in a sign of disrespect. Sibilski smiled.

"Something funny, Sibilski," King asked.

"No, Lieutenant, just thinking about that long
walk in the dark. Not gonna be an easy walk," he
answered.

"You men have been trained, you know how to do
it, and we'll get where we are going."

"Yes, sir," Sibilski said.

"You men get some rest. We'll head out in a few
hours," King ordered. "Jackson, I want you to sit on

the edge of the trees and stand guard. Throw a stick or rock back our way if you see anyone or any of those patrols."

"Yes, sir," Jackson replied.

CHAPTER 12

"Where no hope is left, is left no fear."

—John Milton

Brian and Rahn met along Highway P just before dark. Stopping at the intersection of where a road turned off the highway, the two men stepped out of their vehicles and spoke between the two Hummers after an exaggerated stretch of their bodies. Brian stretched again, placing his hands in the small of his back and bending backward. "I think I'm getting too old for this shit," he remarked.

"Yeah, too old. What are you, all of thirty-two or something like that," Rahn commented.

"I'll have you know I'm thirty-seven, and an old beat-up thirty-seven at that," Brian replied.

"Uh-huh, try forty-two. That's ancient," Rahn said.

Brian laughed, then immediately got serious. "You think those guys are out here, Top?"

"Oh, they're here," Rahn said, looking past Brian. "They could be sitting inside the tree line watching us right now."

"Then we'd be the perfect target, wouldn't we."

"Yup, and we two old soldiers should know better. Mark my words, Chief, they're out there somewhere nearby. They aren't on the roads. My guess is they're inland a bit. Jake's boys will most likely find them. We, on the other hand, will only find them if Jake's boys flush them out and we catch them running."

"Hmm… That gives me an idea, First Sergeant," Specialist Johnson chimed in. He had exited his vehicle, stretched, and walked over to the two leaders, listening in to their conversation.

"What's that, Johnson?" Rahn said.

"Maybe we should do an old-fashioned deer drive," he replied.

"A deer drive?" Brian asked.

"Yes, sir. We used to do one on the last day of deer hunting. A couple of guys would set up in a deer stand or two by a field or large opening in the woods. The rest of us would get in a line and start walking toward them. Our going through the woods would scare the deer into moving, and we'd drive those moving deer right into the guys waiting. Bam, we'd get venison."

"That's not a bad idea, Johnson," Brian said.

"No, it isn't," Rahn agreed. "You've outdone yourself, Johnson."

Johnson smiled. "Thanks. It's all that E-4 mafia experience, First Sergeant. Nobody can make a job easier better than an E-4 who's probably going to have to do most of the work anyway."

"The E-4 mafia strikes again," Brian chuckled, remembering when he was an E-4. As it had been explained to him, the E-4 mafia was a collection of senior Army Specialists and a couple of Corporals who know what is really happening, know what will eventually happen, and almost always know another E-4 who is in a position to influence what needs to get done because most likely, they will be doing it. Outside the military, it was called networking and being truthful, Brian recognized. It had become a bit of a military urban legend that soldiers joked about while also wondering if it really does exist. "Let's head back to Fort Home, call most of the patrols in and plan this out. I think we can make this happen."

"Worst case, Chief, we can get a couple of deer out of it," Johnson remarked.

"You betchya," Rahn said with a large full-faced grin.

"Is that how you reply to a Specialist, First Sergeant?" Johnson asked, his eyes sparkling in amusement.

"Get in the Hummer, Johnson," Rahn replied.

Johnson quickly turned and jogged back to the vehicle, chuckling as he went.

"I think there's hope for that boy," Rahn quipped to Brian.

"Maybe we should promote him to Sergeant," Brian said.

"And make him cry?" Not waiting for a reply, Rahn said, "See you back at the cabin."

"You betchya, on the porch," Brian replied.

Rahn gave him a casual salute, which Brian returned with equal casualness, moving his hand somewhere in the vicinity of his forehead.

···◆◆◆···

King and his men completed their move just before the sun came up. Exhausted, and with a few scrapes and bruises from the journey, they made camp inside the tree line across the large field in back of the farmhouse.

"You men get set up and get some rest," King said. "Sibilski, you come with me. I want to check out our surroundings now that we have better light."

"Yes, sir," Sibilski replied.

As the other men picked out a spot to lay down and catch some sleep, King and Sibilski approached the edge of the trees, dropping down on their hands and knees to crawl forward. As they got to the edge, King took out his binoculars and scanned the field, starting first with a look at the white house at the far end, almost a thousand yards away. He could see smoke coming out of the chimney and two people walking outside toward a structure behind the house to what he thought might be a garage. Or maybe an outhouse. He continued to scan the field and the surrounding area. He saw little of interest—some scattered piles of small machinery in the field and a mound of dirt, but nothing more. Setting the binoculars down, he turned toward Sibilski and said, "Looks quiet. Is there a water source nearby?"

"There's a creek a couple of hundred yards behind us. It's slow-moving but probably clean enough."

"Good, but nobody drinks from it without using the water purification tablets. We don't need anyone getting sick out here," King said. "I'm going back with the others. Stay here, and in about four hours, I'll send someone to relieve you. If you see anything I need to know, come back and tell me. No yelling."

"Yes, sir," Sibilski replied.

···◆◆◆···

Rahn and Brian found me on the porch. I was sitting where I always sat and wasn't hard to find most days.

"You two look mighty chipper," I said as they stepped up on the porch. They both took a seat, grinning broadly.

"Yep, we're mighty chipper," Brian replied. "The E-4 mafia came through once again."

"That still exists?" I asked.

"It does," Rahn said in a serious tone. "Johnson must be one of the leaders. He came up with a great idea, and we want to run it by you."

"Okay," I answered. "Let's hear it."

Brian began to explain the idea of using a deer drive to speed things up and save time to find the FEMA scouts. I had to admit; the plan was a good idea.

"My only concern is safety," I said. "People have to make sure that they know what's behind any targets they might see. We don't need any friendly fire incidents. Especially if you guys drive a few "deer" out ahead of you, and you take advantage of those targets of opportunity."

"We're planning to use the Guard and Hummers as the blocking force," Brian said. "Jake and his people are better set up to go on horseback through the trees. We have the SAWs, and that gives us a better range and, if necessary, fire superiority."

"I'm sure the deer won't know the difference if they get shot by a SAW or an MP4," I quipped.

"Good point. I'll make sure the guys know only to use the SAWs against any human targets in FEMA attire if we find any," Brian said.

"When do you plan on having this little hunting party?" I asked.

"First thing in the morning. I left two patrols out there for the night along the county highway. They'll be stationary and are only looking for visitors coming our way. We'll swap them out when we head out," Brian said. As he finished, Jake walked up and joined us.

"I hear we're going hunting in the morning," he said.

"Word travels fast," Rahn said. "So much for OPSEC."

"I don't think we need to worry about Operational Security with these guys, Top," Jake said, laughing.

I noticed the word "Top" caused Rahn to grimace, but he had lightened up over the use of the word in the last weeks.

"So, what's the plan for this deer drive?" Jake asked.

Brian and Rahn spent about ten minutes explaining the idea, how Jake and his people would fit in, and then asked him if he had any questions or ideas.

"I think the idea's sound," Jake said. "I have no doubt we'll find deer, and we can argue over who's dressing them out. The Hummers can haul them back. But do you really think we have FEMA people in the area?"

"Sam heard them on the radio," I answered before anyone else had a chance to reply. "He said the signal was strong, and they talked about seeing my truck. He also said that he heard a little bit coming from Antigo. Maybe our boy Wolfe is there. Too bad, I'd hoped we had run him off after his last disaster. So put all of that together, and they are probably here somewhere. How many and where is the bigger question."

"It'll be hard to find a small group. This won't be like that group at the hatchery," Jake said.

"That's my thought, too," Rahn said. "In Iraq and Afghanistan, we sent out small teams to scout and see what they could find. They'd radio back in, and then we'd set up a strike of some kind."

"Does Sam have their frequency so he can monitor them?" Brian asked.

"He does, but he can't monitor 24/7. He has regular talks with people around the state, and he gets news from around the country. He can't spend all his time listening to dead air hoping he catches a transmission," I said.

"So, we start in the morning," Jake said.

"Early morning," Brian answered. "I want to be in place and ready to start before sunrise."

"Let me go tell my boys," Jake said. He stood and stepped down off the porch. "I hope we get some deer, we're gonna need a feast to quiet all the grumbling I'm getting ready to hear." He waved over his shoulder and headed toward the barn.

"Yeah, I better get the troops ready, too," Rahn said as he stood.

"I'll be along directly, First Sergeant," Brian said to him, watching Rahn head off to gather his men. "Think this bullshit will ever end, Dad?"

"I hope so, son. It is getting old, isn't it."

"Too old," he replied. "I hope we catch these guys, wipe them out, clean out the armory, and they leave us alone forever."

"If wishes were horses, and horses were men," I said. Before I could finish, Brian interrupted me.

"What?" he asked, confused.

"An old saying about wishes. I hope that your wish comes true, but I fear it won't. It won't until all of this returns to normal, and I don't think that will be anytime soon."

"I hope you're wrong, Dad. On this, I really do."

I nodded once in agreement. "Me, too."

CHAPTER 13

"Never let the future disturb you."

—Marcus Aurelius

The sun was beginning to set as King rounded his men up and began to brief them for the evening's activities.

"As soon as it's dark," he instructed, "we'll go out in two teams. Check your watches for the time. Leonard, you'll go with me. We'll take the north side of the road, in front of that house over there, and head east. We'll patrol till midnight and then return here. That's the direction you said you saw the truck drive away."

"Yes, sir, they pulled out of the driveway at the house and headed down the road that way," Leonard replied, pointing toward the east.

"Sibilski, you and Jackson, get close to the house. See if they have any guards out and where they are. Also, and this goes for everyone, no contact. You don't touch anyone, you don't talk to anyone, you don't get seen. Am I clear?"

"Yes, sir," all the men said softly.

"What do you want me to do, Lieutenant?" Gully asked.

"I want you here and alert. Make sure no one goes wandering on our site. As best you can, keep a watch on Sibilski and Jackson. Once it gets too dark to see, I want you set up on the edge of the field and listen."

"Listen for what, Lieutenant?" Gully asked.

"*Lord, help me.* Anything and everything. I want you to listen for those people who are looking for us. Listen to the nightbirds and insects. The best alarm you can have is when everything goes quiet," King explained. "Now, everyone chow down, no fires and no heaters for the MREs. I don't want any cooking odors drifting anywhere."

"Those things taste like shit when they're cold, Lieutenant," Leonard said.

"Most of 'em taste like shit when they're warm, Leonard. So eat 'em cold and be happy we have food," King replied. "We move out in an hour; get yourself taken care of and assemble back here. Gully, you might as well start your watch now. Keep an eye out, and let me know immediately if you see anything. I want a headcount of how many people you see."

"Yes sir," Gully mumbled, and grabbing his kit and an MRE, headed for the edge of the tree line, situating himself at the base of a large tree.

The rest of the men did as instructed, and afterward, gathered together, ready to begin their night patrols. All of them kneeled in a tight circle around King.

In a low voice, he said, "All of you know your instructions. There will be no contact with anyone. I don't care what you think might happen—do not be seen, do not talk to, or otherwise get close and personal with anyone you see. Am I clear?"

"Yes, sir," the men replied.

"Okay, Leonard and I are leaving now. Sibilski, you and Jackson head out at midnight. Get close to the house but don't get caught. Your primary mission is sentries. I want to know where and how many. How disciplined are they? Any questions?"

"Seems easy enough, Lieutenant. That's all you want us to do?" Sibilski asked.

"If you find no one outdoors, or what you find isn't worth worrying about, make your way into the town on the southside of the road. Do not cross over to the north side; that's where we will be. See if you can locate any OPs they may have in town. Remember, Major Wolfe told us about one of the patrols getting ambushed in town, which reminds me, stay off the road."

"Yes, sir," Sibilski said. "Lieutenant, what's an OP? You have to remember we ain't infantry grunts. We don't know all of those tactical words."

The remark brought a quick smile to King's face. "It's an outpost or observation post, Sibilski. Kinda like an early warning system."

"Oh, okay, Lieutenant," Sibilski replied.

"And Sibilski, I'm Air Force; we have better manners than the grunts." King's comment brought a chuckle from all of the men. Grunts were what Marine and Army infantrymen referred to themselves as. It had as much to do with the sound they made when carrying heavy loads on their backs as it did them spending so much time wallowing in the mud. "Any other questions or comments," King asked.

After a moment of silence, he said, "Okay, let's move out. Leonard, you lead the way; this is your show tonight."

Silently, Leonard picked up his weapon, and holding it in a low ready position as it hung from the two-point sling, he walked off into the darkness, followed by King.

· · ◆ ◆ ◆ · ·

It wasn't long before either man could be seen.

"When do you want to head out?" Jackson asked. The tremble in his voice showed he was scared or, at best, very nervous.

"Relax, kid," Gully said. "It will be a piece of cake. Those goobers over there in that farmhouse will probably all be asleep by the time the two of you get over there and check things out. It's when you head into town that things might get dicey."

"How's that?" Jackson asked wide-eyed.

"If one of those OPs are there, those people know what they are doing. Those Henry people are all trained and experienced. Look what they did to Major Wolfe's people. You heard what Edmiston said. It's those people you need to be nervous about, not those goobers in the farmhouse," Gully explained.

Jackson just swallowed and nodded his head.

"Leave the kid alone, Gully," Sibilski said. "This is his first time, and we don't need him scared shitless over anything."

"Fuck you, Ski," Gully said, causing Sibilski to glare at him until Gully turned his head and went back to where he was supposed to be watching the field from.

"Don't let him scare you, kid. Just stay alert, do what I tell you, and all will be fine," Sibilski said.

"Thanks, Ski," Jackson said softly. *But I am scared shitless.*

•••♦♦♦•••

I was in the dark, enjoying the quiet with just a soft glow of a lantern next to me for company when the creak of the screen door announced that I was no longer alone. Linda came out onto the porch, stopping long enough to slow the screen door's closing and avoid the telltale smack as the spring on it pulled it shut.

"Hi, John," she said as she walked over and handed me a glass.

"What's this?" I asked before sensing the telltale aroma of whiskey, most likely my Rebel Yell.

"I figured you'd need a drink," she answered.

"Why would I need a drink, and where did you find my whiskey?"

"Brian told me where it was," she explained.

"Brian told you?" I said, my face showing a bit of frustration. "Lovely, I'm going to have to hide it again. Now tell me, why do I need a drink?"

"Because you and I need to come to an understanding, and I don't think you'll like it."

"And what is that?" I asked.

Linda was starting to get more ambiguous, something she already did with great expertise. I have found many women do this, and I don't know if it's learned or natural. Either way, I didn't like it.

She sat down in the chair beside me and looked my way. "It's about what you did this morning. I didn't care for what you said to Zach and how you felt that you needed to rescue me. I'm a single mom, John, and I'm perfectly capable of taking care of myself and my two boys on my own."

"Okay, I get it. What would you have me to do in the future?"

"Nothing. You don't need to do anything. You're my friend. You aren't my boyfriend, my significant other, or my husband. Even if you were, I am perfectly capable of defending myself. I'd appreciate you butting out unless I ask for help."

"I see. So why do I need a drink?"

"Because you're taking me back over there in the morning," she replied.

"No, I'm not. We have an operation going on, and no one is going anywhere tomorrow except those involved in the operation."

"What do you mean? What operation? Everybody knows the men are looking for the FEMA people. It's been going on for days."

I explained the deer drive to her and how we were using a coordinated effort between the horse patrols and the Hummer patrols to try and find them.

"So, what makes it all that different than what you've been doing?"

"It's a more active push to try and flush these guys out of hiding. We know they are here. The other way we were searching for them required that we get lucky and stumble across them. This way, they get flushed out into the open, and then we manage the problem."

"You mean you shoot them," she said. Linda rarely raised her voice or changed her tone, at least around me. Even in the dark, I could tell she was angry with me, and it wasn't by hearing the tone of her voice.

"That's probably what they will do," I said, confirming it. "They don't belong here, we consider them a danger, and we will shoot them for that very reason."

"So what's changed? You've done that since I got here. Why can't you take me to see the refugees? Either you take me, or I'm walking. It's your choice."

"Dammit, Linda, why can't you, for once, just listen and do as others ask?" Now I was getting angry. "Why do you have to be so damn stubborn?"

"It's just who I am, John," she said, her voice softening. "I'm stubborn, and I've been stubborn all my life. It has served me well."

"It may have served you well and you may consider it a strength, but it can quickly become a weakness, ya' know."

She shook her head, her hair moving about her shoulders. "It's not a weakness. It's how I get things done. When I worked, when I ran a business, being stubborn meant I didn't quit. I have to help those people build that greenhouse. I promised I would. Time is ticking. You're always telling me how you keep your word and how you do everything you can to keep your word. Well, I'm doing the same damn thing. I am keeping my word. So, are you taking me or am I walking? Either way, I'm going there tomorrow."

"Damn, you *are* stubborn," I said. Then, I started laughing. That probably wasn't the best thing I could do. I almost spilled my drink, which would have been a sin.

"You're starting to piss me off, John," Linda said as she stood up, all five feet, seven inches of her towering over me.

"Sit down, Linda," I said. "I'm not laughing at you. I'm laughing at me."

With a confused look on her face, she sat down again. "Why are you laughing at yourself?"

"I'll take you over there tomorrow. I'm just as stubborn as you are, that's why. You win, okay?"

"Now was that so hard," she said, patting my arm with her hand.

"Yes, yes, it was. But the alternative is unacceptable, and I believe you're pigheaded enough to do it, too. You aren't walking over there alone, and that's final. So, I'll give in, which is what you wanted, and take you over there. You just need to understand one thing."

"What's that?" she asked, meeting my eyes.

"If Zach puts one hand on you in a way I decide is abusive, I'll beat his ass to a pulp. I will not compromise on that."

"Relax. He doesn't mean anything."

"I'm serious, Linda."

"So am I, John," she said as she stood up. She let the screen door swing closed naturally, the double *"whack"* as it bounced against the door frame ending our conversation.

I sat back and took a sip of the whiskey she'd brought me. *Women are hard to figure out sometimes.*

"Ahem," a sound in the dark startled me. "Is it safe to come up now?" It was Craig.

"Yes, it's safe," I answered. "How long have you been listening?"

"Long enough to know that woman is pissed at you, and you don't want to get on her bad side."

"It wasn't that bad, Craig."

"You weren't listening; you were just hearing. You said that to me a lot while I was growing up, Dad."

"I heard *every* word she said."

"Well, I'm not gonna argue with you," Craig said. "All I'm sayin' is, things aren't what you think they are."

"Whatever. So, what brings you up here? I thought you were out on patrol?"

"I am, or at least I was. We came back in to get ready for tomorrow."

"So, what do you think about the plan?"

"I think it's a good plan, but a few days late. We probably should have done it a week ago. Those people know we're looking for them now. They've probably left the area and moved on by now."

"Did you share your thoughts with Brian?" I asked.

"Yes. He said I had a point, but that we needed to do this his way. I can't say I disagree, but I still don't think this will work effectively."

"All we can do is try, son. I'm sick and tired of those people coming here. I just want to be left alone. I don't understand why they think they can run our lives, and I don't like the fact that they are trying. The things they've done, the…shit, you know. It's time for them to go and stay gone."

"Yup," Craig replied.

"So, did you just come here to tell me that?" I asked.

"No, I'm worried about Addie. Being pregnant has changed her. Shoot, being married has changed her. She worries more than she used to."

"We all worry, son. When women get pregnant, their bodies change, and some of them do act different. Hormones. Wait till the birth. You'll really understand *different* then."

"What do you mean?" Craig asked.

"I'm guessing you'll want to be there when Addie gives birth, right?"

"Yes."

"Well, when she's pushing and her labor pains are getting stronger, she may start cussing you. She might call you every name in the book and swear like a sailor."

"Oh," Craig said softly.

"Then after the baby comes, everything changes. They get all nice again."

He looked at me with hope in his eyes. "Really, Dad?"

"That's what happened with all three of you boys. So yeah, really."

"Lovely."

"It will be, son. Being a dad is the greatest thing in the world. You'll see very soon what I mean."

CHAPTER 14

—Hermann Hesse

King and Leonard slowly made their way across the field, planning to pass the farmhouse to its west side. Several times, they almost tripped over debris in the field that King identified as parts of motorcycles.

"Somebody must have had a bike repair shop around here," he whispered to Leonard. "Why they'd throw their garbage out here in the field makes no sense to me."

"That's common out here in the country, Lieutenant," Leonard whispered back. "They don't have garbage pickup, so they burn it, bury it, or toss it."

"Amazing," King replied. "You'd think out here in the country they'd think more about the environment than to throw garbage in a field."

"Oh, they care, Lieutenant. They just care different than those who are from the city."

"If you say so, Leonard. Let's get out of this field before someone sees us."

Leonard nodded his head and continued to lead the way across the open ground. "Shit," he exclaimed, and then realizing that he spoke a bit too loudly, said "shit" in a softer voice.

"What is it?" King asked in a low voice.

"Barbed wire fence," Leonard replied. "Tore my pants up a bit, too."

"You can take care of that later. Keep your voice down and your eyes open. We have a lot of ground to cover, and I don't want to spend the night hiding because we made too much noise."

"Yes, sir," Leonard replied. "There's a road here. Once we get across, we're back in the woods, and we can head east toward town. That's the direction I seen that truck go."

"Lead the way," King replied.

Leonard bent over and ducked under the fence. He then stopped and held the top strand up so King could get through it. They made their way across the road and back into the woods. The pine trees weren't very thick, leaving a clear pathway for them to head in the direction they needed to go.

"Should we keep going?" Leonard asked.

"Yup, the town should be up ahead a bit. Stop when you get there. We'll figure out which way to go then," King said.

"Yes, sir," Leonard said as he stepped forward into the darkening woods.

··◆◆◆◆··

Zach stepped out of the garage carrying a wood-framed double-hung window. Walking across the yard, he placed it on the ground next to the others.

"That makes eight," he said aloud to himself. "That should be enough."

Stepping away from the stack of windows, he placed his hands in the small of his back and rubbed the stiffness out. After stretching, he stared at his pile of windows. Stacked next to them were several 2X4s, an old wooden door, and some longboards.

Gonna be a busy day tomorrow. I'm not convinced this will work, but for everyone else's sake, I hope it does.

He stretched his back again, then began to cross the yard. Several others were gathered in the corner of the yard and starting a fire in the firepit.

"Hey, Zach," one of the men shouted to him as he approached. "You ready to start making that greenhouse?"

Laughter erupted from the group.

"You'd better hope that the damn thing works," Zach shouted back.

Then, dropping his tone to a normal level as he reached them, he continued, "Because without that greenhouse, we'll all be eating perpetual soup, and that's gonna get old real quick."

"What's perpetual soup?" one of the men asked. "Is that something the Henrys dreamed up for us?"

"Perpetual soup is when you start a pot on a stove, and it never stops cooking. You just keep adding water and whatever you have into the soup as you eat it. So, it's soup for breakfast, soup for lunch, soup for supper."

"That don't sound too good," the man said.

"It won't be after a while. We'll end up with venison, rabbit, squirrel, and any other animal we shoot in the stew," Zach said. "Their guts and stuff, too."

"How do you know all that shit, Zach? You're just a carpenter," the man said.

"I read about it in a book once. About how some people had to survive all winter long and then the summer until the gardens came in. Almost a year living off of the same crap," Zach answered.

"That don't sound too good at all," the man said. "I don't know why we just don't go to Wausau and the FEMA camp. They have food."

"Because Wendy and the almighty and knowing Henrys say those camps are just slave labor camps. That people are locked up for objecting to the camps, and some are killed because they wouldn't go into them willingly," Zach explained.

"You believe that?" the man asked.

"I don't know. Seems kinda far-fetched to me, but the Henrys sure believe it. My friend told me about some FEMA camps in Green Bay that were bad," Zach answered. "I'm tempted to go find out, though."

"Wendy would have your ass if you took off," the man said.

The others started to laugh.

"She ain't gonna do shit if I take off," Zach said angrily.

"Then why don't you go?" one of the men asked.

"I ain't ready to go. I want to see what happens here first."

"Yeah, he's got his eye on that woman who is friends with the Henrys. That's why you're stickin' around, isn't it Zach?" an older man mocked him.

"Fuck you, guys. Although I'll admit, she's good lookin'," he said with the beginning of a grin on his face.

"Wish we had something to drink around here besides water," somebody said.

"That would be nice. Anyone know how to make a still? I'm sure we could figure something out if we could make a still," another said.

All of the men started talking at once in their new excitement over the possibility of making a still and forgot about Zach and his fascination with Linda.

···◆◆◆···

Sibilski and Jackson exchanged a silent look. With nervous sweat streaming down their faces in the cool night air, the two men began to slowly crawl away. Each man inched quietly backward, deeper into the dark of the field, and away from the group at the fire. It seemed like an eternity to crawl the twenty or so yards they had traveled.

In a soft whisper, Sibilski said, "Did you hear that? I think there's people here who don't like the Henrys."

"What are we gonna do about it, though?" Jackson whispered back. "The lieutenant said no contact with these people."

"We'll have to tell him about it. He needs to know this," Sibilski replied. "We should move toward town. I don't think we'll see anything here for a while. Let's crawl back a bit more and head that way."

Jackson nodded his head, and they began their slow journey toward town.

···◆◆◆···

"Shit," King said softly.

Leonard stopped and quickly looked around.

The two men had entered the town and were across from the burnt remains of several buildings and a gas station. Concealed by the darkness, King dropped to a knee and pointed across the road. There, barely visible, behind a pile of burnt wood and branches, was a Humvee. The silhouette of a man standing in the turret next to a SAW was barely visible.

King motioned for Leonard to move back, and slowly the two men made their way into the pine woods behind them.

"What?" Leonard whispered.

"There, hiding behind all that debris," King whispered as he pointed.

Leonard followed his pointing finger and saw the Hummer. "Shit," he said.

"That would not have been good if they saw us. We have to be close to the Henry place," King said. "That's probably a forward scout position. You can bet they have radio contact, too."

"Now what?"

"Let's get deeper into these woods and head east. We've got to be close." Looking at his watch, he said, "We've got about an hour before we have to start heading back."

"Okay," Leonard answered.

"Hopefully, we don't run into any more scouts," King said, almost unnecessarily.

··•◆•··

Sibilski and Jackson made their way into town and stopped behind the burned-out remains of several buildings. They sat by a large garbage bin behind what appeared to have been a restaurant.

"Now what?" Jackson asked.

"Let's sit here for a while and watch. If we don't see anything, we'll head back to that house, watch and see if they have any guards out, and then go back to our camp," Sibilski answered. He reached around for his canteen and took a sip. "Besides, I'm hungry, and I'm gonna sit here, eat, and take a break."

"All I've got is some beef sticks from my MRE," Jackson said.

"Sucks to be you," Sibilski said. "I've got pretzels and peanut butter. Lucky me."

The two men sat silently as they munched on their meager food. Neither spoke as the night sounds, silent when they moved into the area, began to return tenfold.

"Kinda loud out here in the middle of nowhere," Jackson said.

"It's the best warning device you'll ever have. The crickets and other animals stop making noise when something unnatural starts moving around. That's why we don't hear anything when we are moving. If they stop making noise, something is close, so shut up and listen," Sibilski said.

Doing as he was told, Jackson sat there, eating his beef sticks and listening to the sounds of nature around him. It didn't take long before he heard Sibilski quietly snoring.

Settling his back against the garbage bin, he did the only thing he knew how to do. He sat there nervously, waiting for the noises to stop.

··✦·✦·✦··

I decided to stay up. I couldn't sleep anyway, and with Jake's people, which included Craig, Rick, and Sajan heading out well before sunrise, I decided I wanted to see them off anyway. It had been some time since I sat on the porch in, as my favorite singer Frank used to say, the wee small hours, but I did. The night noises were everywhere, and an old hoot owl kept me entertained. The scream of a rabbit being caught by something added to what the new day could bring.

Max and King were curled up across from me, and I debated getting a light jacket as the night air was a bit cool. Fall was closing in, and my choice of clothing was going to have to change soon. Being here by myself gave me time to think things over and have some quiet time. I glanced over at the door a time or two, just waiting for the creak of its hinges to tell me my private time was being interrupted. It didn't, and for that, I was glad.

Much had happened since spring. It was well beyond what my sometimes overactive imagination would have ever thought could happen. Of course, the effects of the EMP on all of our lives was first and foremost at the front of my mind. Having Brian, Nancy, and Mike join me here was beyond perfect. I'd have been worried sick over them being so far away and not knowing anything about them. I still worried about my oldest son, John, but I'd accepted that I couldn't do anything to help him. To try would be suicide. Instead, I hoped for his safety. I missed Carol. We had something special. We weren't in love or anything, but what we had was something I would never forget. She was avenged, and Brian and Craig handled that.

It's a hard thing to admit that you're proud of your sons for killing other human beings, but they did, and it was, truth be told, for more than just Carol. Craig had found a wife. The last thing any of us ever expected out of this, and I was soon to be a grandpa again.

Then with Rahn and his men joining us, Jake and his people added, it showed me that in our darkest times, we can all come together and stand up for what we believe is the heart and soul of our community. None of us would have survived as well as we had without each other.

Then there was Linda. My conundrum. A very attractive woman. She and her boys fit right in with the rest of the group. Ten years ago, I'd have thought something could come of a relationship between us. I doubted her plans included me. We were alike, but not enough of each other's type for anything other than blunt friends. Regardless, she was a gift sent by the Gods to help us. She had skills none of us had and a spunk that set her apart, even from Donna, who could be quite willful.

The women were a tight group, and they all worked well together. We wouldn't survive without them, and there was little they couldn't do.

I remembered back to a time when we were all sitting on the porch, sharing stories. Donna and Carol were talking about their time in the service. Donna was army and Carol was air force. In the middle of all of it, Linda gave the classic line, "I almost joined up, but…"

In days past, those of us serving or who had served found people humorous who said that. Linda made the story different only in the way she could. She wanted to enlist and be a sniper, but at the time, they wouldn't let her. Everyone was silent for a moment, not knowing whether to believe her or not.

Leave it to Brian to break the silence when he said something along the lines of, "Well, it's a good thing you didn't cuz we could have met in Iraq, and you'd have never been the same."

I thought Nancy was going to kill him, probably literally, too. Brian's humor was such that his comment could have meant anything. From innocent to tawdry, he was good with the double entendre.

I wish we could have more of those gentle evenings, sitting around and telling stories. That thought no sooner entered my brain when a clattering of activity over by the barn told me Jake and his people were forming up. Things were about to start happening. My quiet time was over.

CHAPTER 15

"The advantage of obtaining the earliest and best intelligence of the desires of the enemy…have induced me to trust the management of this business to your care."

—George Washington

Colonel Wayne Harrigan's short, stocky body moved quickly down the hall. He didn't like what he had just learned, and he was going to put a stop to it. Turning left down the hall, he entered the assembly room and stopped. With his hands on his hips, he glanced across the room. His breathing was heavy, as much from his rapid pace as from the anger swelling inside of him.

"Where is Major Wolfe?" he bellowed across the room.

All of the men stopped what they were doing and stood up. No one spoke.

Platoon Sergeant Mark Thomas hurried across the room and stood in front of the colonel. Saluting, he said, "Sir, I believe the major is outside by the vehicles."

Returning the salute, Colonel Harrigan took a breath and said, "Thank you, carry on." He quickly turned and stormed out of the room. *I'm going to find that devious little son of a bitch.*

He found Major Wolfe and Edmiston leaning against the hood of one of the black Humvees in the parking lot. It was clear the loud banging of the door startled them, and both men looked toward the armory. "WOLFE!" he shouted.

"Shit," Wolfe muttered.

"I'd better go, Major," Edmiston said as he moved quickly away from the approaching colonel.

Colonel Harrigan reached Wolfe and, placing his fists on his hips, glared at the major.

Breaking the silence, Major Wolfe said, "Yes, sir. How can I help you?"

"You can stand at attention, Major. That's how this will begin," Harrigan said loudly.

Wolfe slowly moved himself into a position resembling being at attention. The silent insolence was not lost on Harrigan.

"What is your problem, Wolfe?" Harrigan asked, his tone demanding.

"I don't know what you mean, sir," Wolfe answered.

"You know damn good and well what I mean, Major. Just what in the hell do you think you are doing putting together a secret assault team? I did not order you to do that, did I?"

"Sir, I was putting together a team that was prepared to move once Lieutenant King notified us he had found the Henry camp."

"Bullshit, Major. That's bullshit, and you know it. Did I not tell you that King would come back here, and we would then plan our assault on the camp? Did I not say that?"

"I was using initiative, sir. A good infantry officer uses initiative…"

"A good infantry officer does what he's been told to do, Major. We don't need your special team. You know just as well as I do that your man Thomas is still training people. That will be the team."

"Yes, sir."

"Yes, sir, my ass, Major. You are *not* in command here. I am, and you follow my orders. Is that clear?"

"Yes, sir."

"Good. Now, I don't want to hear any more about you forming up your own team. So help me God, if you keep this up, I'm sending you back to Wausau and putting you in confinement with those other soldiers back there. Understand?" Without waiting for an answer, Harrigan spun around and walked back toward the door to the armory.

"Yes, sir," Wolfe replied, mostly to himself. *Other solders? Confinement? What the hell?*

·· ◆ ◆ ◆ ◆ ··

King and Leonard had gone as far as they dared for the night. "I can smell wood smoke," Leonard remarked as they stopped for a quick break before turning around and heading back to their camp.

"So do I. We've got to be close. Smoke can travel quite a distance, and I don't want to spend the night out here away from our camp where no one will know where we are," King said.

"Not like the old days, is it, Lieutenant," Leonard said.

"No. If it was the old days, I'd be in a nice comfortable bed right now or working in a nice comfortable office. I wouldn't be eating dehydrated food out of a plastic bag," King replied with a grin. "We should start heading back now. We've a long walk, and that guard post we passed is in the way."

"Following you, Lieutenant."

·· ◆ ◆ ◆ ◆ ··

Sibilski and Jackson crawled across the field. They could see the embers and an occasional flame pop up from the fire where they had observed the group talking. Even though neither man could see anyone outside or guarding the property, they knew to be cautious. *I can't believe these fools don't have any guards out,* Sibilski thought. *But with my luck, the second I stand up, some clown is going to see me, and then we're caught.*

Sibilski reached for a small stick that was lying in front of him. He tossed it toward Jackson and said, "Psst."

Jackson turned his head and faced Sibilski.

Without speaking, Sibilski pointed toward the field, indicating he wanted Jackson to move further away from the house and into the middle of the field. After a few minutes, the two men lay with their heads together.

Sibilski whispered, "Do you see anyone in the yard or around the house or garage?"

"No," Jackson whispered back. "I don't see a thing. Do you think they have guards out?"

"It doesn't look like it, but I'll be damned if I'm gonna stand up and be the one that gets seen. Let's crawl further out, and then we'll get up and head back to the camp."

Jackson nodded his head, and the two men headed deeper into the darkness as far away from any possible prying eyes as possible.

···◆◆◆···

The noise of men and horses seemed loud as the teams formed up to head out. Easing myself out of my chair, I went to the barn. The dogs took a look at me as I ambled away, then went back to their snoozing. I'd ignored them these last few weeks, and the way they reacted to me showed. The young kids still gave them a lot of attention, though. I guess you could say they were put out with me and my seeming ambivalence toward them. Dogs teach us a lot. When we ignore them, over time, they will ignore us, too. I planned to spend more time with them when I got back.

The men's activity at the barn now wasn't up to the amount of noise I'd heard before. Mostly chatter and the occasional nicker of a horse. Searching around, I found Craig and Brian. They were talking with Jake, and it looked like they were in good spirits. I caught the tail end of their conversation as I approached.

"So, once you are in place, we'll move the Hummers into a blocking position," Brian said.

"Yep," Craig answered. "Jake and I'll be on opposite ends of the line of riders, and we'll move toward you."

"I put Rick in the center. He knows this area the best, and he can get some experience by having everyone guide on him," Jake interjected.

"Guide on?" Craig asked.

"Yep, fuzzy," Jake said as he reached out and tugged on the beard Craig was growing. "Guide on. It's an army term. It means we line up on him to the left and right, parallel to the direction we will be going, and he sets the pace."

"Why didn't you just say that then," Craig said as he good-naturedly swatted Jake's hand away.

"'Cause it sounds cooler when you talk army shit," Jake said.

That was my cue to interrupt. "Mornin'," I said.

"Mornin', John. We get more work done before 9 a.m. than most people do all day," Jake replied with a chuckle.

"That old army commercial was funny back in the 80s, Jake. Like you and me, it's old now," I responded.

"So, what's the schedule?" I asked, switching the conversation to business. I was nervous for the men. I still feared someone getting shot by friendly fire, plus we didn't know if anyone was still out there or not.

"We're heading out in about 15 minutes," Jake answered. "We'll ride to just west of the hatchery, around where the highway makes that big S. We'll then go into the woods, line up facing northeast, and start driving them toward town."

"So, you'll be west of the river and have to cross that," I said.

"It's a shallow river," Jake said.

"Lots of trees," I replied.

"It's a pine forest, lots of ground, too. We'll be fine, John," Jake said. "Relax, we got this."

"We got it, Dad," Brian said. "After sunrise, we'll head out with the Hummers and line up near Carol's field."

"The biker battlefield," I interrupted.

"Yeah," Brian answered, giving me a look that held many stories, all best left for another time. "I'm taking that group. We'll sit there and wait for Jake and his men to drive whatever they can to us."

"What are your rules of engagement?" I asked.

"Simple, we don't shoot unless fired on," Rahn said. "If the riders engage, they call in the cavalry."

Rahn, Johnson, and Schwartz had walked up on us as we spoke.

"Funny, Rahn," Jake said. "Last I checked, we don't call the cavalry for rescue. Tends to turn out badly for us."

"You forget, Jake, I'm one of you, too, now," Rahn said. The wrinkles around his eyes as he smiled showed he was joking.

"Okay, you two," Brian said without a twinkle in his eyes. "Worst case, at the end of the day, we have fresh meat."

"A couple of deer *would* be nice," Craig said, interrupting.

"As I was saying," Brian said, clearly not liking the interruption. "Worst case, we bag some deer and can stock up the smokehouse. Best case, we catch these guys and wipe them out."

"You going with them, Chris?" I asked.

"Not this time," he answered. "We're heading out to meet Yerks and Captain Handy about phase two."

"You still think it's a good idea to attack the armory again?" I asked.

"We have no choice. If you want peace, we need to run them out of here. We need to make sure they never come back again. I only know one way to do that, Dad," Brian answered.

"He's right, John," Rahn said. "They won't stop. Ever. They have no choice, they have to destroy us, or we destroy them."

"I just remembered something from a long time ago," I said.

"What?" Craig asked.

I looked at Craig. "That just because you've killed a man doesn't mean you've converted him."

"What does that mean?" Craig asked.

"It basically means that you are going to have to kill every one of them, every FEMA or guard member that lines up with them. After that, there will be others. That's what it means," I answered.

"It's going to be that way for a long time," Brian said. "That's our new normal."

"Fear, like a living fire that only death might one day cool. The fire of death we saw that horribly consumed him while he crumbled and said nothing," I muttered.

"John, don't go getting all intellectual on us now," Jake said, laughing. "He did that when we were in the army, too. When he got frustrated, he'd start getting intellectual like that."

"What's that, John?" Rahn asked.

"A poem by Edwin Robinson. It's about the destruction of a man's life because he was consumed by hatred," I answered.

"Never heard of him, or it," Jake quipped. "But then, I never heard of most of the people you quote. He likes those old poets and things."

"Doesn't matter. It's just how my mind works. If I'm not mentally creating a song or music to go with what's happening, I remember an old poem. A poem is what brought me here, remember."

"Yeah, I remember you telling me about that right after you got up here," Jake said. "Something about a house on a lake or something like that. Look around, John, no lake."

"Enough jabbering," Brian interrupted. "You guys have to head out."

"Rick!" Jake shouted.

"Ya' know, other people are sleeping," I said.

"If I whispered, he wouldn't have heard me," Jake said, smirking. "Rick, get 'em mounted up."

Shaking my head, I extended my hand to Craig. As he took it, I said, "Be safe out there. Watch your perimeter and listen to Jake. He knows what he's doing."

"You betchya, Dad," Craig said.

I saw Rahn grinning and shaking his head from the corner of my eye. He'd mellowed over the last few months.

"Good hunting, Chief," Rahn said as he began to leave.

"We aren't leaving for an hour or so," Brian replied.

"We, on the other hand, are leaving now," Rahn said. "Johnson, Schwartz, go get the vehicle ready." The two men jogged off to do as ordered.

"We need to start thinking about our fuel problem, too," Rahn said.

"I talked with Hart about that," I said. "He's sending a team out to find whatever containers we can find, and then we'll pump out the Quik Mart. We should find some other gas stations around here and get into their underground tanks, too."

"Sounds good. We'll get on that when I get back," Rahn replied. "Right of the line, Chief."

"Climb to glory, First Sergeant," Brian replied.

"You two and your 10th Mountain Division shit," Jake said as he walked away.

"It's who we are," Brian said, grinning.

"It was our division and brigade, John. It meant a lot back then," Rahn said. "Still does."

"You don't need to explain that to me," I said.

Rahn saluted Brian casually and walked off. I stood there with Brian, neither of us saying a word as we watched eight men ride off on horses into the early morning and the unknown.

CHAPTER 16

*"I have never made but one prayer to
God, a very short one: 'O Lord make my
enemies ridiculous.' And God granted it."*

—Voltaire

King and Leonard had made it past the observation post at the burned-out gas station. Putting a couple of hundred yards between them and it, King said, "Let's take a break. We've about half a mile to go before we have to cross over the road into the field and get to the camp."

"No argument from me, Lieutenant," Leonard said. "What do you plan on doing next, sir?"

"I think we were real close to where those people live. Depending on what Sibilski and Jackson have to say, we may move closer to where we are now and then find them. I think if we head north of here and then patrol to the south, we'll find what we're looking for."

"Then what, Lieutenant, are we gonna attack them?"

"We'll see, Leonard. I want to know as much as I can before I make any plans. But you can bank on my words. If Sibilski and Jackson have a negative report, we are moving tonight to a new location."

"What about those people in that house?" Leonard asked.

"What about them. For now, they aren't our concern. We can deal with them later. Once we finish with the Henrys and those guardsmen, we can move in and get those people into the camps where we want them."

"Yes, sir."

"We'll sit here for about ten minutes and then head on back the rest of the way. We need to be back in camp before sunrise."

"What's that sound, Lieutenant?" Leonard had turned his head back to the east, toward the direction where they had come. A clattering of noise broke the still quiet of the night. Then a shout, "Helloooo."

"What the hell," King said as he dropped onto his stomach and crawled toward the road. There, in the distance, he saw a man on horseback talking with another man on foot.

Must be checking on the observation post, King thought. As he lay there and watched, he saw more riders join the man. *What the hell?*

The group began moving forward on the road toward where King was lying. Daring not to move, King buried his face into the dirt below him. Not wanting to chance any light reflecting off of his face, he remained still as the steady clop-clop-clop of horses walking on the road resonated through the otherwise quietness of the town.

As they passed, King could hear quiet conversations as the men joked with each other. Someone with a voice of being in charge told them to quiet down, and the chatter stopped. It seemed like an eternity before the sounds of horses and men disappeared into the distance.

Taking a chance, King lifted his head and looked down the road. Down the road, in the direction he and Leonard must go. *Shit.* Crawling back into the woods, he rejoined Leonard. "What did you see?" King asked.

"From back here, Lieutenant, I saw a lot of armed men on horseback," Leonard answered.

"Did you manage to get any kind of a headcount?"

"No, sir, it was just a lot."

"Okay, let's head out. Be real careful. They are somewhere in front of us, and I don't want to walk up on them."

Leonard placed his rifle in a low ready position and followed King into the dark.

·····◆◆◆·····

Brian and I talked until it was time for him to head out. He put Hart in charge of the three Hummers that would provide the successive blocking for the drive, and he took the one that would, to use his words, "play Safety in Carol's field."

As he drove off with his team, I headed for the cabin and walked in through the back door. Nancy was in the kitchen, drinking a cup of herbal tea and talking with Linda. Beyond the soft murmur of their voices, the cabin was silent.

"Morning, ladies," I said as I walked in. Nancy said good morning, but Linda said nothing. I don't know if she didn't hear me, which was doubtful, or if something else was going on. Perhaps leftover anger from our conversation about Zach. I wasn't in the mood for these kinds of games, but I also wasn't in the mood to be ignored in my own home. Nancy and I made eye contact, and she gave me that look that said she didn't know what was going on. Nancy and I didn't always agree, but we could communicate easily.

"Is the water on the stove still hot?" I asked.

"Yes, I just took it off the burner," Nancy replied.

I grabbed a tea diffuser and put in the makings for the herbal tea Nancy had out. After adding it and water to my cup, I moved over to the table and sat down. "What time were you wanting to head out?" I asked Linda.

"I don't know," she answered. "Whenever you're ready. I don't want to impose."

That was a 180 from last night. What the hell was going on now? "Okay, I'll grab something to eat, and we'll head out. Get what you need to take with you," I said.

I went to the stove and began to get together some things for a breakfast of scrambled eggs and venison sausage. I would have preferred to have made a sandwich, but we were saving the flour for winter and using it sparingly right now. I had seeds for wheat, but it wouldn't be until next year that we'd have a harvest. So, for now, it was scrambled eggs and venison sausage.

After breakfast, Linda and I got in my truck, and we headed toward Wendy and the Shawano refugees. As soon as we were on the road, I decided I wasn't going to put up with the silent treatment any longer.

"So, what's on your mind?" I asked.

"Thinking about the greenhouse," she replied.

"What about it?"

"How big will it be? How many we should have? Simple things."

"You seem angry," I said.

"I'm not angry."

"You seem like it."

"John, I'm thinking about the greenhouse, okay?"

"Fine," I replied, and we continued the short drive in silence. As I pulled into the drive, I saw Wendy talking with Zach near a pile of wood and old windows. A deep hole had been dug and squared off. A pile of large rocks was next to the mound of dirt from the hole. They'd been busy. A work team was crossing the road, axes and saws in hand—obviously, a firewood detail.

I waved at Wendy as Linda and I walked toward them. Wendy came near us and said, "Good morning."

Linda and I both replied. Giving Linda a look of frustration, I said, "Wendy, let's go for a walk."

"Good, I want to talk with you, too. We can start with why that military vehicle with the machine gun is in the field." She gestured out across the field where Brian and his crew were walking around a parked Humvee, the SAW up in the turret clearly visible from here.

"We have people driving through the woods looking for those FEMA people I told you about."

"The ones you said were sneaking around here in the woods," she replied.

"Yes, those men. The vehicle is there in case they come this way."

"What happens if they do?" she asked, alarmed.

"We make them leave," I replied. I left the rest unspoken, but I'm certain Wendy understood. In the distance, I saw Zach and Linda talking. Linda had her hand on Zach's arm as she led him around, and even from here, very animatedly showed him what she wanted for the greenhouse. I shook my head. She didn't get it.

"How's the wood gathering going?" I asked, using my head to point across the road where the sound of axes against trees was clearly heard.

"It's going well. They've managed to cut quite a bit, but we'll need more. Our next challenge is getting it across the road and over here," she answered.

"I think we can help you with that. We've a wagon and team we can hitch up to haul wood over here. Should take a good day, but we can get it done," I said.

"Thank you, John. I'm still concerned about food, though."

"I get it. The greenhouses will help once we get them established and warmed up. We've got seeds for

you for some things, and we can provide a few others. It may turn into perpetual soup and wild herbs
and so on until then."

"Zach has already warned everyone about the
soup. They didn't seem too pleased."

I flinched. "Not much we can do about that. We're
stretched pretty thin with all the people we have, and
while we can maybe do some trading with the folks
still on the rez, it will be a lean and most likely very
soupy winter."

"If soupy winter is supposed to be a joke, stick to
your day job, John. You'll not make it as a come-
dian," she said, chuckling.

"Nobody appreciates my humor," I replied. "Let's
go see the plan and progress for that greenhouse."

··◆◆◆◆··

"Lieutenant. Lieutenant." The whispered calling of
his title awakened King. Opening his eyes and staring about him, he saw Gully kneeling next to him, a
look of concern etched on Gully's face.

"What is it?" King asked. His voice was thick from
having just awakened.

"We've got company, sir," Gully replied.

King rapidly sat up. As if on a swivel, his head
turned from side to side, searching for the "company" Gully had mentioned.

"Not here, sir. Out there," Gully said, pointing toward the edge of the trees and the field beyond.

Standing quickly and then crouching down, he followed Gully toward the tree line and then, dropping onto his stomach, crawled forward. Plainly visible, about a hundred and fifty yards away, was a National Guard Humvee with a turret-mounted SAW.

"Shit," King muttered. The word was rapidly becoming a major part of his vocabulary. "How long have they been there?"

"Maybe twenty minutes, Lieutenant," Gully replied. "At first, it looked like they were just driving past, but then they stopped and got out. That's when I figured I should wake you."

"Stay here and keep an eye on them. If it looks like they are coming this way, let me know. I'm going to wake up the others and tell them. We might be moving out."

"Yes, sir."

King crawled back and woke the other men up, instructing each of them to be quiet and to keep themselves low to the ground and out of sight. Gathering all but Gully around him, he said, "We have company."

Startled looks and heads turning rapidly was the response to his words.

"Out there in the field is a Humvee with a SAW and a crew of three. They don't appear to know we are here."

"How do you know that, Lieutenant?" a sleepy Sibilski asked.

"Because they have a SAW, Sibilski. If they knew we were here, we'd be dead," King replied. His words dripped with sarcasm driven as much by a lack of sleep as by his frustration over a stupid question. "Last night, Leonard and I think we got real close to where the home of these people is. We're gonna move closer to there, but we have to be careful. Not only do we have our friends out there in the field, we found an Observation Post in the ruins of an old gas station."

"We were real close to there, Lieutenant," Jackson said. His wide eyes seemed to register the surprise he felt at this discovery. "They were there, and we watched them. We also saw a lot of people on horseback riding down the road last night. Coulda been a dozen. We didn't get a good count."

"What the hell's going on, sir?" Sibilski asked.

"I think they are looking for us. If I had to guess, I think they're going to move through the woods on horseback and try to get us out into the open," King replied.

"But we ain't there, sir," Sibilski said.

"Exactly," King said. "And we aren't going to be here much longer, either. Pack up your stuff and get ready to move out. We're heading south for about a mile, and then we'll turn east, coming in behind the town. I want to be between that old gas station and where we think these people live by nightfall."

"Thought you only wanted to move at night, Lieutenant," Leonard said.

"That is what I said, Leonard. But we can't stay here with those people making a hard move to find us. I'm not willing to sit here and wait to see if they do. We move out in ten minutes."

"Yes, sir," the men quietly replied.

··•✦•··

The greenhouse, or I should say houses, because they were making two of them, were progressing rapidly. The holes dug, their floors, and some of the walls lined with rocks were deep enough. The walls for the greenhouses were getting framed, and the windows would be facing south. I didn't much care for Zach, but I was impressed by his work. He and Linda seemed to be getting on like best friends. That troubled me. It wasn't because I was jealous or anything even remotely like that. I think it was because I cared, and I'd seen far too many women get taken in by the smooth antics of a jerk and then end up getting hurt. Linda was a nice person, and she'd had a lot of crap happen to her in the last few months. She didn't need any more trouble.

"Looks good, John," Wendy remarked. She smiled at me in that way that says, see, I told you it would be okay.

"It does, I have to admit, it does," I answered. "I didn't think you'd find enough materials to make more than one," I said loudly.

"I'm not very good at what I do, Mr. Henry. Just dumb old me fumbling around not knowing what I'm doing," Zach said, his tone and intention obvious.

"That's enough, Zach," Wendy quickly said. "It was meant as a compliment."

Zach shook his head and went back to work.

Linda smiled at me and started laughing with Zach. They were sharing some private joke, apparently.

"They seem to know what they are doing," I said to Wendy.

"That they do, John. Let's leave these two alone and go see how the woodcutters are doing. Maybe swing by the garden plots to make sure those are being set up for later. You said something about winter wheat. Maybe we can start with that soon. Be nice to have flour for fresh bread before next fall."

I knew what she was doing, and she was right to do it. My dislike of Zach would have inevitably started something, and we didn't need that. We all needed to work together.

··✦✦✦··

"He doesn't hate you," Linda said as Wendy and John walked off.

"He's an ass," Zach replied as he drove another nail into the greenhouse frame he was working on. "He talks to me like I'm some kind of idiot."

"He just has a strong personality, Zach," Linda said. "I wouldn't make anything of it."

"You're really nice to me," Zach said. "I like that."

"We're friends, nothing more. Don't go reading more into this than what is there."

"I know, it's just that… Never mind. Friends, it is," he replied.

··◆◆◆··

Jake had the men line up along an approximate third of a mile stretch. He held the north end closest to the road, although that would change as they headed north by northeast on their drive. Craig anchored the southern end of the line with Rick in the center. He would set the pace. By agreement, Jake would fire one round, signaling the men to move forward. That had been a matter of some debate. Some felt it would alert who they were looking for, causing them to run or go into hiding. Others felt that it was okay because the purpose of the drive was to make them run. In the end, Jake made the decision. "I'm firing a round," he commanded. That ended the discussion.

"BAM!" One round echoed across the fields and through the woods. All of the men moved slowly forward, prodding their mounts with their heels. They all carried rifles. Some had ARs, and a couple had deer rifles. It was supposed to be a deer hunt, they reasoned. About a half-mile in front of them, Hart had lined up three Hummers facing west, each with a turret-mounted SAW and a crew of three. It was probably overkill, and the fields of fire risky if anything to shoot was between them. This first field was little more than a practice run to get the men accustomed to what each was to do and to find any flaws in their plan, such as fields of fire that made friendly fire casualties a possibility.

Standing outside of his Humvee, Hart watched the men slowly make their way across the field. Turning to his driver, PFC Travis, he said, "They look like they're on parade out there."

"Looks like fun, Specialist Hart," Travis replied.

"It's fun if at the end of the day you want a sore crotch. I also see a problem," Hart replied.

"What's that?"

"If whoever we are looking for was between us, and we both started shooting, we could have friendly fire casualties. I need to talk to Jake and work out a better ROE protocol."

"Good idea," Travis said in almost a whisper.

CHAPTER 17

*"Being a family means you are a part of
something very wonderful."*

—Unknown

It had been a long day. I spent much of it pacing around home. I think I inspected everything at least twice, visited with Gary, Sam, checked the guard posts in the tree stand in the back, the bunker in the front, the pigpen, the barn, and just about everything else I could think of. I caught Donna and Nancy watching me from the porch, whispering. I think they were wondering just what I was up to. Mike, Caleb, and Ethan were running around the yard kicking a ball. After the bear incident, they were forbidden to go in the woods without the equivalent of a full combat infantry squad, and at the moment, we had those occupied.

I checked on them every now and then. I expected the ball to be "accidentally kicked into the woods," and they having to look for it several hundred yards into those woods. Boys will be boys, and those three liked to push their limits.

I made my way to the porch and parked my behind in my chair. I stretched out my legs and took a deep breath. In the grander scheme of things, we were okay. We weren't great, but we were okay. The biggest thing was we had enough. Enough in the sense that we had plenty to survive and not worry too much about tomorrow. Our only real concern, the fear, if you will, was our safety and security.

The guys out doing their deer drive were, in my mind, out on a lark. I really didn't expect much to come out of it except a few deer for the smokehouse and maybe a huge barbecue. Even that had me concerned, as I was worried about a friendly fire incident. I trusted Jake to keep the drivers in line. With Brian in the position of last resort, the Safety position as he called it, the plan seemed viable. Brian loved his football metaphors. I was comfortable we had done all we could.

Getting Wendy and the Shawano people set up before the snow started to fly was also an issue. Again, we were doing the best we could, but was it enough? I'd already decided they were going to get at least one of the deer; I was confident we'd have more than one, and that would mend any potential hurt feelings about feeding them. I had little confidence in the greenhouses working come winter, even with my idea of building them below the frost line. It just got too cold here, but maybe, maybe the pits would work. Linda was of the opinion that it would work. In my mind, all it would take was a couple of days of solid below-zero weather and clouds to kill off anything inside them. We'd have to wait and see. I hoped she was right.

I heard giggling behind me and thought I was about to get ambushed. Preparing myself, I folded my hands across my stomach, closed my eyes, and faked a real loud snore.

"ROAR!" Instantly, two boys made it onto the porch and proceeded to attack. They were joined a few seconds later by a third.

"Whoa," I shouted as I jumped up and pretended to be scared.

"We got you good, Grampa," Mike said a bit loudly.

"We got you, Mr. John," Ethan said. As usual, behind him, a smiling but quiet Caleb stood.

I fell back into my chair and put my hand on my chest. "You boys scared me good. You shouldn't do that to an old man," I said, pretending to breathe heavily and act as scared as I could.

The screen door creaked. We were not alone. Nancy and Linda came out on the porch, and like a singing duo, said, "What's all that racket out here?"

"We scared Grampa real good, Mom," Mike explained.

"Yeah, we did. We scared Mr. John real good," Ethan said.

"You okay, FIL?" Nancy asked, a huge smile crossing her face.

"I think I'll live," I replied. "Those boys scared me good. I think we need to find some work for them to do."

"Noooo," the older two said together. "We're playing."

"We didn't mean to scare Grampa too much," Mike said. "We're just playing. Aren't we, Grampa?"

"I don't know," I said. "You have an awful lot of energy that we could put to work."

"I have just the thing in mind," Linda said. "You three come inside with me right now."

"Aww, Mom," Ethan said.

"Now," she exclaimed.

I couldn't help but notice a slight grin as she tried to be serious.

"Yes, Mom," Ethan said.

The three boys trooped inside after Linda. Mike, the last one through the door, turned, and smiling at me, gave me a thumbs up. I gave him one back.

"I'm worried, FIL," Nancy said after the boys were inside.

I looked up at her, catching the grim expression on her face. "What are you worried about?"

"Everything," she answered. "I don't know what I'm doing out here, and I feel lost."

"You're doing great, Nancy. We're all figuring this out as we go."

"It's still scary. Sometimes I can't sleep at night from worry."

"I sit out here a lot at night," I said, moving my gaze to the yard. "If you ever feel you need company, just come on out. I'm probably here."

Before she could answer, the roar of multiple Hummers came up the drive and four of them, one right after the other, filed into the yard. I saw the deer across the hoods before I noticed who was in which vehicle. We had six of them to hang and dress out.

Getting out of my chair, I said, "Looks like dinner is here." I reached down and squeezed Nancy's shoulder.

She put her hand on mine and gave it a gentle squeeze. "Time to get the stove started up," she said as she rose and headed into the cabin.

··•◆•··

We spent the night finishing dressing out the deer. I announced that we were going to take two of them to the Shawano people, we'd cook one up for a barbecue, and the rest would go in the smokehouse. I had some strange looks from people, but Nancy spoke up and made it clear that we had plenty, plus the means to get more. She was not going to stand by and have us hoard too much. So that was that.

The next morning, Nancy and Linda got into the truck after I put two dead deer into the truck bed. We then headed toward town. The drive was quiet, and none of us had much to say.

As we entered the drive in front of what was once Carol's house, I saw little activity. A couple were starting a fire in the firepit that had sprung up in the back yard, not far from where the greenhouses were being built. They turned and gave us a casual glance before returning their attention to the firepit.

We all got out of my truck. Nancy and I headed for the back door to the house, and Linda walked silently toward the greenhouses, which looked to be almost completed. I started up the few steps onto the small, raised back porch and reached for the doorknob.

Nancy's voice stopped me. "FIL, what are you doing?"

"I'm going inside. Why?" I asked.

"We don't live here. You should knock," she answered.

I guess the look on my face told her I was not amused.

"FIL, knock, please."

I started to knock on the door when it suddenly jerked open. I jumped slightly and looked into the grinning face of Zach.

"Did I scare you?" he said.

The grin on his face was starting to irritate me. Keeping my calm as best I could, I replied, "No, but that's a good way to get shot springing up on a man like that. You need to think."

"Whatever," he replied.

He must have looked behind me because he then shouted, "Hey, Linda," and squeezed himself by me to come down the porch and head her way.

I shook my head slightly and walked inside. Nancy followed me and made a tsking sound as she did. I figured he opened the door, and that was good enough for an invitation.

It was quiet inside, but I heard footsteps heading my way, so I stopped and waited. It was Wendy.

Startled for a second, she quickly composed herself and said, "Good morning, John Henry, what a pleasant surprise. What brings you here?"

"We have a couple of deer for you. Compliments of yesterday's drive through the woods," I replied.

"Oh, John, thank you. It is so appreciated," she answered. Then, seeing Nancy behind me, she asked, "And who is this lady?"

"This is my daughter-in-law, Nancy. Nancy Henry. You met her husband, Brian. He's the commander of the soldiers we have with us."

Walking toward Nancy, Wendy extended both of her hands, taking Nancy's hands into hers. "It's a pleasure to meet you, Nancy; I'm Wendy Slovack. I guess you could say I'm the leader of this band of refugees."

"Nice to meet you, too, Wendy," Nancy replied. "We've already dressed the deer and removed the hides. I made sure these guys saved you the hearts, livers, and kidneys. They'll do good with starting soup, which I think we'll all be eating before long."

"Thank you again. I cannot tell you how much this will help, and it will definitely soothe hurt feelings and relations some," Wendy said.

"Hurt feelings?" I asked.

"Nothing major, John. These people are still in shock, and when they aren't working themselves half to death cutting wood and digging gardens by hand, they talk. Tired, scared people talk, and it isn't always about puppies and flowers."

"You sound a little irritated yourself," I said.

"FIL," Nancy cautioned. Then she gave me the look that all men know when they've been perceived as doing something wrong.

"It's okay, Nancy," Wendy interjected. "I am, John, but like the rest of them, not at you. You've been very helpful. I'm just irritated at our situation. I'm tired, and I need a bath, clean clothes, and a decent meal. We all do, John, and I'd bet you are, too."

"I get it," I replied. "Sorry if it sounded otherwise."

Wendy made a motion with her hands that said it's nothing. Then she said, "We'll have to do something with those deer. It's not cold enough to hang 'em up to freeze, so we'll have to smoke or cook them. Let me get some people on that."

"I can help, Wendy," Nancy said. "That's why I came, to help."

"Thank you, Nancy. Let's go get some of these sleepy people up and moving. We can trade venison recipes or something."

Nancy smiled. "As my husband Brian always says, that sounds like a plan."

·····◆·◆·◆·····

King's team had made it through the woods, circling well to the south of Lake View, and went back toward the east of town. Setting themselves up about a hundred yards back from the road into town, King told the men to get some rest.

"Gully," he said and motioned the man toward him.

Crawling across the ground on all fours, Gully reached Lieutenant King and said softly, "Yes, sir."

"I'm thinking we are not far from where those people live," King said.

"The Henrys, Lieutenant?" Gully interrupted.

"Yes, those people. I want someone down by the road 24/7. You and I will start watching today. Let the men rest. We'll send out a patrol tonight on the north side of the road and head east. We can't be more than a mile or two from them."

"Okay, Lieutenant," Gully responded. "You want me to go first?"

"No, I'll take the first watch. I'll be down there two hours. Tell the others to rest up, and then, when two hours are up, you come relieve me," King said. "We'll alternate like that every two hours until dark, and then the others can take turns."

King stood up and stretched. Then, he reached down and picked up his kit, putting it on. Grabbing his weapon from where he had leaned it against a small tree, he said, "I'll see you in two hours," and slowly made his way toward the road.

"Yes, sir," Gully said quietly.

··◆◆◆··

The day had gone well. We had unloaded the two deer with the help of a couple of the men from Wendy's group and taken them inside the garage. We spent the next few hours cutting the meat into usable parts for smoking, and the scraps, Wendy took inside to start making venison stew. Nancy had made sure we brought along boxes of dehydrated carrot, onion, and potato chunks. Her doing that surprised me more because I hadn't thought of it. I wasn't sure I'd have been that kind.

It wasn't going to be just venison and water, she'd announced.

I spent most of the rest of the day helping make a small smokehouse out of some boards and screen fencing that was piled in the back of the garage. I sent a couple of people out to the woods to find some dried oak, which I then had two of the men cut into short split logs. That took most of the morning.

"I'm impressed, John," Wendy said to me. "This will really help us."

"It's a good start," I answered. "If you smoke it for a couple of days, it will last a good month. Once the weather gets colder, it will last longer. When we start to get freezing temperatures and you can freeze it, the meat will last even longer. We'll have to get more deer, and I know there are plenty of them around here."

"We don't have a lot of guns, John, and I have no idea how much ammunition we have."

"We might have some ammo we can spare if I know what caliber the guns are," I replied, using her word instead of calling them weapons, which I was more accustomed to. "I suggest you get a couple of men to start hunting in a couple of weeks. I figure two deer every month will be good. I suspect, though, that after a while, they'll get tired of venison."

"Are there any other options?" she asked.

"Possibly. You could send people out to some of the farms around here and look for stray animals like chickens and goats. Most of the farms around here are abandoned, and the people didn't take their animals with them when they went to the camps."

"You still think the camps are a bad idea?" she asked.

"Yes, I do. If the actions of the FEMA people around here aren't enough to convince you of that, I can have a couple of the guard boys come out here and explain what they experienced," I replied a bit too testily.

"Don't get cranky at me," she said with a grin that softened her message. Wendy was good at that. "It's just so hard to grasp. We were always told that FEMA would be here to help in any emergency. This is still hard."

"It's become a sore subject with me. I'm sorry," I said. "Our experience with them after the first few weeks was not good."

"Anyway, thank you for your help. I don't know what we'd do without it."

"It's no problem. You help us, too. Your people give us the manpower all of us will need to survive, and worst case, to help defend our little community here if we need you."

"Is that the catch," she asked. "To add to your army?"

"It's not a catch, Wendy. It's reality. It isn't just the FEMA people who have caused us trouble. We've had looters and rogue motorcycle gangs to deal with. Recently, and right out there," I said, pointing out toward the field behind the house. "They kidnapped my grandson and tried to ransom him. It didn't bode well for them."

"They couldn't have been trained for that, John."

"Most of the people we have with us weren't, either. Nancy was wounded fighting off the Looter band, and we've lost people, too. It's a sad reality that we have to face, and staying free, something I'm dead set on, means we have to be able to defend ourselves. We can teach them as time goes on."

"We'll see. It just concerns me, is all," she said.

I didn't want to debate the issue now. I figured when the time came, and I had no doubt the time would come soon, we'd talk about it then. Their options wouldn't be good; help or move on. I figured I'd talk to them about that when we had a more active threat.

I gave her a tight-lipped smile, nodded my head, and walked away to find Nancy. I knew we'd talk about it again.

Finding her busy, I spent the rest of the afternoon wandering around. I chatted with a few of the people in the wood chopping detail and looked at the garden plots. They were ready, but we wouldn't be planting anything till late spring. Doing it now, as we had, kept them busy while they got used to their situation and would help make it easier when it was time to plant.

I was sitting on the edge of the bed of my truck, looking around at Carol's yard and remembering different times I'd had there when Nancy brought me a bowl of soup.

"Try this," she said.

I took the spoon that was resting in the bowl and gave it a taste. "That's pretty good," I said.

"Yup, not bad for dehydrated vegetables and fresh meat," she said.

"You've changed, Nancy," I said. "You seem very comfortable with our circumstances."

"I don't know if it's change or acceptance," she replied. "I can't do anything about it, and I'm still scared of whatever is coming. But at least I can make something taste good."

"We'll get through it," I said. "We're much better off than we were when this all started."

"I don't even want to think of that," she replied.

"This soup is good," I said, changing the subject. "Let me finish this, and then we'll head back to the cabin." I didn't take long wolfing down the soup. It was about two bites, and then I tipped the bowl up and finished it.

"Did you taste that?" Nancy asked.

I chuckled and said, "Yup," then hopped off the bed of the truck, wiped my mouth with my shirt sleeve, and headed toward the house with the bowl. "Can you tell Linda it's time to go?"

"Sure," she answered.

I got inside, once again forgetting to knock. Old habits die hard, I guess. When I got inside, Wendy was stirring the stew and one of the Shawano women was ladling it into bowls. Wendy saw me enter and said, "We'll have to find things to add to this to keep it going."

"Yeah, perpetual stew means perpetual add whatever you've got," I replied. "You'll want to start that foraging we spoke of."

"I'll start sending people out tomorrow."

"We're heading back to our place now," I said. "We'll be back in a day or two. Did you find out what caliber ammunition you need?"

"Yes, for deer, it's all 30.06 and a few 30.30 calibers, and if you have any .22, we can use that to hunt rabbits," Wendy answered.

"We've collected a lot of different calibers. I'll see what we have and bring some for you."

I remembered the lecture I had been given about sharing some ammo, and while I didn't like giving it away, it was the right thing to do. These people had to learn to supply their own food, and we couldn't feed them all winter.

"Thanks again," Wendy said, and followed me out the door. That's when we heard the argument.

"I said NO, Zach. We're just friends."

The shout had very clearly come from Linda. I looked over toward the greenhouses she and Zach had built. She was standing in front of him.

Wendy quickly put her hand on my arm, gently restraining me. Taking a deep breath, then another, I silently agreed. Linda had made it clear that she could take care of herself. Zach did not appear threatening, and I decided it was her fight. Wendy took off at a speed I didn't think possible. I'm not even sure her feet touched the steps of the porch.

"Zachary Strayker!" she shouted. She said no more until she got in front of Zach, nudging Linda out of the way. I saw Wendy wagging her finger in Zach's face as Linda walked away toward the truck.

"I told you to leave that woman alone," Wendy shouted. "Didn't I say that?"

Zach said something and turned as if to walk away. He took two steps and turned around again, facing Wendy. "You just don't understand," he shouted. Then, he turned and walked away from her.

Wendy watched him go before she headed back to me. "I'm sorry about that, John. Zach has always had problems understanding no means no," she said.

"I have a hard time with men who think they can lord over women, Wendy," I said. "I think it best you keep him away when we come here. I don't know if I can put up with him."

"I'll take care of it. It will be fine. Again, I'm sorry," she said.

I shook my head and stepped off the porch. I stopped at the bottom and said, "We'll be back in a few days. I'd make sure they keep the smoke going on that venison for at least two days, three would be better."

"I will," Wendy answered. "We'll see you in a few days."

I waved good-bye as I went to my truck. Once I climbed in the driver's seat, I saw Wendy going off toward where Zack had gone. I started the truck up, and that caused Nancy and Linda to get in the truck. Nancy was next to me, and Linda was in the shotgun seat, the one by the window.

Nancy whispered, "Don't say anything, John, please."

Nodding once, I put the truck into gear and headed home.

CHAPTER 18

"To live is to war with trolls."

—Henrik Ibsen

We arrived home without incident, and Nancy and the still silent Linda went into the cabin. I followed them, but only as far as my room. From a new hiding place in the wall—*a damn shame a man has to hide things in his own house*—I took a cigar and a bottle of Rebel Yell from behind a secret panel. I grabbed a glass off of my dresser, poured about three fingers of the whiskey into the glass, put everything away, and walked back out to the porch.

I sat down in my chair. Brian called it my throne one day, for which I cut him off from my whiskey. I bit off the end of the cigar. I then took a book of matches out of my shirt pocket and lit it. A deep drag on the cigar and a strong sip of the whiskey, and I finally relaxed. *What a frickin' day.*

Laying my head against the back of the chair, I closed my eyes for a second. A click, click, click on the porch floor made me look up. Max and King had decided to wake up and come see me. King, the older of the two, laid his head on my thigh.

Placing my glass on top of the flat armrest of the chair, I reached and scratched him behind the ear. "We haven't spent a lot of time together, have we, King?"

Max, in true Max form, sat there and looked at me. He didn't like cigar smoke. I could tell he wanted petting, too, so I leaned forward, reached out, and scuffed the top of his head.

Seemingly satisfied, the two dogs wandered back to the far side of the porch, laid down, and placing their heads on top of their extended front legs, stared across the yard.

My curiosity aroused; I looked in the direction they were staring. Of course, I saw nothing. I decided I'd keep looking. These two seemingly lazy dogs sensed something. What, I couldn't tell, and they weren't telling me anything, either. I sat there, sipped my whiskey, and smoked my cigar. It didn't take long. Soon, around the corner of the porch, came Rahn and Brian.

As the duo came up on the porch, I asked, "Was it the whiskey or the cigar you smelled that made you show up?"

"If you're offering," Brian said.

"A taste would be nice, John," Rahn piped in.

Staring, no *glaring* at the two men, I sighed and started to stand up. "I'll be back. You can each have some."

As I got closer to the door, I heard Brian say, "Got an extra cigar?"

I stopped, started to respond, and decided to say nothing but shake my head. After I got two more glasses, generously poured, along with two cigars in my pocket, I went back outside.

I handed each of them a drink and then a cigar. They each went through the ritual of biting off the end of their cigars. Then, both men proceeded to pat their pockets, looking for something.

"Jesus, Mary and Joseph," I muttered as I pulled my book of matches out of my shirt pocket and handed them to Brian. He and Rahn finished lighting their cigars, and Brian put my matches into his pocket.

"Ahem," I said, extending my arm, palm up and fingers wiggling in a "gimme" gesture.

Brian gave me a grin, took the matches out of his pocket, and handed them back to me. "Sorry," he muttered, "force of habit."

"Uh-huh," I replied. "So, what's up?"

"We're heading out to hit the armory tomorrow," Brian answered.

"Tomorrow," I parroted. "You think that's a good idea right now?"

"We're not even sure the FEMA guys are still in the area, or if they ever were," Brian said.

"Jake and his team didn't find any evidence at all, John," Rahn added. "Unless they are real good at what they do, they weren't here."

"I can't argue with that," I answered. "But what if…"

"Dad, you always used to say that if a bullfrog had wings, he wouldn't bump his butt every time he jumped."

"Brian, what the hell," I said. "What does that have…?"

Brian cut me off with a smiling reply, "It's all about *if*. If this and if that. We can't live or operate on if. We have to act. We have to get those people to back off."

Realizing they were going regardless of what I said, I asked, "When are you going?"

"We're leaving late tomorrow afternoon, John," Rahn answered. "We'll assemble at the same place we went the last time, only we'll have two teams."

That surprised me. "Two teams? How many people is that?"

"We'll have twelve, Dad. Six will be in two Hummers, and six will be a breaching force on foot. We'll take four Hummers altogether. Oh, and Donna. We'll want medical support, if necessary."

"So, what's the plan?" I asked. "And what about Rhinelander, those engineers?"

"The engineers aren't coming. Not this time," Rahn answered.

"Before you get all testy and shit, we decided we weren't going to ask them," Brian added.

"Why?" I asked.

"The simple answer is, we don't need them. This is an enhanced hit and run. We want to hit the FEMA guys hard, create maximum casualties with minimal exposure, and get them to leave and not come back," Brian said. "I'm not looking to kill them all, and they aren't here in our home."

"So that's the difference between Antigo and the fish farm?" I asked.

"Pretty much," Brian replied. "Over there, they are just a threat. Here, they are invaders. Different rules and different outcomes for either."

"Okay," I said, accepting the explanation. "So, what's the plan?"

"The breaching force, led by Rahn, will approach the armory from the rear. We will plant some of the C-4 the engineers gave us against the back wall and blow it. Obviously, that's going to get their attention. We have no intention of ever entering the armory. We hope that once they recover from the blast, they'll rush outside and try to find who did it. At that point,

I will rush in with the cavalry, our Hummers, and light them up with SAWS."

"So, besides you, Rahn, and Donna, who else is going?" I asked.

"Johnson and Schwartz will be with Rahn, and I'm taking Roop and Owens. Three more guys in the other Saw vehicle, Hart, Klotz, and Myer. Jake's giving us two guys and Craig will go with Rahn."

"Craig? You're taking Craig? After all Addie went through the last time, you're still taking Craig," I said.

"Yes, he asked to go, and the guys respect him. They've even given him a nickname," Brian replied.

"Oh, this I have to hear, Brian. What nickname did the soldiers give Craig," I said in a tone that might've been a bit too sarcastic.

"BAC," Brian answered. "They call him B A C."

"BAC," I said. "What the hell does that mean?"

"Bad Ass Craig," Brian said, smiling. "They call him Bad Ass Craig. They just shortened it to BAC."

"Jesus Christ, Brian. He isn't trained for this shit. We've had this discussion before," I almost shouted.

"He did very well the last time he went. Jake said he was like a pro. Face it, Dad, Craig's a warrior and probably a better one than you or me."

"He's a kid. A kid who until a few months ago was playing video games," I said.

"Most of the U.S. Army, until a few months ago, was playing video games."

"Dammit, you know what I mean," I said, standing up. I was furious.

"John," Rahn interrupted, "he's as good a soldier as we have, probably better than a few of my men. He wants to go. He said this was his home and his family is here. He feels a duty to defend it."

I sat back down in my chair and glared at Rahn.

He glared right back but neither of us spoke. Rahn was a professional NCO, a career Non-Commissioned Officer. He knew about duty and how I felt about it. He hit me on a core value. Brian stood by silently. He knew I had to process this.

When I finally trusted myself to speak, I said, "He's my youngest. I admit I'm overprotective, but he's my *youngest*."

"The guys have been showing him how to do things. Jake's taken him into the woods and shown him things, too, as have his guys. Craig learns quick, John, and he's a natural at it."

"I can't stop him. I don't like it, but it is what it is."

"I'll keep an eye on him, Dad," Brian interjected. "He'll be on my team when we go in."

"Fine," I said with resignation.

I'm proud of my boys. Craig will always be the baby; he's the youngest. It's his burden and my cross to bear. I should have expected this; been more prepared for it.

"When are you leaving again?" I asked.

"After lunch tomorrow," Brian replied.

· · ◆ ◆ ◆ · ·

Zach walked along the dark road, mumbling to himself. "I don't know where Wendy gets off, talking to me like I'm a child." Before long, he stood on the road in front of a burned-out building.

I must really be pissed to have walked this far.

Wendy had almost rushed at Zach as the Henrys were getting ready to leave. "I told you to leave that woman alone," Wendy had said loudly. "Didn't I say that?"

"She likes me, Wendy. That's all there is to it," he said back and then walked off.

I don't understand what she expects of me. Obviously, Linda likes me. I'm just trying to get her to realize it. I'm not a bad guy.

He kept walking east, out of town. He passed the burned-out gas station. A military vehicle was parked behind some of the rubble; two soldiers were with it, watching him as he walked by.

Soldier boys, where the hell were they when we were being attacked in Shawano? What are they doing here where nothing is happening? Aren't they supposed to be protecting us?

He kept walking and muttering. Sometimes, angry, he shook his fist at nothing, and other times he stopped, turned around as if to head back, but he'd turn right back and continued to follow the road to the east.

I'll just go to the Henry's place and talk to her. I know she'll listen. I bet they'll let me stay the night, and I can go back and explain things to Wendy tomorrow.

The only sounds were of his muttering and the steady rhythm of his footsteps on the blacktop of the road.

··✦✦✦✦✦··

Jackson had relieved the lieutenant at the roadside observation point, and now he had nothing but time on his hands to think.

We've got to be close to those people. Maybe we'll find them, go back and bring everyone else here to do whatever it is that the lieutenant and colonel want. I'm not a soldier, these woods are irritating, and I need a shower. I don't even know what I'm doing here.

He sat down, leaned his back against a large tree, and watched the road. The lieutenant had already told him that the truck that was obviously owned by the Henrys had driven by. John Henry and two women were in it. He was to keep watching to see if any more people came by. *Women, it would be nice just to talk to a woman.*

A noise coming from down the road startled him. Instinctively, he stood up and watched as a man came down the road.

That guy has got to be crazy. Who's he talking to and who is he shaking his fist at? God?

Jackson continued to watch the man as he made his way along the road. Without warning, the man stopped and stared right at Jackson.

"What the hell," the man exclaimed. "Who are you?"

Jackson immediately raised his weapon and pointed it at the man. "Halt right there, buddy," Jackson ordered. He slowly made his way toward the man who had now raised his hands in the air but stayed about ten feet away.

He's nuts. Shit, the guy saw me. The lieutenant is not going to be happy.

With his weapon pointing at the man, Jackson said, "Walk slowly to me. Keep your hands in the air and walk toward me."

The man, keeping his hands in the air, followed instructions and walked slowly toward Jackson. Reaching just a few feet away, Jackson ordered softly, "Stop."

The man quickly complied and then stuttering, asked, "Who-who are you? Why are you stopping me?"

"Be quiet," Jackson replied.

Now, what do I do with him? The lieutenant said for me to stay out of sight and watch the road.

"What are you doing out here at night alone?" Jackson asked. "Where are you going?"

"I'm walking to see my girl, I'm walking to a friend's house," the man answered.

"Who?" Jackson asked.

The man stood there silently.

"Who are your friends?" Jackson asked again. He gritted his teeth, trying to look and sound menacing.

"The Henrys," the man replied.

Using the muzzle of his weapon to point toward the woods, Jackson said, "That way, walk slow and don't try to run. My finger's on the trigger."

CHAPTER 19

"You have conquered and you will conquer still, because you are prepared for the tactics that decide the fate of battles."

—Giuseppe Garibaldi

Jackson and his prisoner walked through the woods back to where the rest of the scout team was resting at camp. The prisoner walked in front, hands held in the air as Jackson held his M4 pointed at him.

I am in so much trouble. The lieutenant is going to be pissed, but the guy saw me. What was I supposed to do?

As they approached the team, Jackson, at first, didn't see anyone. His eye caught some movement as one of the men, Gully, sat up.

"What the hell?" Gully exclaimed.

The prisoner stopped as the man spoke, turning his head back toward Jackson.

"Lieutenant," Gully said in a low voice. "Lieutenant," he repeated, and a shape started to move, then sat up.

Lieutenant King glared at Gully, and Gully pointed toward Jackson and the prisoner.

"What the hell?" King exclaimed. "Jackson, what are you doing? I said no contact."

Before Jackson could reply, Gully stood and unsheathed a knife he had on his belt. "Want me to take care of this, Lieutenant?" he asked.

The prisoner backed up a few steps only to be stopped by the muzzle of Jackson's M4 as it made contact with his lower back.

"Just hold on a minute, Gully," King said. "What's going on, Jackson? Who is this person, and why are they here?"

"I was on guard, sir, and he saw me. I had no choice," Jackson replied.

"I can take care of this right now, Lieutenant," Gully said menacingly as he stepped toward Jackson and his prisoner, the knife visible in his hand.

"Knock it off, Gully," King said. "Now is not the time."

Gully lowered the knife to his side but continued to glare at the prisoner. The words between the men had awakened Leonard and Sibilski, who sat watching the events unfold.

"Bring him here," King ordered. He then pointed to his right at a large tree. Jackson and the prisoner walked toward the tree and stood waiting for instructions. Fear was strongly showing on the man's face, and he started to tremble.

"Put your hands down," King instructed.

The man dropped his arms but continued to be visibly afraid. "I, I, I wasn't doing anything," the man said in a trembling voice. "I was just taking a walk on the road."

"What happened, Jackson?" King asked.

Before Jackson could reply, King pointed at the man and said, "You, shut up."

The man nodded his head up and down vigorously.

"Go ahead, Jackson," King said.

"Well, Lieutenant, I was on guard, and I saw this guy walking down the road. He was mumbling like he was talking to someone, but no one else was with him, so I thought he was maybe, you know, crazy. He'd walk forward and then turn around and then he'd go back down the road and walk some more. I was just sitting there watching him and then he saw me. I didn't know what to do, and you said not to shoot anyone, so I did the only thing I could think of, I brought him here. To you."

King pursed his lips slightly, nodding his head. He looked at the man and asked, "What's your name?"

"Zach, Zach Strayker."

"What were you doing out there, Zach Strayker?" King asked.

"I was going to see someone. To make things right," Zach replied.

King sat there thinking. He worked his mouth a bit, twisting his jaw as he thought through what he was going to do. "Who is this someone, and where do they live?" he finally asked.

"Linda, her name is Linda. She lives down the road."

"She live by herself?" King asked.

"No, she lives with a bunch of other people."

The men began to stir and look at each other. Excited curiosity on their faces was becoming apparent.

"He said he was going to the Henry's place, Lieutenant," Jackson offered. "I should have said that before."

Raising an eyebrow and with a look of mild exasperation on his face, King turned his eyes toward Jackson and said, "Yeah, you should have." Turning his attention back toward Zach Strayker, he said, "You know these Henrys?"

"Yes, I do," the man said. "They come to where I am staying, not far from here, on the other side of the town."

"If they are on the other side of town, what are you doing here?" King asked.

"I'm sorry, I meant they come to where I live on the other side of town. They live just down this road a little bit," Zach answered.

The words made all of the men sit up and pay more attention. Gully put his knife back into its sheath, and crossing his legs, sat down. As he sat, he exchanged glances with Sibilski and Leonard.

"Sit down, Zach," King ordered. "Leonard, give him some water. Zach, my friend, we have lots of questions, and you are going to answer them."

··•◆•··

As much as I loved mornings—early mornings—out here on the porch, there was something to be said about evenings. I could hear noises inside the cabin; somebody doing something in the kitchen and not happy about it. Banging and muttered voices said it was wise that I *not* go investigate. Mike, Caleb, and Ethan were kicking a large pinecone around the yard as if it were a soccer ball. They had a soccer ball, but King and Max decided to fight over it, and the slow hiss of air escaping from it told everyone who heard it that its days were over. Brian and the others were in the barn, most likely preparing for tomorrow's trip to Antigo.

I was relaxed but tense. It's hard to explain if you've never experienced it. The tension of knowing that people you care about are going into battle; the relaxation of feeling safe at the moment with nothing threatening you. The laughter of three boys playing contributed a lot. To be that young and unaware, I thought, although I suspect they were too aware of the dangers and, like most kids, had adapted to the new reality.

I was experimenting with a new drink, coffee made from roasted and ground-up acorn shells. I had remembered reading somewhere that during the civil war, Confederate soldiers had made coffee this way. I feared that our real coffee would run out eventually and we needed to find a substitute. There was no caffeine in it, at least none that I knew of, but the taste was tolerable. It would do in a pinch.

I watched the boys play and sipped at my ersatz coffee, another term from my years of reading everything. Out of the corner of my eye, I saw Brian and Rahn walking toward the porch, more than likely to see me.

"What's up, gentlemen?" I said, raising my cup in a salute.

"Got any more of that?" Brian asked.

"On the stove, unless someone else either drank it or tossed it out," I answered.

"Be right back," Brian said as he headed for the door. "Who the hell would throw out brewed coffee?" I heard him mumble as he went inside, the creak of the door and the accompanying slap of its frame as the spring drew it closed, accompanying him into the cabin.

I saw Rahn smiling and asked him, "What's so funny?"

"I don't think that's coffee you're drinking. It isn't liquor, either, and it's not tea. You haven't gotten that desperate yet," he answered.

"It's acorn coffee."

"What the hell is acorn coffee?" he asked.

The words had no sooner left his mouth when a shout from inside the cabin exclaimed, "What the hell is this shit?"

Laughing, I said, "It's a coffee substitute made from roasted and ground-up acorn shells."

"Where did that idea come from? Sounds like something Jake would suggest."

"A book I read once," I said as Brian came back outside.

"I thought you had coffee," he said with a tone that suggested he was less than pleased.

"I do," I said, raising my cup. "Acorn coffee."

"What the hell is acorn coffee, and why aren't you drinking the real thing?" Brian replied.

"Coffee is gonna run out, son. This time next year, you'll be drinking this concoction and be glad that you are."

"Are we out now?" he asked.

"Nope, just an experiment," I said. Then quickly, before he could say anymore, I added, "And you can have some tomorrow before you head out to Antigo."

"We aren't going to Antigo tomorrow," Brian said.

"Oh? Why not?" I asked.

"Bad fuel," Rahn explained, sitting down on a step. "We need to siphon out what's in the tanks, filter it, and put it back in."

"How long is that going to take?" I asked, curious.

"Tonight and most of tomorrow. After that, we'll filter what's in the storage tanks just to be sure. Hart's gonna make a filter for when we take it out of the underground tanks at gas stations. This shouldn't be a problem again until we run out of fuel totally," Rahn said.

"Hmmm," I said, "how long do you think before that?"

"Probably a year, and that depends on how good the gas in those underground storage tanks is after winter," Rahn replied.

"Guess all those apocalyptic books I read weren't as accurate as some said they were."

He gave me a look. "What do you mean?"

"Those books all had people with a steady supply of food, gas, ammo, and so on. A couple didn't, and they were pretty realistic. Others, not so much," I said.

"And back to the subject at hand, all the more reason to use our advantage and take out the armory," Brian interjected. "And to answer your next question,

Dad, we are going the day after tomorrow. Same plan, just a day later."

···◆◆◆···

Zach had spent, what to him seemed like an eternity, answering questions of what he knew about the Henry compound.

These guys are serious. I think I can use them.

"Lieutenant," Zach said, "I can help you get to their compound."

"We know where it is now. Why would we need your help?" King asked.

"They know me, I can get in there, and they wouldn't be suspicious," Zach answered.

"Why? What's in it for you?" King said.

Zach stared at King for a moment, he seemed to be the one in charge, and then said, "I have a friend there. I need to see them and explain some things."

"I'm beginning to think you and the Henrys aren't as friendly as you are leading us to believe, *Zach.*" King's tone seemed ominous.

"It's a girl, a woman. I kinda made her mad. She likes me, and well, you know…"

"No, I don't know."

"We had an argument. That's why I was going there. I wanted to explain myself," Zach replied.

"That doesn't tell me why you want to help us out," King said.

Zach sat tight against the tree, his face contorted as he thought his answer over.

"I'm running out of patience, Zach," King said as he started to stand.

"Okay, okay, it's the old man. Henry, he caused the problem between us by sticking his nose into it. If it wasn't for him, the woman and I would be together."

"This woman have a name?" King asked.

"Linda," Zach answered. "Her name is Linda."

CHAPTER 20

*"Let us have faith that right makes might,
and in that faith let us to the end dare to
do our duty, as we understand it."*

—Abraham Lincoln

It was dark and I couldn't sleep. I decided I wanted some alone time on the porch. Me with my two companions, Max and King, faithful German shepherds, and we had deposited ourselves there to relax. In their case, it was where they were usually found, more often than not, curled up on the far end closest to the barn. I could hear the men off in the barn, their chatter and laughter bringing back memories of my own time in uniform—those exciting evenings in the quadrangles behind our barracks or the boisterous times we had horseplaying inside.

The crickets were loud tonight. People who haven't lived in rural America don't often understand just how noisy they can be. The steady and noisy chirping of crickets can sound as loud as a traffic jam in Chicago. What's different is that when the noise suddenly stops, it means something is in the area that could be a problem. I often referred to the noise of all the creatures in the Northwoods as a security alarm. When they suddenly stopped making noise, that meant I needed to be more alert. Something was in the area that I needed to be on the lookout for.

"What ya' thinking about, Dad?" the voice in the dark said.

It startled me, and I realized that nature's security alarm had failed me. My hand had instinctively gone to my side where my always present Glock hung in its holster. Recognizing the voice, I moved my hand back to its place on the arm of my chair.

"What's up, Brian?" I said with an irritated tone.

"Thought I'd come over and see what you were up to, that's all."

"Not much," I said. "I was sitting here and remembering better times."

"Better times," Brian quipped. "What's wrong with these great times we are having now?"

"I was remembering more peaceful times. Times before this."

"Ahh, the good old days."

"Sometimes I think about back when I was a kid, growing up on base with your grandpa and grandma. Other times, it's when we were on base and listening to you kids running around. Or that day I watched all you kids line up in front of quarters and watch the retreat ceremony across the street at the Fort Headquarters."

"I remember that. Travis got us all in line like a squad. We saluted and everything."

I smiled. "And yes, Brian, those were the good old days."

"They weren't all good, Dad. When you came back from Korea, that was hard."

"Yet, here we are, losing the bad memories and remembering the good ones. Some of all of this will be good memories one day, too," I said.

"If we live long enough to see those days," Brian said flatly.

"So now you know what I was up to," I said, changing the subject. "Is that the only reason you came here, or is something on your mind?"

"We're putting the mission off for another day," Brian replied.

"Oh, why's that?"

"These guys need rest. We've been running them ragged, and they need a day to unwind. Those people in the armory aren't going anywhere until we get done with them."

"That's probably wise," I said.

A loud noise, laughter, and youthful shouts came from the direction of the barn.

"Sounds like they are already unwinding, son."

"Good, they need it. I think I'll spend some time with Nancy and Mike. They need that, too."

"Mike may be disappointed. He was planning on going hunting with Caleb and Ethan."

"Seriously? After the last time, and he still wants to go hunting?"

"But Brian, nobody died," I said, failing at subduing a chuckle.

"That was funny. It wasn't, but it was."

"Bears good eating."

"Bullshit. That shit's awful," Brian said.

"A lot of fat and protein. Come winter, we'll need it."

"Bears hibernate in the winter. We should hibernate, too. I know how cold it gets here. Brrr…" He shook himself.

I rolled my eyes. "Aside from security and meat hunting, we'll probably do just that. We need to make more firewood. We'll burn a lot staying warm, and we have a lot of places to heat and a lot more people to keep warm this year."

"I'm gonna snowbird. I'm going to Florida for the winter."

"Yeah? Good luck with that, son," I said, laughing. "Send me a postcard."

"You betchya, Pops," Brian said.

He stood up, stretched his back. "Time to go play with Momma. Don't stay up too late, Dad." He walked toward the door, and with its always present squeak as it opened, he went inside.

I sat on the porch and waited for the night creatures to start playing music again.

···✦ ✦ ✦···

Zach had shared his knowledge of the Henry compound, all based on a single trip there in the back of a pickup truck to get tools and supplies for the greenhouse he was building. When he had finished, he drew his legs up closer to his chest and hung his head between his knees.

"So, you'll lead us there?" King asked Zach.

"Sure," Zach said, his tone defeated. Raising his head, he looked King in the eyes. "When I do this, I get Linda, right?"

"Of course, Zach, we're friends now," King replied.

For some reason, Zach didn't get a comfortable feeling from the way King said that. The way the other men looked at him wasn't very friendly, either.

Without waiting for Zach to reply, King looked toward his men. Locking eyes with Gully, he said, "Let's get everyone kitted up. We're heading out. Our friend here is going to guide us the rest of the way."

Gully nodded his head, showing he understood. The four men—Jackson, Leonard, Sibilski, and Gully—stood up and began to put on their MOLLE-style vests, a vest, in their case black in color, with horizontal bands where they could attach various pouches and other equipment using small straps they had been carrying on their mission. It had a zippered front and was loaded with carriers for the magazines for their M4s, PFAKs or Personal First Aid Kits, and small pouches carrying a compass or a multi-tool of some other small piece of equipment. Each man picked up his weapon, an M4, a 5.56 mm Carbine compact version of the M16A2 rifle equipped with a collapsible stock. It could fire automatic or in 3-round bursts, depending on a selector switch on the side of the weapon. Each weapon had a single point sling, meaning the sling was attached to the weapon by a single point, making it easier to carry and use when needed. Each man then put their rucksacks on their backs and waited for King to give the order to move out. Each man was little more than a silhouette in the dark woods.

"Gully, you take point," King ordered. "You follow him, Zach, and I'll be right behind you."

Zach felt an icy chill course through his body. *Zach, my boy, I think you need to find a way to escape these people.*

"Okay, let's move out," King said.

· · ◆ ◆ ◆ · ·

The soft laughter and mutter of voices from the barn caught my attention. Like a moth drawn to a lightbulb, I wandered over. As I stood by the barn doors, I could see the horseplay of the soldiers and a few of Jake's people. Like all soldiers, they were engaged in a combination of playing grab-ass and teasing each other, most of it of the irreverent kind. Seeing one of them sitting on a straw bale to the side, I headed that way. I soon recognized him as Specialist Johnson.

"Hello, Johnson," I said.

Glancing my way, he replied, "Evening, Mr. Henry."

"I thought I told you I was John," I replied. "Mr. Henry is your boss." Every soldier knew Army Warrant Officers are addressed as Mister or as Chief.

"I keep forgetting. Besides, I've got manners, and you always say mister to your elders."

"Touché, Johnson. Touché. Why aren't you joining in?"

Johnson glanced my way. "I'm the First Sergeant's driver, Mr., I mean, John. I have an image to uphold."

"You do that well. These men respect you."

"I don't know about that," he said softly. "I'd like to think they do, but I think mostly it's because I'm Top's driver."

"Don't let him hear you call him Top." I chuckled in response. "Nothing sets off a First Sergeant faster than being called Top."

"You were a First Sergeant, weren't you?"

"No." I laughed, perhaps a bit too obviously. "I was a Master Sergeant. A First Sergeant and a Master Sergeant are the same rank and paygrade, but a First Sergeant has a diamond in the middle of their chevrons, three stripes on top, and three rockers on the bottom. I was smart enough not to wear the diamond."

"When you were in the army, was it like this? I mean, did you experience anything like this?"

"No," I said. "Never anything like *this*." My mind briefly wandered back in time to the bases I served on and my deployments to Honduras, Panama, and Korea. The uniforms were different, but the bodies inside of them were the same. "In an odd sort of way, it was more sane."

"You were in World War II, right?" Johnson asked, barely suppressing a chuckle.

"Go to hell, Johnson," I said, patting him on the leg. "It was the Civil War."

We both sat there silently, enjoying the humor and the activity in front of us. After a moment or two, I stood up. "I think I'll wander around a bit more. Check-in on Sam and see what's going on in the world."

"Okay, John. Have a good evening."

"You, too, Johnson."

I then headed into the barn and to the steps leading up to Sam's radio room. I had recently told him it reminded me of the basements we derisively defined as the place aimless young people hung out in before this. He didn't think it was funny.

······◆······

They arrived at false dawn, about an hour before sunrise, when ambient light from the sun was just below the eastern horizon and began to make objects more visible. Zach had led the team through the woods to the north and west of the Henry family compound to the north end of a large open area. From that position, they were able to observe across the field and see the buildings and the movements of people.

King positioned the men about five meters inside the tree line, telling them to stay there and be quiet. He motioned to Zach and had him crawl alongside him to see what, if anything, was going on in the compound.

Laying where the woods and brush met the edge of the field, King placed his binoculars to his eyes and began to scan the compound. The dark shapes of buildings could be seen in the distance, as well as trails of smoke rising from the main cabin and some smaller cabins nearby. Turning to face Zach, King whispered, "How well do you know the compound? What am I seeing over there?"

In a low voice, barely qualifying as a whisper, Zach replied, "I was only there for a short time. We had gone to get tools and supplies for some greenhouses

I was building. What I remember is a large cabin, a barn, and some smaller cabins behind the main cabin. They had a garden behind the cabin and a couple of smaller buildings, too. I saw horses inside a fence and a bunch of army vehicles, but that's about all that I remember."

Turning and looking through the binoculars again, King said, "Did you see any guards or guard posts?"

"I saw one in front by the road, but I didn't see anything else."

King continued to observe and was mentally cataloging the identity of each of the buildings. Then, lowering the binoculars, he whispered, "Okay, I've seen enough. Let's crawl back." The two men, staying low on the ground, crawled back inside the trees. Once they were sure they could not be seen, stood up and walked back to the others.

King pointed to a large tree and said, "Sit over there."

Zach, thinking King meant him, went over to the tree and sat down.

"Circle up," King said to the others.

Jackson, Gully, Sibilski, and Leonard scooted across the ground and formed what kindly could have been called a circle and waited for King to speak.

"What I've seen so far is a cabin, a barn, and some other buildings." Scraping away the leaves and twigs in the ground in front of him, King sketched a diagram of the Henry compound into the dirt. "Our friend, Zach says they have horses, a bunch of army vehicles."

Interrupting, Leonard said, "Those must be the Hummers they have."

"Obviously," King said. His tone made it clear he did not like the interruption.

"Sorry," Leonard muttered.

"I have no doubt there are more there. What we don't know is how many people they have, how many vehicles, and most importantly for now, if they have any guard posts, lookouts, or roving patrols that would come back here."

"What's the plan, Lieutenant?" Sibilski asked.

"I was just getting to that, Sibilski, now if you'll allow me to continue," King replied, glaring toward the man.

"Sorry, sir," Sibilski said.

These men are tired, King thought to himself. *I need to keep that in mind. They aren't soldiers; they are guards. Not very good guards at that.*

"What we will do is the same thing we've done before. One man will crawl up to the edge of the field, keeping themselves concealed and observe any activity. I want to know how many people, if they have guards or an observation post, a lookout, anything like that. If they send patrols our way and you won't be seen, I want you to crawl back here and let us know. Absolutely no one is to stand up more than 10 feet from here toward the field. I'll give you my notebook and a pen. You'll write down what you observe and the time when you saw it. Any questions?"

"Sir, I don't have a watch," Jackson said.

"You don't have a watch?" King asked. "Who else doesn't have a watch?"

All of the men raised their hands.

"Jesus Christ," King muttered. Raising his left wrist, he unstrapped his watch and said, "Each of you will leave this and the notebook at your observation point. When we leave, I want it back. Sibilski, you were so interested in the plan, you get first watch. I want you there for four hours. Then Leonard, Jackson, and Gully, then myself."

Reaching across the short distance between him and the men, King handed Sibilski the notebook, pen, and watch. "Don't lose any of this, Sibilski," he said.

"Yes, sir. I mean no, sir, I won't," Sibilski replied, taking the items from King.

"While one of you is on guard, the rest of us will sleep, check our weapons to make sure they are clean and operating, and eat. No one leaves our perimeter without permission from me. Zach, I'm trusting you to stay here. If you try to leave, it will be the last thing you do. Do I make myself clear?"

"Yeah," Zach replied, rapidly nodding his head up and down.

King reached into his rucksack and pulled out an MRE. Glancing at it, he saw that it was elbow macaroni in tomato sauce. *I hate this stuff.* He tossed the tan package to Zach and said, "If you get hungry, eat this."

Catching the bag, Zach looked at it with curiously and shook his head in the affirmative.

"You know the rules. Don't betray my trust. Remember that," King said.

"Okay," was all Zach could say.

King puffed up his rucksack like a pillow, took off his floppy patrol cap, and lay down, his head resting on the rucksack. Placing his hat over his face, he remarked, "I'm going to sleep. You may want to do the same."

CHAPTER 21

*"The angel of death has been abroad
throughout the land; you may almost hear
the beatings of its wings."*

—John Bright

I had my morning coffee on the porch as I listened to the sounds of everyone waking up. Noise from the barn and inside the cabin told me that I wasn't the only one awake. As I nursed the last of my cup of real coffee, not my acorn experiment, I thought over the day to come.

In a few hours, Brian and Rahn would head out for their planned assault on the armory. I was left leading the home guard. I decided I was going to change that role today. I wasn't going on the raid with them, but I was still taking a leadership role, if not the top leadership role for this entire group. There were many more people here than just soldiers, and worse case, my devious mind concluded, I would invoke the Constitution and state that civilian control over the military was how it was going to be. Brian and Rahn were going to have to accept that.

Right about now, I wished I had a cigar. I was down to three unopened and well-hidden boxes and one open one stashed in my room. I was limiting how many I had a week and was down to one every couple of days.

I'd shared with Craig that we may have to become raiders and go out and try to find some more cigars. I think he took me seriously, as I saw him a few minutes later talking with Jake and pointing back toward the cabin as he animatedly shared something with him. Regardless, I cut Brian off from my cigars, and he gave in too easily. I suspect he's secretly looking, though. The whiskey situation had better potential.

Jake and some of his group had built a still. While the raw materials were a bit of an issue—sugar was impossible to get, and all we had was honey; the product was getting better with each bath. Jake insisted on calling it firewater, and the first few batches were perfect for just that purpose—starting fires.

Finishing my coffee, I stood up and headed for the barn. The activity over there was increasing, and it was time I began to step up and get more involved. No time like just before a mission, one that I was still not comfortable with, to start.

As I got closer, I could see Brian and Rahn standing near the side of the barn in deep conversation.

They seemed oblivious to the activity around them. Rahn had his arms folded across his chest, nodding his head as Brian spoke.

"Good morning, gentlemen," I said, startling the two men.

"Morning, John," Rahn replied.

"Morning, Dad."

"How are the preparations going?" I asked.

"Good," Brian said. "Everything seems to be ready."

"I'm going to do another walk-through in the field with the men," Rahn said. "We already did a couple. I wanted to wake them up and get the juices flowing."

"You were quiet then," I said. "I didn't hear a thing."

"Don't say that too loud, Dad," Brian quipped. "You'll give the First Sergeant a bad reputation. They are supposed to be loud."

"Bullshit." Rahn laughed. "I've never been loud in my life."

"Even I don't believe that, Chris," I replied. Then, changing the subject, I asked, "When are you heading out?"

"Late this afternoon," Brian said. "I want to watch the walk-through and then give them some time to rest up or take care of any last-minute things. It will be a long night."

"You still think this is a good idea?"

"We've been over this, Dad. It has to be done."

"And what happens when you are gone? What happens if something comes up here? You've got most of the trained people we have."

"Not everyone is going. Some of the guard people will stay here, plus most of Jake's people," Brian replied.

"What's up?" a cheery voice asked. Craig had walked up on us, then took a step back. "Did I interrupt something?"

"No," Brian said quickly.

"Just talking about your mission," I quickly added.

"Well, that explains why everyone is looking all serious and shit," Craig said. "Speaking of serious, when are we heading out?"

"This afternoon," I said and walked away.

··◆◆◆◆◆··

"He still doesn't want us going?" Craig asked.

"That pretty much sums it up," Brian said. "We'll have to talk about all of that when we get back."

"That should be fun," Craig said, rubbing his hands together.

"Before we get all chummy and family-focused, we should get these guys set up for the last walk-through," Rahn interjected. "I want to spend some time with the sand table and walk everyone through that. Then, we'll take a couple of vehicles and do a dry run in the field."

"Okay, First Sergeant," Brian replied. "Make it happen. Craig, let's take a walk."

"What's up, bro?" Craig asked as they walked across the yard toward the main cabin.

"This shit's about to get serious, and I don't want you joking around. I need you to be serious about this," Brian said.

"You think I haven't been serious? I've been in the middle of this shit since almost the beginning."

Brian put his arm around his brother. "It's more than that, Craig. I know you can do it. I know you've done it. What I'm worried about is your attitude about it."

Craig shrugged away from him. "What's wrong with my attitude?"

"You treat this like a video game, bro. You're so damn cavalier about it, and if you aren't careful, you're gonna get hurt, or worse."

"I admit, it seemed like a game at first. I remember when Dad came to Appleton to get us, that was the first time I saw anyone get hurt or threaten us, and it seemed like a game to me then. It wasn't real. It was...*surreal*."

"How so?"

"Don't you know the story? Dad had come to Appleton to get me and my mom..." Craig summarized what happened, and how he had reacted by firing from the upstairs room.

"You killed someone?" Brian asked.

BAM! I awoke with a start as two shotgun blasts broke the silence. I was instantly mad at myself for falling asleep, and then the door swung open, swinging toward the recliner I was in. "BAM!" Another shot sounded as I saw someone rush into the living room and go past me. Instinct took over, and I didn't even hesitate. Pulling up my AR and squeezing the trigger, I put two quick shots into the back of the intruder. He took another step and fell to the floor, sliding forward and into the chairs around the dining room table. I heard more footsteps rushing up the steps and rolled out of the recliner, putting it between me and the front door.

"DAD!" It was Craig coming down the stairs. "Stay there," I shouted back. I heard him going back upstairs and could hear footsteps on the floor from up there. I crawled around the chair toward the front door. "Bam! Bam! Bam!" Three more shots rang out. This time from some sort of rifle. Rolling toward the door, I fired back with three shots of my own.

"We know you have food in there; now give it to us!" a voice rang out from the front yard. I heard others, too, how many I wasn't sure.

"FUCK YOU!" a male voice rang out from upstairs, followed by a flurry of shots that could only have been from Craig and Donna. The firing was so fast it had

to be two weapons. I rolled further across the room and placed myself by the front window on the opposite side of the door. Peeking over the windowsill, I saw a body sprawled on the porch and two more in the yard, a man and a woman; the clear sky and full moon making it easy to see a lot of detail. At least I thought it was a woman given the long hair and flip-flops. They both laid on their backs, arms and legs splayed out. Neat holes in the center of their chests showed the aim of Craig and Donna had been true. Several other holes in the bodies suggested it was more a case of fire supremacy.

"Yeah. That's what happened. I felt nothing at the time. A little later, it started to sink in what I'd done."

Craig just stood there. I could see the shock starting to show on his face as I walked back toward him and his mom. Setting the two rifles down, I got closer to him, putting my hand on his shoulder.
"Are you alright?" I asked again softly.
"I shot them," he said.
"Yes, you did. You done good, son."
"Are they dead?"
"Yes."
"Is everything okay down there?" Donna said from behind him.
"Yeah, looks like it."

Craig slowly sunk down, stopping on his knees, and let out a sob. I sat down next to him, saying nothing but keeping my eyes on the neighborhood. Donna came out on the porch and sat down beside him, putting her arm across his shoulder.

"I had to do it," he said. "I had to."

"Yes, you did, son. I fear it won't be the last time, either."

"Is it going to be like this? Are we going to have to do this again."

"Most likely. Things are going to be bad for a while."

"Craig, are you alright?" Donna asked.

Sitting next to him, I could tell she was trying to protect and comfort him. Her AR was leaning against her. She might be a Southern California girl by birth but her life and her time in the Army still gave her the cajónes needed to get through something like this.

Craig stood up without saying a word and went back inside the house. I followed him, and Donna followed us both. She reached out to him, but he brushed past her hand aside as he slung his rifle over his shoulder, went over to the body lying by the dining room table, and drug it outside by its foot. I went over and grabbed his other foot, and together we drug him out, past Donna, and down the steps, putting him next to the man and woman lying in the yard. As he stood there looking down, I went and grabbed the man by the steps. Donna came down and helped me drag him to the others.

"We'll leave them here," I said.

Craig took in a deep breath, accented by a sob. Donna looked at him, her concern very evident, but she knew he needed to process this.

"Okay," he replied as we all walked back into the house, closing the door behind us.

"Why don't you go to sleep Dad, I'll stay up."

"You sure? I can do it."

"I can't sleep. I'll be okay. Besides, you are driving in the morning."

"Well then. I'm sleeping in your bed."

"G'nite, Dad."

"Nite, son."

Donna went to him and hugged him. She whispered something to him, and I heard him say, "I'm okay, Mom."

"I'm here if you want to talk," she said.

"I'll be okay. I had to do it; I'll be okay."

"I love you, Craig."

"I love you, too, Mom."

I went over and hugged him, too. "You did the right thing, son. I know it was hard, but you did the right thing." He said nothing. What he'd just done was tough, and I knew he'd most likely have to do it again. I let him go and trudged up the stairs with Donna. "He'll be okay," I said.

"Now the fighting just seems like a part of life. We have a family to protect, and I need to help do that. It's what we all have to do, and if we get soft, we lose. If I get too serious about it, I'll get depressed, and then I lose. If I lose, then Addie has no one. So if I seem 'cavalier,' as you put it, lighten up, bro, I can handle this." He grinned.

"I just want you to know how serious this is, that's all. I can't lose you; we don't know what has happened to John and his family in Indianapolis and never speaking again. You guys are all the family I have."

"We aren't ending up like the Winstons, Brian. That won't happen, I promise you that."

"Still the badass, aren't you?" Brian tousled his brother's hair.

"You ain't seen badass yet," Craig said with a serious look on his face. "Let one of those fuckers come here, and I'll show you badass. We'll both show them badass."

"Yes, we will, bro. Yes, we will."

CHAPTER 22

Leonard watched as soldiers and a few others, who were not in uniforms, moved back and forth across the field. With binoculars pressed tight against his eyes, he saw them charge, drop to the ground, get up and charge again.

Wiggling himself into a more comfortable position, his elbows resting on the ground and the binoculars tight to his eyes, Leonard continued to watch the people perform their movements.

He set the binoculars on the ground, and sliding back into the woods, he hunched over and made his way to where Lieutenant King and the others were sleeping.

"Lieutenant," Leonard said softly.

King stirred on the ground in front of him.

"Lieutenant," Leonard said a little more loudly.

"What? What the hell? Leonard, who's on watch?" King said, irritation in his voice as he sat up and rubbed the sleep from his eyes.

"I am, sir. You need to come see this," Leonard answered.

"See what? Why aren't you at your post?"

"They're up to something, sir. I thought you should see it."

Raising himself up onto his knees, King took a deep breath and said, "Okay, show me."

Stooped over, they made their way to the tree line. A few yards before reaching it, they dropped to their bellies and crawled the rest of the way. Leonard handed King the binoculars he had left lying in the grass, and King, raising them to his eyes, watched the soldiers maneuver about the field.

After a few minutes, he whispered, "Leonard, I do believe they are up to something. It looks like they are practicing an assault."

"Assault on who, sir?"

"If I had to take a guess, I'd say our base in Antigo."

"Jesus, Lieutenant."

"I need to get word back to Antigo, and our radios won't work from this far. Stay here and keep watching; I'll send Jackson back until he's in range. They need to know this," King explained in a low voice. Handing the binoculars to Leonard, he slid backward a foot then stopped. "Good job, Leonard."

"Thank you, sir."

··•◆•··

Rick Stepanik stood in the tree stand observation post near the rear area of the main cabin. From here, he could see everything the National Guard soldiers were doing.

This is almost better than TV. Man, I miss watching things on TV…

Sitting in the stand, he leaned back against the tree, holding his rifle across his lap. Unlike the others, Rick preferred a .308 Winchester. It had been given to him by his grandfather, Quint Stepanik, when Rick lived with him while his dad was fighting in the Middle East. When Rick's dad didn't return from the war, he continued to live with his grandfather. Quint was killed by one of the looters when the Stepaniks and Henrys had to defend themselves against an attack, and John Henry had allowed Rick to stay with them.

Rick enjoyed the view and all the activity. He knew he wasn't going with them, and that upset him. He wanted to do more. The youngest of "the grownups," as he thought of them, he wasn't a kid anymore like Mike, Caleb, or Ethan. He was a grownup, too. He sat there, commiserating with himself, watching the guard's movements and occasionally glancing around the field and the woods.

What's that?

A flash of light, white in the trees on the back edge of the field, had caught his eye.

There it is again.

Reaching above his shoulder for the field phone, one of John's many items he had stashed in the basement, Rick took the case down, pulled out the handset, and turned the handle on its side. He could hear the ratcheting and buzzing travel through the line as the call went to the cabin.

"Cabin," the voice on the other end answered. He recognized the voice. It was Donna.

"This is Rick. Is John there?" he asked.

"Hold on, Rick, I'll get him."

It took a few seconds, and then John spoke, "What is it, Rick?"

"I'm in the stand out back. I just saw something in the tree line at the back end of the field. It looked like a scope flash. You know, when sunlight hits a scope lens and makes it flash."

"How many times did you see it?" John asked. I knew what a scope flash was, but it wasn't necessary to say that. Rick was doing his job.

"Twice, not too far apart. Just a few seconds between flashes. It might be those people we were looking for."

"Stay in the stand and don't do anything. Keep watching, and do not use your rifle scope to check it out. Just be calm. Where are Brian and Rahn?"

"They're in the field training."

"Okay. Like I said, just stay there and don't do anything."

"Okay, John."

· · · ◆ ◆ ◆ · · ·

King slowly made his way back to where the men were sleeping. He moved cautiously until he stood next to Jackson. Using the toe of his boot, he nudged him.

Jackson stirred and then opened his eyes, blinking rapidly to get accustomed to the lack of light. "Yes, sir," he said, the sleep heavy in his voice.

"Get yourself awake and bring your stuff. The radio, too," King ordered.

"Yes, sir," Jackson mumbled.

King went to his kit and sat down. As he rifled through the various pouches looking for his notebook, he saw Zach watching him. "Something I can help you with, Zach?" he asked with an amused look on his face.

"Nope, just watching you guys. What's going on?"

"Nothing special. You just sit tight and behave like you have been."

Jackson walked over and stood next to King. Before he could speak, King said, "Sit down, Jackson. Let me write something down for you. You're going on a hike."

There is something going on, Zach thought. *King seems nervous.*

King block printed a short paragraph.

SITREP: LOCATED HENRY COMPOUND. LOTS OF ACTIVITY. APPEARS THEY ARE TRAINING FOR AN OPERATION. BELIEVE TARGET ARMORY. WILL CONTINUE TO ADVISE. KING.

He handed the paper to Jackson. "I want you to head west until you can reach the armory by radio. Then, read this message to them. Return here with any instructions they give you. Any questions?"

"What if they ask me what's going on?" Jackson asked.

"Tell them I observed a large group of military and civilian forces practicing assault tactics. You can also tell them how they made us leave our original area by putting scouts out. Explain the challenge we have with the radio and distance, and then return here."

"When do I leave?" Jackson asked.

"Right now. Get your stuff and head out. I have no idea when they are planning their next move, and we need to get this information to the armory ASAP. Should take you no more than a day there and back tops."

"Yes, sir. On my way."

"Good man," King said as Jackson headed off into the woods and to his destination.

········◆····

I made my way to where Brian and Rahn were observing their teams practice assault techniques. The soldiers were in full uniform, the classic pattern of the U.S. Army Camouflage Uniform or ACU, their plate carriers and MOLLE gear, each of the tiny straps on the MOLLE gear holding a pouch or other equipment and ballistic helmets. Those who were not soldiers were dressed the same, except none of them wore ACUs. As I approached, I scanned the tree line across the expansive meadow area behind the cabins.

"How's training going?" I said as I approached the two men, also wearing fatigues.

Brian, not taking his eyes off of his men, said, "Going well, they'll be ready when we leave."

"How'd you like a live-fire exercise first?" I asked.

"We don't have the time for that, Dad," Brian answered.

"What do you mean?" Rahn asked, seeming to sense more from my question.

"Don't look, but we might have company. Rick said he saw something flashing in the tree line."

"Shit," Brian remarked.

"What are you suggesting, John?"

I answered with another question of my own. "Do they have ammo?"

"Yep. They always do when kitted up," Rahn answered.

"Well, my idea is to send a group around behind them as a blocking force if they are still there. Then, we get everyone online in three groups. We move toward the tree line with the left and right ends acting like the horns of a bull. The center will be the head of the bull. The left and right flanks will move forward faster than the center and encircle them. The force behind will work like your deer drive exercise and will either prevent a retreat or drive them toward the head. The head will smash them," I explained.

"Whoa, Dad. That's pretty good, slick as shit as Grampa used to say," Brian remarked.

"Well, I can't take full credit for it. Saw it in a movie once about British soldiers and Zulu warriors. It's a common battle tactic."

"I saw that movie. It's a good one, old but good," Rahn said.

"Then I say we make it happen," Brian said. "First Sergeant, you want to take the group around to their rear? We'll give you time to get in position. You can signal us by breaking squelch on the BaoFeng radios," Brian said as he patted the one hanging from his belt.

"No problem, Chief. I'll take a team back toward the Stepanik place, and then we'll swing around and get behind them. Give me 30 minutes."

"Who are you taking?" Brian asked.

"Johnson, Schwartz, and Roop. That should give us enough firepower to either hold them up till you bite 'em in the ass or push them out toward you."

"Sounds good. I'll take the right flank, Dad. Can you take the left?"

"Yeah, I can do that."

"I'll put Hart in charge of the middle. He's senior man," Brian said. "Dad on the left, Hart in the center, and me on the right of the line."

"Right of the line, Chief," Rahn said, the motto of their old unit in the 10th Mountain still held strong for these two.

"Climb to Glory, First Sergeant," Brian replied with a grin. "I do not miss the 10th Mountain Division, but I wish we had them here."

"Roger that, Chief," Rahn replied. "Johnson, Roop, Hart, Schwartz," Rahn yelled, twirling his hand over his head, using the hand signal for 'assemble on me.'

The three men trotted over to where Rahn was standing. Rahn briefed the three men and instructed them not to look toward the tree line. "Johnson, Schwartz, Roop, follow me. We're getting a Hummer and heading out. Hart, stay here."

"A Hummer, First Sergeant? It's just a short walk in the woods," Brian quipped.

"A good grunt never walks when he can ride, Chief," Rahn said. He trotted off toward the barn with Johnson, Roop, and Schwartz following him.

Hart asked, "What do you want me to do, Chief?"

"Just stand here and chat with my dad and me. We've got company, and in case they are watching, I want to try a little deception. Can't have them thinking we've seen them and are up to something."

"Yes, sir," Hart replied. "So, Mr. Henry, how are you?"

I laughed. "It's John, Hart."

······◆·◆···

Leonard continued to watch the soldiers practice in the large field in front of him.

Soldier boys sure like to play at it.

There were three groups of men rushing about in the field, acting as if they were attacking something. The soldiers were in full uniform, the classic pattern of the Army Camouflage Uniform or ACU, their plate carriers and MOLLE gear, each of the tiny straps on the MOLLE gear holding a pouch or other equipment and ballistic helmets. Others he suspected who were not soldiers were dressed the same, except none of them wore ACUs. Behind him, Leonard could hear Lieutenant King, Gully, and Sibilski stirring about. That guy that Jackson had captured, Zach, was there, too.

I don't care for that Zach guy at all. The lieutenant should have just let us off him once we got here. We could've found this place on our own.

A change in activity instantly caught Leonard's attention. The three groups now stood spread out, facing in his direction. All of the men in front of him were armed.

Leonard quickly crawled to where King and the others were. "Lieutenant. Lieutenant. Something's up."

King made a shushing sound. "What are you doing here, Leonard?"

"I think they're heading for us, sir," Leonard answered.

"Show me," King said, and grabbing his M4, he followed Leonard rapidly back to the edge of the woods, dropping to his hands and knees to crawl unobserved toward the edge.

Sibilski and Gully grabbed their weapons and followed. Crawling along the ground, the two men joined King and Leonard, watching the line of soldiers approaching them.

· · + ◆ + · ·

"What in the hell are these people up to," Zach wondered aloud as he sat leaning against a large oak tree. He watched as first King and another man left and headed toward the Henry homestead. He then watched as the other two men followed them, leaving him unguarded.

I don't know what's going on, but it's time for me to get out of here.

Zach started to stand up and stopped.

They're crawling for a reason. I've got to get away from these people and find Linda.

He dropped to his hands and knees and began to crawl away.

· · + ◆ + · ·

Rahn and his team had driven to the Stepanik farm and then behind it as far as the Hummer could take them. He had explained the situation to them on the way. They stopped at the edge of the back pasture in line with what would be about 30 yards behind the tree line of the main cabin. All four men, Johnson, Roop, Schwartz, and Rahn, exited the Hummer.

They stood together, and Rahn said, "Okay, we are heading west from here. It's about a half mile, maybe three quarters, and we should be behind where we think our intruders are. Schwartz, you take point and do not get us caught."

"Roger that, First Sergeant," the young man replied with a face-splitting grin. He turned and scanned west toward their objective.

"Everyone, lock and load," Rahn said.

Each of the men ensured they had a round chambered in their weapon.

"Keep your selector switches on safe and fingers off the trigger." It was an unnecessary command as each of the men had been trained and retained numerous times on proper weapon handling procedures, but Rahn said it as a reminder every time. He didn't want anyone to get hurt because of friendly fire. "Move out, Schwartz," Rahn commanded, pointing forward with his finger. Without a word, the small team headed into the northwoods.

The woods, while dense, were not impassable as the team moved quickly and silently through the trees. A crashing noise to their left made them stop; something or someone was moving quickly through the trees.

Each of the men dropped down on one knee. Schwartz kept looking forward to the west while the other three searched their front for whatever was making noise. Whatever it was, it continued to move easterly, and after a while, the sound diminished.

"Must've been an animal," Johnson said softly.

"As long as it's not two-legged, that's fine by me," Roop replied.

"At ease, gentlemen, we have a mission to conduct," Rahn interrupted from the back.

The two men nodded their heads, acknowledging the correction.

"Move out, Schwartz," Rahn said.

After a brief and tense fifteen or twenty minutes, Schwartz held up his hand, stopping the team. Slowly standing, he looked toward where the main cabin should be and tried to peer through the foliage. Unable to see anything except trees and bushes, he dropped into a squatting position and made his way to where Rahn and the others were kneeling just a few feet away.

"I can't see a thing, First Sergeant," the young soldier said. "I can hear stuff in the distance, so I know we're close, but I can't see 'em."

"Okay, spread out in a line about 8 feet apart, parallel to our front. Get prone behind a tree, get comfortable, and stay alert. Johnson, you go to my left, Schwartz, you are the far right, and Roop, you split the difference between Schwartz and me."

"I'm right of the line," Schwartz said with a grin.

"Yeah, but you ain't 10th Mountain, Schwartz. You hold that line, and we might let you join us," Rahn replied, smiling. "Move out, gentlemen, and get ready. I'm not sure what is waiting for us."

He watched the soldiers deploy into their positions and then removed the radio from a pouch on his vest, turned it on, and slowly pressed the push to talk button three times. Each time broke squelch, letting Brian and John know his team was in position.

⋯⋄⋄⋄⋄⋄⋯

The radio on Brian's waist came to life. The three slow clicks of the radio quickly got his attention.

"Showtime," Brian said to Hart and me. "You know what to do."

We each headed to our assigned positions—Brian on the right, Hart in the middle, and me on the left.

"Assemble in your groups," Brian ordered loudly.

The groups of soldiers joined each of us.

Brian and Hart were quickly getting their men in a line.

I told my team to do the same. On the far left of this long line of soldiers, we stretched across a front of almost 40 yards. My plan was coming together. I noticed we were now one straight line.

Walking in front of my section, I said, "In those woods, just inside the tree line, we think we have visitors. Lock and load your weapons. We will advance on Brian's command and stay in line. We will not move to the center. When we get to the trees, we will swing like a gate to the right as we advance into the woods. First Sergeant Rahn is behind them, so make sure of your target if you have to fire. Only fire if fired on or if ordered to shoot."

The nodding of heads told me they understood. I reclaimed my position on the extreme left and waited.

"Forward," came Brian's command. With almost parade-ground precision, the line moved forward.

··•◆•··

Sibilski and Gully crawled up behind King and Leonard.

"What are you two doing here?" King asked sharply.

Neither man spoke when King said, "Who's watching the prisoner?"

Sibilski and Gully exchanged a glance, and before either could say anything, Leonard said, "They are moving toward us, sir."

King looked toward the field and saw the line of soldiers moving toward them. "Time to bug out, men; I think we've been found."

All of the men moved back toward their camp on hands and knees, standing as they got further back. Grabbing his equipment, King said, "We'll move back into the woods and then head west. Let's go."

He took the lead, and the men followed.

A few steps into the trees and brush behind them, a voice barked, "HALT!"

A brief hesitation followed, and then, raising his weapon to his shoulder, King fired toward where the voice came.

BAM, BAM, BAM.

It was answered by a fusillade of weapon's fire as both sides engaged.

·· ◆ ◆ ◆ ··

Brian ordered his men forward, and at a run, they followed him. Taking his lead, I did the same with my team, waving at Hart to halt and to drop in place, prepared for anything to leave the woods. He was in the most direct line of fire and could also overshoot and possibly hit Rahn and his team.

My team had swung completely around inside the woods, and we now effectively held a blocking position to the west of our target. Each of my group had found shelter behind a tree and pointed their weapons toward where we believed our eavesdroppers were.

A weakness in my plan quickly became evident. We were in danger of shooting our own people if we started shooting, too.

I shouted, "Don't fire unless you have a clear target."

A few of my men found targets, and three-round bursts exited the muzzles of their M4s. The intensity of the gunfire in the woods was increasing with each second, and then it suddenly stopped.

An eerie silence surrounded us.

A moan came from our frontside.

I whispered to the man to my right to cover me, and dropping to the ground, I snaked my way through the underbrush. It took just a moment before I found the first body. I didn't recognize the man. He was one of the people we were seeking, shot multiple times. I don't know if the moan was gas leaving the body, the last breath before death, but he was obviously dead. No one could survive wounds like that.

···✦✦✦···

Zach heard the gunfire in the distance and quickened his pace. *I don't think things are going well for them.* He continued toward the cluster of small cabins in front of him. *She's got to be in one of these.* As he approached, he could see a small band of people standing behind the large cabin beyond him. Each was armed and milling about, plus two women and a young boy. A Black woman was saying something to a child near her, gesturing toward the cabin.

Zach could hear her shouting but couldn't make out the words. He walked onto the porch that connected two of the cabins. Both had open doors and were empty. He peeked inside and saw a shotgun rested against a bed in one of them.

He walked in, picked it up, and checked to see if it was loaded. Smiling with the satisfaction that it was, he left the room and walked to the next cabin.

····◆◆◆····

Linda was in Gary's cabin reading to him. He'd been feeling better but still had trouble getting around. The willow bark tea she had made helped him some, and he was drinking a glass of it that had been allowed to cool on a nearby table.

Addie was playing checkers with Ethan and Caleb, and both of the boys got frustrated every time her checkers jumped one of theirs. Without missing her reading, Linda remarked, "It's good practice for you. When your little one gets that age, you'll be ready."

"Gee, thanks a lot. But they are sweet boys," Addie said.

"Don't say that too loud. They'll use it for all it's worth."

"We *are* sweet, Mom," Caleb quipped. "Seeee," he continued with a huge tooth-filled grin.

The quaintness of the moment was interrupted when the door burst open.

Addie shrieked and reached for the two boys.

Jumping to her feet, Linda shouted, "Zach, what are you doing here?"

· · + ◆ + · ·

I walked around the wooded area, looking at each of the bodies on the ground. All were dead, and there was no doubt where they had come from. The four black uniforms and their equipment gave them away.

The others had started to gather around. The few who had not yet seen any combat were swallowing fast as they tried to keep from vomiting at the sight of what a 5.56 round can do when exiting the human body. No one said a word, which made the shout from the trees beyond even louder.

"FUCK! Chief, Chief," the voice in the woods cried out. "NO, NO, NO!"

I took off at a run toward the cry.

I found Specialist Johnson kneeling over a body on the ground.

I swallowed hard. I knew who it was but didn't want to believe it.

"They killed him," Johnson said, tears streaming down his cheeks. A trampling of heavy feet in the brush to my right announced the arrival of Brian.

He glanced at Johnson. Looked at me, and then quickly did a check of all he could see. I knew, like me, he was trying hard not to accept who lay on the ground before us, his blood seeping into the forest floor.

First Sergeant Chris Rahn lay there, shot through the head. It appeared he had died instantly.

I put my hand on Johnson's shoulder and squeezed. His face showed the anguish we all felt.

· · ◆ ◆ ◆ · ·

"I said, what in the hell are you doing here, Zach?" Linda shouted.

"I came to get you. We're leaving this place," Zach said, using the gun to gesture toward the door. "You and me. Now. We're going to Wausau; it will be better there for all of us."

"No, I'm not going anywhere, and I'm especially not going *anywhere* with you."

A movement on the bed caught Zach's attention, and aiming the shotgun toward it, he said, "Don't try anything, old man."

From the corner of her eye, she saw Gary grimace in pain as his hand noticeably slid under the pillow underneath him as he reached for his gun and aimed.

Bam! A shot fired from Gary's gun.

BOOM! The shotgun in Zach's hand seemed to explode; the pellets shredding the man in the bed.

"ZACH! What have you done?" Linda screamed. "Oh my God, Gary."

Bam, Bam!

Two shots added to the noise inside the small cabin. The boys were screaming and crying, Linda was shouting at Zach to stop. Her ears were ringing from the loud report of the shotgun.

Spinning around, Linda saw Addie standing by the checkerboard table, the boys behind her. Addie, trembling slightly, held a pistol in a two-handed grip, pointing it in Zach's direction.

Zach was on the floor bleeding profusely from a head wound and another to his chest. A splattering of blood had spread across Linda as the bullets from Addie's shots had struck Zach.

Ethan and Caleb raced across the small room, grabbing onto her tightly. She squatted down and held them as the tears flowed.

Addie set the gun down on the table and walked over to Gary. There wasn't much recognizable of his face and head. She reached down, grabbed a blanket, and gently pulled it across him.

Pounding of feet on the porch floor and a loud bang as the door was pulled open suddenly was the next sound Linda heard.

Nancy, Donna, and Sajan stood there, weapons ready.

"What happened?" Nancy asked.

"Gary's gone," Linda said softly, tears streaming down her face.

··•◆•··

Gunshots disrupted the solemn gathering in the woods. "What the hell was that?" I asked.

"The cabins!" Brian shouted, and he ran toward them. Craig joined him as they ran at a neck-breaking pace toward the cabins.

"You men, take good care of the First Sergeant and bring him to the barn. A couple of you follow me," I shouted, and I ran after Craig and Brian.

As I ran through the field and toward the cabins, my mind was racing everywhere.

Was there an attack? Who was shot? Who did the shooting? So many questions and, for the moment, no answers. The panic of those thoughts kept me going, providing the adrenaline I needed to make the run. Craig and Brian were far in front of me, and I saw them both turn toward the cabin where Addie and Gary lived.

When I finally arrived, Nancy and Donna were sitting on the porch near Addie. Craig was next to her with his arm held tight around her. Brian stood in the cabin doorway, his hand above his shoulder and resting on the door jamb. I saw Linda off in the yard with her boys.

As I approached Brian, he said, "Gary's dead."

"What do you mean, he's *dead?*" I couldn't gulp air into my tired lungs fast enough.

"I'm sorry, Dad. That guy from the Shawano refugees shot him," he said with more sincerity.

Footsteps behind me caused me to turn. Sam and Allen had joined the growing crowd, along with a couple of Jake's men.

Rahn's death was hard enough, but to lose Gary, too. That broke me, and I leaned forward on my knees. Brian caught me before I fell. "I'm okay. I'm okay."

"John, what happened?" Sam asked. "I heard gunshots."

I took a breath and stood up. Looking Sam in the eyes, I said, "Gary's dead, Sam. That punk refugee killed him."

Sam staggered a bit. He and Gary had been friends for decades. Tears formed in his eyes as he stared at me. He went to enter Gary's cabin, but Brian stopped him with a light hand to Sam's chest.

"You don't want to go in there, Sam. The guy used a shotgun."

"What, what happened?" Sam asked.

Brian replied, "Seems that guy from the Shawano group that took a liking to Linda snuck in here and tried to convince her to leave. He had a shotgun. Gary tried to defend her. The guy shot him. Addie had a pistol on her, and she used it to shoot the guy."

"Zach," she said from behind us. "His name was Zach. He thought he was in love with me and that I'd want to go away with him." Linda spoke calmly as she walked up on the porch. Caleb and Ethan each held one of her hands. "I guess I didn't understand how serious he was. I should've known."

Her voice was almost monotone and without emotion. The blank look on her face, spattered with blood from either Zach or Gary, told me she was probably in shock. I turned and asked Donna to take care of her. Donna and Nancy guided Addie, Linda, and the boys to the main cabin. I had no intention of following.

"Rahn's dead, too," I said, shaking my head at the loss.

Sam and Allen were visibly stunned. "How?" they both asked.

"I guess one of those things that happen in battle," I answered with a cold numbness that startled everyone. "I need to talk to Johnson about it. Find out what happened."

"Anyone else?" Sam asked.

"The bad guys," Brian said. "Four of them. They won't be a problem anymore."

CHAPTER 23

"At the end of the fight is the tombstone white, with the name of the late deceased."

—Rudyard Kipling

Brian and I talked with Johnson. Through his tears, he explained Rahn was killed by a round with his name on it that found him. It was a straight shot through the forehead. If there was any good that came from it, his death was quick. Rahn never knew what hit him.

A darkness had come over Johnson, and I told Brian to keep an eye on him. Brian seemed okay, but only time would tell. He'd lost comrades in battle before, but he and Rahn had been close in these last months, keeping us safe, planning together as if they knew what each other was thinking. Rahn's and Gary's deaths had hit us all hard. In some ways, they were like Carol's death. Unexpected and sad. We knew the way things were now, that we would lose people. People we cared about or even loved, but it didn't make it any easier.

After we'd cleaned up, Linda, Donna, and I returned Zach to the refugees. When we arrived, Linda asked if she could talk to Wendy alone and explain what happened, and we agreed. She went inside Carol's old house.

"John, are you okay?" Donna asked.

"No. Yes. I will be," I said.

After a few moments, she came back outside with Wendy. I got out of the truck and tried to talk with Wendy, but she said, "Not today, John. Perhaps tomorrow or in a few days. I know this isn't your fault."

Two men came and took Zach's body out of the bed of the truck. We had sewn him inside an old flat bed sheet, and blood had seeped onto it in large patches. The two men were silent and gave us expected angry looks as they took him away.

I told Wendy I'd be back in a couple of days to check on her. Donna, Linda, and I got back into the truck, and I started to drive away.

As we backed up, Linda stared at the greenhouse, almost completed, and remarked, "All we did was build that." The three of us drove home in silence.

Zach had been obsessed with Linda. A death was a death, and Zach's meant nothing to me.

We buried Chris Rahn and Gary Jones the next day. It was a slightly warm and sunny day. A light breeze moved through the grass, making it sound like gentle waves beating on the shore of a pond. It was a sound I had wanted to hear when I first moved here, hoping for a home on a small lake. Now, it wrapped itself around us and helped us take them both to their final resting place.

Two graves had been dug alongside where we had put Carol and Grady. I had an odd thought that not only was our cemetery growing, but wondered how much more it would grow in the days and weeks ahead.

Brian had the National Guard soldiers lined up in two squads. We brought the coffins out in the back of my pickup truck, side by side. Sam and I had quickly built them the evening before from lumber we had salvaged and stored in the barn. I had a large American flag that covered them both. Gary had been a U.S. Marine and served in Vietnam. Rahn was a soldier and had died as one. They'd earned our respect. Even though the country we knew was gone, and neither had given their lives for it, they had both served it. The honor was fitting.

Each of the squads came over and carried a coffin to the grave. We had ropes set aside that would help us lower them, and each coffin was set on boards across the open graves. Jake's people stood in a small group, hats off in respect. The Henry band—Craig, Nancy, Addie, Donna, Mike, Allen, Sam and I were all together as a group. Mike was crying, and Nancy put her arm across his shoulders and pulled him toward her. Rick and Sajan stood guard in the bunker and tree stand, respectively. Linda and her boys stood near us, but noticeably not with us. She had been of few words since the *day*.

I'm not a religious man, but I had a bible. I read from Ecclesiastes Chapter 3.

"For everything there is a season, and a time for every matter under heaven:
a time to be born, and a time to die;
a time to plant, and a time to pluck up what is planted;
a time to kill, and a time to heal;
a time to break down, and a time to build up;
a time to weep, and a time to laugh;
a time to mourn, and a time to dance;
a time to cast away stones, and a time to gather stones together;
a time to embrace, and a time to refrain from embracing;
a time to seek, and a time to lose;
a time to keep, and a time to cast away;
a time to rend, and a time to sew;
a time to keep silence, and a time to speak;
a time to love, and a time to hate;
a time for war, and a time for peace."

I paused and looked around. Without prompting, Brian asked if anyone wanted to say anything.

Sam spoke of his time with Gary and how they used to hunt and fish together. "Good times," he said. There was a long silence when he finished.

I saw Brian chewing on his lip. I knew he had something he wanted to say. He stood there, his hands in the small of his back in the U.S. Army position of parade rest.

I watched him as he stiffened up, and dropping his hands to his side, he raised his right hand with his fingers and thumb extended and the palm of his hand facing downward. The tip of his fingers was just touching his eyebrow. He then commanded the soldiers behind him, "Present, Arms!"

Each of them executed the movement with parade-ground precision of saluting the men.

"Right of the line, First Sergeant," Brian said.

I heard another voice, quieter. It was Specialist Johnson. "Climb to Glory, Top."

The 10th Mountain Division had shown its last measure of respect to one of their own and to one that wasn't.

After a moment, Brian said, "Order, Arms," and each of the soldiers lowered their hands back to their side, standing at attention.

After a moment, I said, "Thank you, everyone." And everyone began to walk back to their cabins. Jake and his people had offered to lower the coffins and fill in the graves.

I caught up with Brian on the walk back. He was talking to Johnson.

"I don't know, Chief," Johnson said.

"The men respect you. You can do the job," Brian said.

"C'mon Chief. I'm the First Sergeant's driver. I can't be the First Sergeant."

"Johnson, I think you can. I need you to step up and do this. I believe in you."

"Can I sleep on it, Chief?" he said, glancing sideways at Brian.

He nodded curtly. "Tomorrow morning, Johnson. Let me know then."

"Yes, sir." He saluted Brian and walked away, his head down and his feet shuffling on the ground.

"What was that about?" I asked.

"I need a first sergeant. I just told him he's my choice," Brian answered.

"I think he'd make a good one," I replied.

"Tell him that. He doesn't think so."

"I will if he asks my opinion."

"You know this sucks, right," Brian said, disgusted. "I mean, Rahn…"

"I know. What are you going to do? Is the raid still on?" I asked.

"It will be in a few days. I've had it with those people. We are past running them off. I'm sick of this shit. Why can't they leave us alone? This time, we are wiping them out."

"Whoa, Brian, slow down…" I said, taking his arm.

"No. Not this time, Dad." He shook out of my grip. "I need you, too. As far as I'm concerned, you're back in the army."

"We'll talk about that later. Right now, I think everyone needs to take some time, get their heads back on straight, and then we'll do what we have to do," I said.

"I'm taking that as a yes," Brian said. "These guys need another leader."

"We'll see," I answered.

·· ✦ ◆ ✦ ··

Jackson stumbled through the thick overgrowth that grabbed at his boots and pants. He had heard the gunfire earlier, but it didn't last long.

The lieutenant told me to send this message by radio, and that's what I'm going to do.

Even though it wasn't hot outside, his clothing was soaked from perspiration. A combination of nerves, exertion, and overall fear was making him move faster than he should have. A sun brightened spot up ahead told him there was a road or a clearing coming up.

I'll try the radio there.

Jackson walked out into the open area. It was a meadow-like patch easily 40 yards across. He dropped his kit and leaned his MP4 against it. Squatting down, he opened up the attached pack and rummaged around inside until he found the radio. He then stood up and turned the radio on.

"Well, well, well, what do we have here?" a voice said, startling Jackson into dropping the radio on the ground.

"What, what, don't shoot," he said, raising his hands into the air without being told. Two Native Americans stood in front of him. One held a deer rifle on him while the other grinned, playing with a small ax.

"What you doin', boy?" the one with the ax asked.

"I'm trying to call my base," Jackson said without thinking. Then he swallowed hard. *I shouldn't have said that.*

"Why are you calling your base for?" the one with the rifle asked.

Jackson stood there, at first saying nothing. Trembling, he said, "Don't shoot. Please. I surrender."

"Oh, I won't shoot, boy. But my partner with the ax is another thing."

Jackson glanced quickly toward the man holding the ax. His eyes widened as he saw the man draw his arm back, the ax flashing in the sunlight. Then everything went black.

CHAPTER 24

"It is natural to die as to be born."

—Francis Bacon

It was not a good couple of days. I sat on the porch as the sun set that evening. The homestead was eerily silent. The usual cacophony of noise from the barn or inside the cabin absent. King and Max were across the porch, curled up and asleep. The silence was both deafening and maddening. Not even crickets seemed interested in their usual chatter.

I needed a walk. With no idea where I was going, I headed toward the barn, stopping and looking inside. I could see Johnson sitting on a straw bale, picking at something in his hands. I started to walk toward him and stopped. He needed his privacy right now. Of all of us, he was the closest to Rahn and now he had been asked to fill what I'm sure he believed was a very big pair of shoes. I could see a few others toward the back of the barn, idly chattering in voices so low I couldn't hear what they were saying.

I turned and walked away, heading toward the cabins lined up behind mine. The beginnings of a path were worn between them. Soft yellow lights from candles or lanterns shone from their windows, and behind them, some of Jake's men were throwing axes at a target.

I kept walking, and after a while, I was at our little cemetery. Dark mounds of freshly turned dirt marked where Rahn and Gary would spend eternity. Their deaths were senseless, both of them. Chris had been full of life, youthful. Healthy. He should've had a lot more years, and Gary, though he had been in a lot of pain, had never harmed anyone. He served the community, helped people. We had yet to make markers for them, and I knew that anything we did make would not be as permanent as the old stone, marble, or granite markers from our past. But we would mark them.

Carol's grave was still the most prominent. I had made an oak plank marker for her. It had her name, *Carol Jensen*, the years of her birth and death. I also included the words, *Dearest Friend*. We were much more than that but had never publicly admitted it. I decided I would respect our privacy and not say any more.

My mind wandered. It wandered to what could have been had none of this happened. It wandered to why I came here and built a home. A home I intended to keep for the rest of my days. People very dear to me now rested in the land I owned. Their presence made it more than just land; it made it more than the words I could ever imagine to describe it. It was more than home; it was deeper than that.

As I pondered those thoughts, the future came into my mind. We were not done with dark days, and I knew, sadly, that more mounds of freshly turned dirt would grace this land. We were now fighting for more than just our freedom to live as we chose, to not be subjected to those who wanted to take that away from us and who now, most assuredly, wanted to erase us from the face of the earth. We were fighting for our very existence.

I knew Brian was right. We had to not only chase away those who threatened us. We had to end their ability to threaten us, and there was only one way to do that. My realization and acceptance of what was to come weighed heavily on my shoulders.

I looked back toward the cabins and our little community. What was to become of them all? I couldn't protect everyone. I took a deep breath and shuddered.

Then, I headed back toward the main cabin. It was time to end all of this.

As I approached the front of the cabin, I heard voices. Heated angry voices. Brian, Johnson and Craig were sitting in the dark.

"This shit has to end," I heard Brian say.

"When we were in Iraq, the First Sergeant and I saw people die. This is different. It shouldn't be happening here, not like this," Johnson said.

"We need to take those people out, every last one of them," Brian said.

"So what are we gonna do, Bro?" Craig asked.

"No more of this crap. We end all of this," I said from the bottom of the porch steps. "We end it forever."

EPILOGUE

A creak of the screen door made everyone look toward it. A young girl, tan buckskin shorts and barefoot, walked out onto the porch. The shuffle of her feet audible across the wood floor. She walked into the center of the group, standing with her hands on her hips and glancing suspiciously at each of the three men sitting there.

"Whatchya talkin' bout?" she asked. Her body language and tone sounded sharp and commanding and innocent as any pre-teen girl might sound.

"We're talkin' about the weather," the bearded one said.

"Uh, huh," she replied. "Drinking moonshine and tellin' stories about things you'll say I'm too young to know about is what I think."

"No sweetie, we were talkin' about the weather, for real we were," the large bald one said.

"I can't wait for snow," she said, pouting.

"Your grampa always said that. He loved the snow, said it made him feel like a little kid," the bald man added.

"I like the snow, and I am still a kid. I like snow-men and snow ice cream Mom makes me." She walked over to the younger bearded man and said, "Mr. Rick, you like the snow, don't you?"

"Sometimes. Not much time for me to play in it, though, with all the work I have to do."

She snorted a laugh and said, "You don't do that much work. You hunt and fish mostly. That ain't work. My mom said so."

"Oh, she did, did she?" He chuckled.

A creak of the screen door announced another visitor to the small group on the porch. "Emma, you leave those men alone. Can't you see they're working hard?"

The three men laughed at the remark. "See, sweetie, your mom knows we're working."

"You gonna tell me more about my grampa now or what?" she asked, glancing at her uncle, the large bald man.

"Tomorrow, sweetie. We'll tell you more tomorrow."

ABOUT THE AUTHOR

D.M. Herrmann is a retired soldier, having spent twenty years in the U.S. Army. Enjoying a rich, adventurous, and non-traditional Army career, he draws on those experiences, crafting them into elements of these stories. He has authored three fiction novels under the pseudonym Evan Michael Martin. *Fire of Death* is the fourth novel in the John Henry Chronicles series. He lives in Wisconsin.